LISTEN TO THE HOUSE

Ratna Rao Shekar

ISBN 979-8-89233-952-0

For Neil and Keya

Our light

"Life is not what one lived, but what one remembers and how one remembers it in order to recount it."

— Gabriel Garcia Marquez

CHAPTER 1

It is the countries, the cities, the streets, the houses we have grown up in that define our lives. How can we ever escape them? We look at our life years later by the streets we have played in, the houses we have lived in, and the cities whose bylanes we crisscrossed.

We are *that* memory finally.

This was Malavika's childhood home. She thought of the house as a mother. No, not a mother, but a mother's mother, a maternal grandmother who had loved and adored her anyway, no matter what she did, or said. A gentle grandmother of a house.

It was this house that had held her in its arms when she was brought from the nursing home, the placenta and blood washed off from her little body. This was the house on whose walls she had drawn with her wax crayons, to have her mother thrash her for ruining the walls painted a week before Diwali. But the house... the house understood her love and let her not just doodle on its walls, but lick its paint too.

Malavika put her tongue out to remember the taste of the house once again. The taste and smell of its freshly painted walls. Not just that, she wanted to feel the coolness of the red oxide floors. She wanted to remember the day she lay crying, her cheek to the floor, unable to tell anyone what was bothering her, when the house and its warm stone had comforted her.

She had had enough of the silence of her sprawling home in suburban Connecticut. She wanted to sit in the courtyard of this old house, watching the moon pregnant and sexual on full moon nights, and listen to her Avva's voice breathing life into stories from the *Ramayana* with mime and gesture. Sometimes laughing aloud like the ugly rakshasas who guarded Sita in Lanka, at other times pursing her lips like Hanuman holding the scorching sun in his mouth, and leaping across trees. Or simply raising her hand in benediction like the benign Rama – that god who sat frozen in a Raja Ravi Varma print in that very house, which became her prototype of a god forever. A green coloured Rama along with a coy Sita, an obedient Lakshmana by their side, and Hanuman perennially in worship at their feet. All of them draped in velvet clothes with jewels sewn into them.

She wanted to search for those crevices in the walls where she had saved up coins and rupee notes to buy herself an electric train whose pictures she had seen in a magazine. A train that went around on a track. She had forgotten about those coins, as she had about the train. If she found the coins, she would give them to her girls to buy themselves an electric train. But they were too grown up now to be playing with trains and toys. Even if they had still played with toys, who would want a simple electric train in this age of cyber reality?

She wanted to hear the voice of her banker father, hear him talk of his own childhood in Madras as a judge's son. The voice of her mother scolding her for not crossing her legs to sit like a young lady, so she wouldn't show her underclothes even by accident, especially when she wore a short skirt and not the pavadas her Avva liked her to wear.

She wanted to listen to the voice of a young Malavika lying on her bed and repeating words, as if they were spirits who had to be invoked and made to come alive with their sounds. *Efflorescence, Emollient, Evanescent,* she would chant. *Tintinnabulation,* she said to herself now, rolling the word and letting it ring in her ears like that – *tin-tin-amb.* There were other words she liked. *Propinquity. Serendepity. Circumambulation.*

She closed her eyes wanting to climb the mango tree in Siraj's house, to peer inside and see him sitting in his study listening to Frank Sinatra on his old gramophone player, or simply reading a gilt-edged book of the collected poems of one of his favourite poets, Yeats or Eliot. How she wished he would look at her from his window now and ask her to come inside, so the two of them could listen one more time to a recording of TS Eliot reading *The Love Song of J Alfred Prufrock.* Mixing memory with desire.

But he had passed away after a brief illness after she had left for America.

She was hungry for the sounds and smells of childhood. The din of steel vessels in the interiors of the kitchen's store rooms, the Fiat car APU 478 honking minutes before pulling into the porch, and the sound of the koel on the guava or some other fruit tree. Or, best of all, the musical voice of a young Suhaasini come to tell her for the tenth time in the month that she wanted to be a dancer, another Anna Pavlova who would perform all over the world and be toasted as *that* beautiful dancer from India.

Her parents passed away one after another. Her father, her dear beloved father didn't even have time to go to the hospital after a heart attack, and had died at the doorstep of this very house.

Others passed on too, Siraj and Vani Atha, all the people who were part of her childhood.

And Suhaasini lived in Paris.

All things she loved had perished in this cycle of time. Except the house. She still had this grandmother of a house. And no builder was going to bring it down for a faceless apartment. No, she wouldn't allow that. Not till she was alive, at least.

This house didn't just hold her history, but her dreams, her self, everything that was important to her from another time.

CHAPTER 2

Many things had changed on this narrow street in Hyderabad. Many of the Telugu families had migrated to booming cities in the United States, to be with their children who had settled there as doctors or engineers. Others had simply died, and their children showed no interest in their ancestral property in the city.

Consequently, many of the old houses here had been brought down, and in their place, builders had put up apartment buildings without character or aesthetics. Hyderabad itself had changed, beginning to expand into the important business centre it was to become. This so altered the city, that Hyderabadis like her would rue the day it would morph into just another megalopolis, like so many cities around the world.

Malavika's family home remained the same. After her parents passed away, she had kept a tenant at one point whom she had finally to evict for non-payment of rent for several months. More recently, she had leased the house to a distant relative who had come to the city for a job in one of pharma companies that were beginning to mushroom here. She let him stay there more as a caretaker than for the rent he was paying her.

When Malavika was growing up, this was a small tree-lined avenue with just a few houses on each side of the road. Even if one end of the street led to an arterial road of Hyderabad, the other was a dead end, so they always felt safe, boxed in the street. In any case, there were not that many cars here those days and children could cross the street by themselves. Not just on this street, Hyderabad itself had such few motorcars that the children could cycle all the way to Public Gardens on school holidays – sometimes up Naubat Pahad, which had now receded into pictorial books of Hyderabad.

In lanes such as these where ordinary middleclass people lived, houses tended to be similar with not much architectural variation. But in this bylane, the owners had let the builders free their imagination, so that each house was different from the others. All of them had large compounds with so many trees that in a time prior to manicured lawns and gardeners who would tend to flowers and cut hedges, some of their backyards resembled forests that gave rise to fantastical imagination among the children.

The street had only three or four houses on either side, but each was a sub-plot that could be explored separately.

Malavika's house was double-storeyed, and since her father was originally from Madras, reminiscent of some of the art deco homes in Adyar and Mylapore. A large verandah ran around the house, unrestrained like little children. Like those old Madras houses, the arch at the entrance had the figure of the goddess Lakshmi painted into it in pink, the crown in gold paint. Mangalore tiled chhajjas protected the windows, unusual in this Deccan city whose zamindars and nawabs were more influenced by the architecture of Europe, than that of any place in India.

There were many rooms in the large house, but Malavika liked to spend most of the time she was at home, either in her own room or in the courtyard adjoining the kitchen, where the dramas of the family were played out.

In the portico of the house was parked the family Fiat, and it was from here that her father and other guests arrived and left. But the front of the house never interested young Malavika, or for that matter an older Malavika.

It was in the courtyard that her mother, Rekha, whom she always thought of as being more beautiful than anyone she admired in books or movies, assigned chores to the staff of the house. What vegetables the cook should make for the day, at what time the driver should go to the school, her husband's office or the market, and what the maid, who lived in her own quarters within the house, should be doing: dusting, washing or mopping. It was here that Rekha sat down to sort out the differences between Vijaya the cook and Lakshmi the maid, or between Lakshmi's husband Govindaiah the gardener and the driver Allaudin, who thought of himself as being superior to the rest of them.

It was in this courtyard at the back of the house that the servants sat in a row to have their chai and dosas, or their lunch (which Allaudin didn't partake of, as it was always vegetarian food in this Brahmin household), gossiped about everyone on the street, or simply reviled Vijaya for the terrible food which they never found spicy enough.

Malavika would sit here, pretending to be doing her homework, while Lakshmi beat her school uniforms to a semblance of cleanliness on the raised platform – a large granite stone that had become smooth after many years of being washed with soap and water. Lakshmi would make swishing noises with her tongue as she scrubbed and beat the bedsheets and towels, contorting and twisting them into long white snakes, as the soapsuds and water sprayed around her like a halo. Drops of water would fall on little Malavika and she would look up, distracted from the homework or colouring that she was engaged in, to let out a delighted laugh.

If Malavika realised her mother or grandmother were not watching, she would run towards the washing stone and play with the bucket of soapy water, dipping her hands in to raise the soapsuds to her mouth and blow bubbles into the air which reflected the morning sun.

It was from the verandah of this house that Malavika escaped to the huge garden overrun with giant trees – mango and tamarind, even a peepul tree under which there was a small shrine that no one knew how it came to be.

Best of all, the young Malavika liked climbing the natural rocks that marked the landscape of this part of the Deccan and which her family never displaced even while making extensions to the house. There were two in particular that balanced one on top of the other. Malavika and Suhaasini were sure they would topple and roll down one day, crushing Lakshmi and her husband, but it never did happen in all of their childhood.

Among the other houses on the street, one belonged to Siraj who lived by himself though it was rumoured he had a wife and son somewhere. No one knew where his family was, but his house had everything that defined a graceful way of life in Hyderabad – old clocks, rosewood furniture with satin cushions, large maps, black and white photographs, and books in every corner of the room. He was a man in love with books. And with typography. He even had some books set word by word, sentence after sentence, in a letterpress, when printing itself was nascent.

Down the road was a tiny playschool run by a German lady married to an Andhra doctor. It was said that one of the big houses on the street, the first one in fact, which had lain unoccupied for decades, belonged to one of the former Presidents of the country who was from Andhra Pradesh.

There was another house, a modest one and an important player in the story. It was Seshagiri Rao's. He had bought the land when he moved from Guntur to Hyderabad for the sake of a government job in the newly formed capital of Andhra Pradesh. This was in the early sixties, when there was a shine to the city and there were many new opportunities in the government and in industry in the state.

The house didn't have too many rooms. The Raos, simple people from a small town, didn't want a fancy or large house, nor did they want to decorate it with endless bits and pieces of furniture. Nor for that matter did they hang row upon row of photographs of scenic beauty or film stars that city people seemed to love embellishing their homes with. No, they didn't want that. The only thing Vani – the lady of the house, who, conservative as she was, knew what was good for her two children – wanted, was a tulsi sapling at the back, and a puja room where all her gods and goddesses could sit in seclusion and peace, where she could propitiate them at the appropriate times of morning and evening with flowers and other bakshanams that gods were believed to be fond of.

Unlike Malavika, who was an only child, there were two children in this house. Dhruv was born nearly seven years after Suhaasini, who herself had been born 15 years after her parents' marriage. Where everyone else had young parents, Suhaasini had ageing parents.

When Malavika and Suhaasini became friends, it seemed as if their houses too formed a bond because of the affection that ran between the girls who lived in them. Even when the girls became young women and went all over the world, they stayed connected because of their childhood in this city. They could never really break the umbilical cord to the house, and to some memory of their life in the city.

To that, and to a friend who was a refuge.

Dear, dear Haasi,

It's such a cold morning in New Haven that I have not wanted to get out of bed at all today. Vikram leaves for work by the crack of dawn so he can make it to the bank by 8 am. You know, people here keep such devilish hours. And as if all this were not enough, he has decided to go for some advanced classes in finance in the evening because of which he returns quite late in the night. I so want to be the good wife, but as you know, I've always had a problem staying up late and am barely awake when he returns. Amma wouldn't have approved, but I am hardly able to stay awake to even heat up his food.

I know Amma and Avva (if she were alive) would have disapproved of my freezing dals and veggies for a whole week and thawing them to make sambar or kootu when convenient, but that's the way it is here, I would have to tell them.

Why food? Even the air we breathe is stale here, I often think, for during these winter months we don't even open the windows.

Before the onset of winter, only a week ago, I saw Vikram sealing the windows. He said that would keep the cold out.

We both went to the mall to buy warm clothes a few weeks ago. It's my first winter here, and maybe I will wear those boots we bought and walk around the snow. Remember how you and I used to watch Hollywood films and hope one day we would lie in the arms of some handsome man on a cold morning, and watch snow fall through the window? All I can say is that I would still like to lie in the arms of a good looking man, but sweet Jesus, I can't really take this cold. Or the dull, dull dreariness of these days.

I miss wearing the starched Venkatagiri saris (our mothers') and taking the university bus hoping we wouldn't be crushed by lecherous and hungry men – that is, hoping they wouldn't crush our starched cotton saris. And I miss shopping for the colourful organdie saris at Finlay's in Abids. If I have to wear my grey sweater or my thick jacket one more time, I think I will scream.

I know I should get a job here, but looks like my Bachelor's degree in English from Osmania doesn't count for much here. I volunteer at the local library – it's fun because the library has a women's book club that meets once a month, and I am making friends with those women. Though when I say friends, it's not what you and I were like – our hearts beating in each other's. (Intense as it sounds when I re-read the letter!)

But I like one in particular – Amy, who is quarter Cherokee Indian, quarter Scottish, quarter White American, and god knows what else. She is a broadcast journalist here, and getting a divorce soon. She's already separated from her husband, I think. This is one thing that amazes me here, their streak of independence and ability to chuck something up when it's not going right instead of hanging on to things as if it was god's wish.

They are all so curious about our customs, and wanted to know why I wear the large bindi on my forehead. They asked if it's a sign of marriage, which I told them it was. And all those who were married said, we could wear one too, but a large diamond on our fingers is so much better! Vikram wears a wedding band. Maybe I should have him get me one as well, and discard this mangalsutra that I wear tucked inside my sweaters. But you are not to breathe even a word to Amma about this. She would kill me rather than hear of such sacrilege.

I have to invite these women for a Andhra meal one of these days, though all that they know is Bombay and Madras. And snake charmers and Mother Teresa. I will call them over when the weather gets better. Anyway, with Christmas coming up all of them are so busy now.

I really miss talking to you, which is why you have to forgive me for these long letters. I know you must be busy with the Madras music season. How many performances are you giving there this year? And where? You must send me all the reviews. You know I love reading all that's written about you, my Haasini.

I still remember how as a young eight or nine-year-old I had pressed my nose to the grill encircling the verandah, to see the commotion in the opposite house where you had just moved. I watched you, thinking what thick, long straight hair you had. You know how I hated these curls of mine. I often wanted to tie my hair to the ends of two doors, to make it straight! Who'd heard of blowdrying hair those days in Hyderabad!

When I look back, I think I was a lonely child, and that's why I was so eager when I heard that someone with a girl as old as I was, was moving across the road.

We are not born with perspective. That comes with age. And so the child in me turned away to other distractions of the day – the birds on the trees, the Little Lotta and Dot comics that I used to devour. But there are moments in life that in hindsight we know were important to to our life, that the historian in us wants to bookmark so we can recall them when we want. That was one such moment, when I saw you, my friend forever. And to think I don't remember the date.

I am being sentimental, I know, Haasi. But I have so much time here, I have all the leisure in the world to look back and write letters to you. I really wish phone calls weren't so expensive.

Maybe I should get myself a job. Or as I know Amma is hoping – have a baby soon. Bah!

Yours ever,

Malavika

CHAPTER 3

Everything about Hyderabad was new to Haasini and her parents. Even the Telugu they spoke in Hyderabad was so different from what they were used to speaking in the Krishna district. Her mother was puzzled when the maid said 'nalla' for a tap, 'bokkalu' for bones, and 'moofalli' for groundnuts. The maid from this region of Telangana would ask Haasini why she had not made any 'dostulu' even though it was more than six months since she had come to Hyderabad.

But the ten-year-old Haasini did not care about not having any friends in the city. She was happy to be going with her grandfather to the City Central Library where, while he sat reading the Telugu newspapers, she read *Chandamama* in Telugu and became immersed in yet another story of King Vikramaditya and the Betal, whose questions and dilemmas never ceased to fascinate her.

What she loved even more was to go to Ravindra Bharathi to watch classical music and dance programmes. Her grandfather, her father's father, who lived with them, was the president of the South Indian Cultural Association, and would invariably take her along for the concerts. Sometimes her mother would wear one of her Guntur saris with a huge zari border, place a coin-sized kumkum on her forehead, and leaving Dhruv in the care of someone in the house, set off with her father and Haasini for the programmes in their modest Standard Herald car. Since Haasini's grandfather would often be called onto the stage to introduce the artist or give the vote of thanks, the family would sit in the very first row of the auditorium to listen to Balamuralikrishna or Chitti Babu, both of whom, if not yet at their peak, were reaching it in the early seventies.

Haasini's mind tended to wander during Carnatic music concerts. But she watched without fidgeting in her seat or barely blinking when it was a Kuchipudi or Bharatanatyam performance. She loved the costumes the dancers wore, loved the way their bodies and faces expressed a story from the *Ramayana* or the *Mahabharata*.

After that, when she came home, she would lock herself up in her room hoping her brother wouldn't bother her, and dance before the mirror, an odhni wrapped over her head. She would walk as if she were Gollabama in Mathura crooning "Madhuranagarilo, challanamma brovvu..." a song famous in the Kuchipudi repertoire.

She wanted to learn dance – Kuchipudi, Odissi, Bharatanatyam – she didn't care what. Her mother herself had wanted to be a dancer, but in the small towns in Andhra when she was growing up, daasi natyam, as these temple dances were called, were only performed by the devadasis or women who were dedicated to the temples. In time, the art gathered disrepute, as these women who were well versed not just in dance but in poetry and music, became the mistresses of zamindars and landlords, even the temple priests.

Seeing that Haasini, young as she was, wanted to dance, Vani decided to find her a guru in Hyderabad – not easy then, as there were not many interested in classical dance in the city. She decided to send Haasini when she was a little older, after she finished high school, to Madras, to that great dance institute, Kalakshetra, where she would be well taken care of even if she was away from home.

When Haasini was not obsessing about dance, or trying desperately to escape the constant chatter of her younger brother, she loved to watch Telugu films in theatres with her grandfather. They would both sneak off on Sunday mornings for the mythological movies that the Telugu film industry was famous for. They were in black and white, even if life itself was in technicolour, and Haasini would be mesmerised by the number of laddoos and murukulu a Ghatotkacha could eat in the film *Maya Bazaar*, singing "Aha, aha vivaha bhojanambu," or how the arrows of both the Pandavas and Kauravas would clash on the silver screen setting the dark sky ablaze in *Pandava Vanavasam*. She watched all this breathless with an excitement that had few parallels in her childhood.

Haasini always imagined Krishna to have a blue face like that of the actor NT Rama Rao and a tantrum-throwing Satyabhama forever to look like the Telugu film actress Jamuna in *Pandava Vanavasam*. They saw the movies in the Ramakrishna theatre, which though far from home was all the rage for it had a special 70mm screen and stereophonic sound, rare in Hyderabad those days.

Before Haasini spent all her time watching movies and going around Hyderabad with her grandfather, she must find her a dance teacher, Vani decided. She would ask Rekha, her neighbour, who had lived in Hyderabad for a long time and knew every little thing about the city – from where to get blouses stitched to where you could get good quality chintakyalu for the pachchadis, or to which schools to send the children. Her daughter, Malavika, would make a good friend for her little Haasini, she thought, resolving to go to Rekha's house that very week with a jaadi of tomato pachchadi she had freshly made.

Dear Malavika (I've always loved the sound of your name),

You are lucky that you don't live in Hyderabad any more, as it is changing rapidly, and all that we once loved in this city is fast disappearing. Remember all those lovely cinema halls – Tivoli, Plaza, Skyline, Embassy and Liberty, where we saw films like The Great Escape *and* Goodbye Mr Chips? *Well, they are all being brought down one by one. And coming up in their place are horrid looking apartments or function halls, which they are even calling Plaza function hall and so on as a tribute to the theatres that no longer exist.*

How would the people who bring them down know what they meant to us? How we sat in hushed silence with Siraj to watch Goodbye Mr Chips *and after that fell madly in love with Peter O'Toole! Or the Telugu films you would sometimes come for with Thatha and me that we saw at theatres like Deepak and Venkatesh. I know you didn't much care for Telugu films but Hanuman flying through the air with his tail on fire and Ghatotkacha eating platefuls of chicken and laddoos was magic realism at its best, don't you think? The Satyabhama of my dance will always be based on Jamuna's interpretation of her. No one to beat her for arrogance or getting into a huff.*

I have been busy with my choreographies and students, it is true. But I have been broken-hearted too. I didn't tell you, as it was too soon after you left, but I was seeing this young man, a poet and a Telugu film critic who shall remain nameless. But he's been acting strange recently and not taking my calls or coming to meet me. This was the same man who would say he couldn't breathe if he didn't see me. What happens to men that they change their mind halfway through a relationship? Why don't they realise love is a woman's life, and the time spent together creates such a deep impress on our internal circuits that we have to live with these painful memories until kingdom come? I can't go to Havmor any more and not remember how we split the ice-cream sundae. I truly felt I was that cherry on top of the ice-cream. Why Havmor, I can't step outside the house knowing that I will be driving alone, and have no one to pick up halfway to Abids.

I've been sleeping very badly, for I miss him so. He was saying he would be going to the US to do his Master's in communications. Maybe he just left, maybe he didn't have time to say goodbye, maybe he lost my number. Maybe he had an attack of amnesia like King Dushyanta.

Or maybe, sadly, I didn't mean all that much to him. Malavika, who knew when we were growing up that life would be full of such heartbreaks? If we knew we would have to confront all this sadness, we could have inured ourselves against them, like the inoculations we took for measles and mumps. At least I haven't lost my sense of humour! Wonderful, is that not, my friend?

Amma wonders why I am not myself, but somehow you cannot tell a parent about heartbreaks. I shall just go deeper into my dance. Dance has the ability to make me transcend my world, any world in fact. I am truly blessed to be a classical dancer. Siraj always told me this. And I know while you love me for what I am, that I am a dancer means something to you too.

I shall put my fury into the Kaliyamardanam *that I am choreographing for an upcoming concert. The indifferent and the evil shall be thus slayed!*

Take care, my friend.

Haasini

CHAPTER 4

If there was one raga that was associated with Malavika's growing up years, it was Bhoopalam, in which MS Subbulakshmi sang the Venkateshwara Suprabhatam. *Kausalya supraja Rama poorva sandhya pravarthathe, uttishta Narasardula karthavyamdhaivamanhikam...* This, her grandmother would play every morning on the gramophone player that she kept on a small wooden stool in her room. She would play this around 5 am every morning so loudly that everyone knew the oldest member of the family had woken up, and the ceremonies associated with her making her filter coffee would soon commence.

Since no one else was awake at this hour of the morning, and it would be a few hours before Vijaya would come to make the palaharam, it was up to Avva to get on with the morning ritual of making filter coffee. She would turn on the lights in a still dark kitchen, and in the brass coffee filter that she had brought from her own home in Bangalore (which she wound up on her husband's passing away and came to stay with her daughter Rekha) heap two spoons of freshly ground coffee, and pour boiling hot water. She would wait for the water to percolate down, meanwhile looking in the steel tins for some Marie biscuits. She was unhappy that in Hyderabad no milkman (or for that matter, newspaperman) came until 7 or even at 8 am. So she had to use the previous day's milk lying in the fridge for her coffee.

"Rekha, can't we send Govindaiah to get fresh milk from the milkman's house instead of waiting for him to arrive here at 12 in the afternoon, as if he were the Nizam himself?" she used to ask when she moved to the city a few years ago, a little after Malavika was born. But she had soon given up demanding this when she realised the futility of such requests in a city like Hyderabad. Among her other frustrations of moving from Bangalore was also the fact the she couldn't get good ground coffee here, like she would so easily in Malleswaram.

When her son-in-law Ram travelled to Bangalore, she would make sure he brought her some Cothas coffee from a corner shop on 18th Cross in Malleswaram. "You just have to tell that man who roasts and grinds the coffee that Vasantha maami wants her special coffee powder, and he will make it precisely the way I like it, with a dash of chicory," she would exhort her son-in-law. He in turn would send the bank's driver to get his mother-in-law's coffee. When she didn't have a ready stock of this coffee, she had to be happy with what Rekha procured from Lakdi-ka-pul or some other pul in Hyderabad which was never as fresh or as aromatic.

"What would Hyderabad people know about coffee? Even these Andhras who have moved from Madras?" she would ask no one in particular. She felt only Bangaloreans knew the authentic taste of roasted peaberry. Hyderabad was a chai drinking city, and she wasn't going to have any of it. Let the maids and drivers drink the brew, she would mutter under breath.

Vasantha would then pour the dark, dangerous looking concoction in a steel tumbler held in another small steel vessel that served as a saucer (no cups and saucers for her – she thought these were for Englishmen and their ladies) and hobble towards Malavika's room, sitting by her bed, sipping the coffee and talking to her, even if the child pretended to be asleep.

The Suprabhatam by then would have concluded, and if Vasantha didn't go to her room to flip the record to hear the Vishnu Sahasranamam sung by MS Subbulakshmi (with an introduction by Rajaji), there would be hissing sounds with the needle going endlessly over the record. And that, if nothing else, was sure to wake up Malavika whose room was just next to her grandmother's.

If MS Subbulakshmi's chanting was the background sound to her early childhood, the aroma of strongly brewed and evil looking coffee, drunk with lots of milk and sugar, was the smell Malavika associated with being woken up. That, and the warmth of her grandmother's voice as she ruminated aloud over this and that with the child, unmindful of her age or experience.

It was an everyday ritual for Malavika to open her eyes to see Avva by her bedside looking bright and happy in her mithai pink or mango green Kanchi silks that Malavika imagined she wore even to bed. She would sip her coffee and talk to Malavika and let out bits of information about her own life. One day she told Malavika how she had got married to her grandfather when she was only ten or eleven years old.

"I was about your age when I got married to your Thatha," she told her, offering to bring her a warm glass of Ovaltine. Malavika liked to drink the badam-flavoured Ragimalt at all times, but her mother and grandmother thought it was only good as an after-school drink and insisted she drink Ovaltine or Bournvita in the mornings.

"But Avva that means you had a friend even at that age at home all the time. That must have been so much fun. Look at me, I have to wait for Haasini to wake up or be free in the evening before I have anyone to play with," Malavika would say fully awake in a manner only children can be, the very minute they open their eyes.

"Thatha was alright when he was young. After that he became obsessed about becoming a physicist and working at the Raman Research Institute. By the time he was 16 years or so he would sit with those huge, fat books all the time. He was a world famous astro-physicist and didn't believe in the panchangam, setting out on his travels without waiting for the auspicious time," she would reminisce.

"Avva, what is auspicious time? Do I also have to follow auspicious time? Should I see Haasini only at auspicious times every day?" Malavika babbled.

"Never mind the auspicious time. I think you should get up right now, get dressed and go to school. Let me call Lakshmi to give you a bath and get you ready. I will oil your hair and plait it with white ribbons as your school wants, I promise," Vasantha said, getting up to go.

She sighed as she went to her room to get ready for the day. She would have to wait for Vijaya to arrive before she could have the morning tiffin of upma. If only Vijaya would roast the cashewnuts in good ghee, her upma would taste so much better, she thought. But there were all sorts of economy measures in this house, she sighed to herself. Sometimes in this household upma was even made with wheat ravva, which was unheard of in her own home! Vasantha decided she would write down her recipe for upma for Malavika, so she at least would know how to make it the proper way when she grew up.

Already, recipe books were becoming popular and being written by all sorts of people, even Americans and Europeans. What would they know how to roast the ravva? Or what vegetables were to be added to make the upma tasty? Or how much karvepaku had to be put along with the onions?

Dear Ms Suhaasini,

Have you forgotten me, or is it your dance choreographies that are keeping you busy? Well, I hope it is the latter because I can't imagine you not wanting to talk to me in the same way as I want to. I really wish we could afford the international calls, because I think if I were to speak to you and Amma at least once a week, I wouldn't be so homesick.

I am trying to grow kothimira and gongura in little pots in the kitchen window now that summer is here.

I know I can buy all the pickles and pachchadis in the Indian grocery stores, but this is a way of being connected to home and Hyderabad. And to all of you. But I have to look for Avva's recipe for gongura pachchadi that she said she got from her own mother. Amma and she would always be arguing about the things that were to go into the gongura pachchadi, and then your mother would add her own two-bit Guntur chillies of wisdom. Vijaya being a Hyderabadi would have no clue about how to make the pachchadi, and would insist on making a gongura pappu – which was nice, when I look back, but didn't have the mouth-watering tang of the pachchadi. Gongura pachchadi with garlic was a definite no-no with Avva, but was endorsed by Amma. We would call them the Gongura Wars, remember! Maybe one day I shall record the story of these wars among Andhra families.

There was something else – the gongura mutton we tasted, you and I, at Siraj's house, made by his cook Abida! We swore we would never tell anyone for it would upset our mothers. But if there is one reason for me to give up my vegetarian ways it is this gongura mutton, surely! As it is I find it so difficult to be a vegetarian in this country. I can't eat much except a vegetarian pizza when we go out.

Vikram, as you know, loves his fish, like a true-blooded Bengali (having lived in Calcutta all his life, even if his family is originally from Vijayawada) but I have told him he can eat fish only outside the house. Sometimes I sound so righteous and horrid even to my own ears. And I really, really need to find something more to do than the three times a week library job. Maybe I should do something at the Metropolitan Museum, go for those art appreciation classes. You were always the more talented one between us, but I am sure I will love learning about European art – Matisse's Blue Period and Picasso's Cubism. Learn more about Frida Kahlo whom I've been fascinated with for years now.

This first year of marriage has been difficult. I don't mean to complain about Vikram but he's so set in his ways, wanting to go to a bar on Friday nights, and on Sundays watching football on the television. He can't understand why I pine so much for Hyderabad, and calls me a small town Andhra girl. The first time he said that, I sat in the bathroom and cried and cried. And guess what? He didn't even notice that I was not around in the kitchen, or in my room, until it was dinner time!

Today, while I sit by the window in my room writing this letter to you, I don't see the apple trees in our garden. Instead, I see the guava trees of my childhood home. I see and smell the half-eaten red guava discarded by a parrot. How angry I would be that the guava that I had waited for to ripen on the tree before I plucked it, should be so mutilated by a parrot who was smarter, it seemed to me, than a young girl. I would pick this half-eaten guava from the ground and fling it across, it would hit Lakshmi or Govindaiah, and they in turn would scream at the invisible parrot. I wonder if the cackle of the parrot was because she was laughing at the comedies of human beings who get flustered over a mere guava.

Our yard and the streets here are littered with apples, and we think of them more as a nuisance than a source of any joy. And to think how grateful and lucky we used to feel when our mothers bought Kashmiri apples from the Mozamjahi Market during the season.

We grow up and think we leave our childhood behind. But do you think childhood ever leaves us?

Let me not bore you with my profound thoughts on apples and pachchadis. Au revoir, my friend.

Yours,

Ever in friendship,

Ms Malavika

CHAPTER 5

The tree-lined lane where Malavika lived was so quiet an avenue that you knew who was passing through, which fruit seller or flower seller was doing the rounds, or whose car was going by. Ramu, the regular flower man, would cycle through the gate in the evening when the children were back from school.

"Mallepuvvulamma, kanakambaralamma!" he would intone in a singsong voice, cycling so fast that even before Malavika could come out with ten paisa coins to buy the flowers, he would be out of the lane and into another, leaving behind a trailing echo of his jasmine voice, "Puvvulu... puvvulu... uvvulu... uvvulu..."

Rekha bought these flowers for her puja the next morning. They were kept wrapped in a damp, white muslin cloth and placed carefully in the fridge. Vasantha however, had no such compulsions and felt even more liberated from piety and rituals after her husband passed away.

Rekha had assured Ramu that in this house, they would definitely buy flowers every day and that he should stop by every evening. But if he didn't see anyone at the gate, this man who was always in a hurry would cycle away with the elan of Dev Anand in a love song.

When Lakshmi was alert in the evenings, and not busy putting things in Malavika's room or ironing clothes, she would waylay Ramu and buy the flowers. She would gossip, flirt and cajole him into giving at least one mura flowers free, after she had bought the two muralu of garlands of mallepuvvu and kanakambaram for the household. If Ramu wasn't charmed into giving flowers for nothing, she would just grab a small garland from the basket tied to the seat at the back of the cycle, and walk away triumphantly.

She would tuck these flowers into her own hair and some into Malavika's, who would be playing Chinese Checkers with her grandmother or reading by herself.

Jasmine in the hair, a young Malavika would look at herself in the long mirror in her grandmother's room turning this way and that way, holding her polka dotted frock with her two hands and putting her tongue out deciding that the girl in the mirror with flowers in her plaits looked plain silly. She would tear the flowers out, her plaits coming undone, and feel displeased with everything that evening.

She would then run out of her room into the backyard and out of the gate into Siraj's house, where no one asked her to do anything. They let her play hopscotch on her own on the large squares of the mosaic floor, or climb the mango tree and read a book, listening to the koel or looking a squirrel in the eye.

As she sat perched on one of the trees she would often hear laughter and arguments from inside the house. She would know then that Siraj must have invited people for a game of rummy and dinner. If, while walking past the driveway they saw her, they would ask Siraj about her. If she jumped down from the tree, the belt of her frock undone, they would pinch her cheeks and call her a waif. She asked her mother what a 'waif' was. Rekha laughed and told her, yes, that's what she was, a little minx who ran away and hid in Siraj's house while they looked for her all evening. And Malavika would wonder why adults never explained anything, but expected you to know every word in the dictionary.

She liked it best on the evenings when Siraj saw her sitting on the tree and asked her to come inside the house. If she ran in, he would tell her to walk slowly. "Young lady, gently. Why are you rushing like an Andhra cyclone into the house?"

While she found a chair to sit on – usually rather big for her small frame – he would summon Abida, the old family retainer and cook, to bring Malavika a plate of badaam ki jaali and a glass of the devilishly pink Rooh Afza she loved so much. He would then walk up to his study, open one of the rosewood cupboards with glass doors and pluck out a book.

Mostly, he read to her what he pleased, quite oblivious to how young she was. Sometimes he would read the longwinded sentences of Lawrence Durrell. At other times the poems of T S Eliot. Even Tolstoy on certain days, unmindful that to the little girl in Hyderabad, the world of Russian Czars would be an unfamiliar, and unreal country.

But one evening her mind wandered to other things in the room: to the old maps on the walls, Roman statues on marble tables that were further burdened with black and white photographs in silver frames, and to the bluebell that had crept insidiously into the room through the open window like curious children. She got up to touch the petals of the bluebells, amused by the pollen that fell on her little wrist that she tried to blow out through the window.

But all of a sudden, the room fell into a hush. Why wasn't she hearing Siraj's deep voice, so comforting that she could hold it and go to sleep with it?

What was he telling her now? Was he angry with her?

"Words, girl, listen to words, listen to the rhythms of words and see how they can intoxicate you. Stop being so distracted. And why are you slurping the sherbet like that, like a herd of elephants drinking water in the lakes of Masai Mara. I know Abida is not the greatest of cooks, but you are a young lady now. Not a savage," he was thundering.

She liked it when he read Rudyard Kipling – the stories of Mowgli in the Indian jungle. When she was younger, Siraj had read out these stories and shown her the black and white illustrations of Mowgli and Sher Khan from his early edition of *The Jungle Book*.

This evening, he tried to bring her mind back to the story of Anna Karenina that he was reading out from a hardbound edition with a green cover edged with gold. He had read the book many times over, but was so carried away by the story sweeping like a storm through the room, by the tragic death of the countess who committed suicide by falling under a train, that for a few minutes there was only the presence of the story, and the voice of a man whom she loved dearly.

When Siraj stopped reading the book and closed his eyes sliding comfortably into his planter's chair, Malavika slipped out of the room into the backyard taking with her the *Little Women* she had left behind on a previous visit.

She climbed up the tree and sat there reading. Everything was still, not even the cries of birds returning to their nests. That's when she heard voices from the new neighbour Haasini's house. Malavika's mother had told her the girl's name and promised to take her to meet her one day. From atop, she couldn't see Haasini but a little boy bending his head over a table. She wished she had a long neck like a heron so she could see everything that was going on in Seshagiri Rao's house, lit by a fluorescent tubelight.

The next moment there was a scream. The boy fled, and a girl who must be Haasini began to chase him, shouting, "My god, this idiot brother of mine has torn pages from my diary again, and scribbled his silly pictures of cars and trains! Where is he? Dhruveeee..."

Dhruv had hidden in the backyard of the house. Haasini, tired of looking for him, sat on the steps of the house and looked up at the trees in Siraj's house. There she saw a girl of about her own age who she guessed was Malavika – the girl her mother had told her about.

What a tall girl she was, Haasini thought, looking at Malavika's long, long legs hanging down from the branches of the mango tree. And what sort of eyes were they that darted around like the little elves that Haasini had anyway imagined lived in the trees and gardens of this street!

Dear Mala,

Forgive me, woman, for not being able to write to you. But will you believe me if I say that I think of you all the time? Please, please believe me. Only yesterday when I looked out of my window, what did I see but Siraj's house being brought down, accompanied by loud crashes and thuds. There was so much dust and such loud noise that I had to shut my eyes tight and close my ears, something I used to do when Dhruv burst crackers on Diwali nights, years ago.

All that dust made me cough so much that Amma rushed to see what the matter was. But when she came into the room, she too stood looking at Siraj's crumbling house. And we thought to ourselves how sad it was that since Siraj passed away, no one had been interested in the house and had let it fall apart. Especially his son Roshan, who lives in Canada and who said he wanted nothing to do with his ancestral home in his beloved Hyderabad. He sold the house to a builder. How quickly they want to erase all memory of its previous owner! I remembered how you loved to spend every waking hour in that house. Especially on the mango tree. So many times, I thought you were an elf, sitting like that on the tree.

Amma and I stood looking at the house for a few minutes, until she touched my shoulder and said, "Haasini, don't write to Malavika about the house being brought down. You know how attached she was to Siraj, and his passing away itself had upset her so." She had seen the letter that had recently come from you, and asked me to stay in touch with you. You must be missing Hyderabad, she said, living as far away as you do from your parents and the city you loved so.

She told me not to tell you about Siraj's house, and look at me, that's the very first thing I am writing about.

But tell me, how are you? How is Vikram? Is marriage all that you wanted it to be? Alas, for me, there is no time for marriage. Life is way too busy for me to settle down. Guess what? The Ministry of Culture sent me a letter last week asking me if I would participate in their Festival of South Asian Arts that is to be held in September in London. Am I excited? Of course I am! I haven't sat down or slept since I got the letter from the Ministry the other evening.

There are others who will be going from Madras, Bombay and Calcutta. Dancers and even musicians. But only I will be going from Hyderabad. It's quite an honour, I believe.

Remember Indira, who was in Kalakshetra with me? Well, she is going too, and I am sure she deserves to go. But she called me two evenings ago just to tell me that when the Ministry of Culture called her early this year and asked her to recommend names of dancers, she had suggested my name. What gall to say that it was she who recommended me, when it was that Sen who saw me perform in Delhi recently who made sure I was invited! When he came backstage he had congratulated me on a fine performance and said I should be dancing at some of the Festivals of India. And Indira claims she suggested my name! Though I am quite sure being a Bengali she must be 'pals' with Sen.

I suppose we will be put up in the same hotel in London and I have to suffer her chatter. As a dancer, you'd think she'd be more dignified. But not Indira. She gossips and complains about some dancer or musician, or tells all of us how some man or the other is in love with her. My god!

That reminds me, I have to tell you something funny, even strange. There is someone who has been following me from one dance performance to another during the music season in Madras. He's always there, sitting in the second row, near the press stand, to one corner. I always expect him to come backstage to talk to or greet me, but he does nothing like that. Wonder who he is – this rasika. Good-looking, you are wondering? Yes, of course, crumpled kurta, light eyes and elegant hands. More about the admirer when I find out something about him.

I promise to write to you from London. A postcard, for sure. I've almost decided what I will be performing – your favourite, Jayadeva's Ashtapadi. What could be more romantic than a Radha looking for her beloved Krishna in London?

Yes, I shall take London by storm. I shall have them stand and applaud me, just like they did Anna Pavlova. Malavika, when and at what stage in life did I get this ambitious? How horrible is that, Siva, Siva.

I'm sleepy now. I will find an envelope for this letter tomorrow morning.

As I look out of the window I see your favourite mango tree, the leaves drenched in the light of the moon, and a tall, attractive girl shouting, "Haasini, don't hit the child." How many years ago was that, Malavika? If I am 26 now, it must have been a good 16 years ago? At least, so far they have not cut the mango tree. When I miss you, I look out of the window and see the girl who loved to sit on that tree and read a book. Such a bookworm she was, my friend.

Amma sends her love to you. Pa, absentminded Pa, read in the newspapers about the elections in America the other day, and thought of you. He wanted to know if you were safe in America and what you thought of Kennedy. Kennedy, now? He has early stages of dementia I am thinking.

Love as always,

Haasini

CHAPTER 6

One evening, Malavika had come back from school and was in her room, sipping her Ragimalted milk and crunching the crisp pakodis laid before her on a steel plate by Lakshmi. Neither her mother nor her grandmother were in the house, for it was a Friday and they had left for the Balaji temple in Chikkadpally. If it were the Hanuman temple in Khairatabad they had been visiting, she would have insisted on going with them and even thrown a tantrum that they had not waited for her return. Hanuman, who could fly across oceans and to whom she prayed at night when she was scared of thieves and murderers, was Malavika's favourite god. So, she was happy for now to be reading a Gerald Durrell that her father had bought for her from the AA Husain Bookstore because she had stood second in the class.

Lying on her four-poster bed with legs hanging down, her little body was tense with the anticipation of all the adventures of the Durrell family and animals, when she felt a sound vibrate from under her bed. She leapt out, and tried to trap the sound under her bare feet in order to see where it had come from. The sound, however, escaped and scurried around the room. Like a mouse.

She realised the noises were coming from Siraj's house. She had known that the house, which looked old and dilapidated, would collapse one day. But not that soon!

Malavika ran out of her room, through the courtyard and the verandah, out of the front gate to the house that was next door, unmindful of the cars and cycles, to Siraj's house, praying to Hanuman to not let him die in the crash. She didn't want Siraj to die – no, she didn't want that. In a child's world, he was her only ally, apart from Avva.

It must have been the witch, Abida, who was crushing Siraj with her grinding stone to rob him of his wealth, she thought to herself. Her mother was always reading about such thefts in the *Deccan Chronicle,* a paper her father dismissed saying it had too much local gossip, preferring to read the more staid, if international paper, *The Hindu.*

But riches and wealth? What did Siraj have? Had she not seen him buy bread and biscuits and give it to the urchins and beggars on Tank Bund when he went there for his early morning walks? These things cost money, and Malavika was sure he didn't have much left after that. Besides, she had never seen him go to work either. He was always sitting on his planter's chair and reading or writing. Once when she had asked him why he never went to work like her father did to the State Bank in Sultan Bazaar, he'd said he gave up his lecturer's job in Nizam College as no one these days wanted to read poetry or classics.

During the summer holidays, on the days she could get up early, she would go with Siraj for morning walks, carrying the biscuits and bread Abida would keep aside for them in a cloth bag. She would feel happy when the mothers of the hungry urchins blessed them, thinking she was Siraj's daughter. She didn't mind being thought of as the child of this man who had the greenest eyes in the world, who showed her books with illustrations and maps, and who loved horses.

Malavika's feet would ache but Siraj insisted that she walk with him the length of Tank Bund from one end to the other, and then take a turn and walk down Lower Tank Bund, almost towards Gagan Mahal. Sometimes he walked her up to the Sailing Club, and since summers were really hot in Hyderabad, she would be glad for the glass of cold lemonade and biscuits he ordered for her, while he himself had a pot of coffee. The bearers at the Club would chat with him, asking him about his horses, while she smiled and looked at the waters of Hussain Sagar where boats sailed around gently.

Most mornings he would run into someone he knew. But once, when they were by themselves at the Club, he told her, "Little one, if I ever fall ill, make sure they don't take me to a hospital. I want to die at home, looking at the mango tree. I have little pills in my clothes' closet that will end any agony. And don't let my son, his name is Roshan – how will you know his name, you've never even seen him – get near me when I am dying. There should be some dignity in death. You have to die elegantly, just as you have to live with passion. Eh, what was that I said? I forget sometimes that you are only nine years old. I know you will grow up into a fine woman. If only you didn't walk like a World War II veteran."

Another time, on one of these early morning walks, he had told her, pressing her young palm into his large, rough hands, glaring at honking cars that wouldn't allow them to cross the road from the Club, "I knew a woman once..."

Unmindful that the child had not reacted, he had continued: "This woman, when she walked into my apartment in Oxford, brought in the fragrance of some flower from an English garden... foxglove, primrose, daffodil, lavender.... When she was happy, and she was always happy when she came to see me, she brought a whole garden of roses with her. A woman must evoke the seasons, the flowers of a garden. Your mother, god bless her, brings the smell of lotuses from an Indian summer. It's such an Indian fragrance that Lillette could not evoke it."

"Who's Lillette, Siraj? Was she your wife?"

"Lillette? Who was she, you are wondering? She was my love, shall we say? She was working on Samuel Beckett. As if anybody even in Oxford understood what he said. Godot? Was he god himself, she asked me once. If only I knew, I said to her. The absurdity of that wait... You have to read Beckett, young lady, one day for sure, you will. But remind me to show you the lovely edition that I have, when you come home. You will come to see me everyday, won't you Malavika?"

"Siraj, can we sit for a while?"

"Eh, what is it that you are saying? That your legs are aching? Now that won't do, Malavika, because young women must have strong legs. And, ah, yes, remember to thank your lovely mother for the kheer that she sent for Ugadi last week."

"Yes, yes, I will thank Ma. Siraj... Why are you telling me all this, Siraj, are you going to die very soon?"

"What is it, Malavika, my heart? You know, you must learn to speak up. This mumbling and chewing of sentences won't do. I don't know what they teach you in school nowadays. Eh, you don't want me to die. But everyone has to die. We must move on and let others live after us. We are of course alive as long as we are remembered. You will allow me to sit quietly in some corner of your memory, won't you Malavika? This old man who has had the misfortune of seeing Hyderabad change and be destroyed within his lifetime..."

"Siraj, will I have a fragrance too...?"

"You are still so very young. But one day you'll acquire your own special fragrance. I won't live to see it. The mild fragrance of the parijat. That's what your fragrance will be. Maybe even champa. No, that's too mild a fragrance, for one as strongminded as you. The tango, lady, not the march past of the war veterans. Remember that, and you'll be alright."

"Are you ill, Siraj?"

"No, I am not ill, young lady. Anyway, let's go home now. I know you are hungry again. Let me see if I can get you muffins. I could do with another cup of strong coffee, not the weak one they give here at the Club. And when I am dying, young lady, make sure you leave a door in the house open for me to look out of. I want to hear footsteps from the cobbled footpaths of Oxford once again. That, and smell of chrysanthemums, and roses."

Having run all the way from her room to Siraj's house, Malavika now stopped to catch her breath. She was glad that the house was not coming down after all.

She was in the verandah but had not entered the house even though the front door was open. She could hear voices coming from within. Was that Siraj's voice? Was he listening to the radio, the BBC talk shows he often heard in the afternoons? Was he giving Abida another lecture? No, it couldn't be Abida because she always argued back, and no one, least of all Siraj, could ever get a word in sideways.

Siraj must be reading poetry to himself. He did like to read poetry aloud. That was when his voice became soft as it was now. He would caress a line of poetry as if it were his favourite daughter.

Malavika walked through the door into Siraj's study. She saw Haasini sitting on a mora close to Siraj's chair. She stood near the door, hiding behind the curtains that she wrapped around herself as if she were a mummy, and eavesdropped on the conversation.

"By the time I saw Meenakshiammal, her body had aged. But even then, she could sit with her spine erect, willing to show you the abhinaya the devadasis were known for. Not the Brahminical nonsense Madras later called Bharatanatyam. She would raise an eyebrow like this and plead with Krishna to appear before her. And indeed, as if she were his mother Yashoda, Krishna could not help but appear before her. Such was the power of her expression and abhinaya," Siraj was telling Haasini.

What was Haasini now asking him in that musical voice she spoke to elders with? Malavika could not hear very well for she dared not move from the curtain that had now coiled tight around her neck. But Siraj was continuing to talk to Haasini.

"Was she beautiful? Of course Haasini, all dancers are beautiful. By the time I went to see her in that little house that she lived in, in Luz, she was well into her seventies. But when I watched her abhinaya, I could see how dazzling she must have been in her prime. How she could not only dance, but sing her own padams, and recite poetry. These devadasis were indeed special women who were much maligned and misunderstood in independent India. It's the British who never understood them."

How many things did Siraj know? How did he know so much about Bharatanatyam too? In fact, she wouldn't put it past him that he'd danced with Uday Shankar and his troupe. So when did he have time to learn dance? She wished Siraj would stop talking about varnams, padams and jatiswarams, words that were alien to her. But the girl Haasini was nodding her head as if she understood everything he was saying.

When, in an effort to hear him better Malavika leaned forward, the curtain and the rod came crashing down, narrowly missing her head. But everyone saw her hiding.

Siraj, Haasini, even Abida.

Siraj beckoned to her kindly as if she were his older daughter. "Come, child. Do you know Suhaasini? She is going to be the world's greatest dancer. I know that. Look at the way she takes those steps, with such grace, head held high. And look at the expressions on her face when she talks! Like the great dancers I have seen. Kamala, Bala, Meenakshiammal..."

World's greatest dancer? So, this girl danced? Malavika too sang and danced to all the songs from *My Fair Lady* and *The Sound of Music*. But not once had Siraj praised her and said that she would be the world's greatest dancer or singer. Well, she would be the world's most beautiful woman, she decided, screwing up her face as she picked herself up.

"Siraj," she said coyly, in a voice that even she failed to recognise as her own. "Will you help me to learn these lines from Shelley's *Ozymandias* for my recitation competition in school?"

"*Ozymandias*, girl? We have read that so many times, you and I. What is there to get worked up over it? And pulling that curtain down so!"

"I am sorry, Siraj..."

"Never mind, young ladies. Malavika, don't slouch like that. Yes, even if the rod has fallen on you. Young women like you shouldn't be slouching. Have I introduced you two? How impolite of me! Eh? What Malavika, you already know Haasini? That's settled then, you know each other. I know you two will be good friends. And friends are more important than even family," he said, and got up to see if there was anything in the biscuit tins that he could give his young visitors.

"What is that infernal noise in the kitchen? If Abida were not so stubborn, we would have had the mutton spewing kitchen somewhere near the outhouse which is where the Burra Sahebs liked it, and I don't blame them. But now she wants a granite slab for her gas stove and mixie. She wanted me to upgrade the kitchen ever since she saw your mother's kitchen, Malavika."

Malavika was distracted for a moment. She looked towards the kitchen and saw that even the floor had been dismantled and realised the source of the noise that had reached her in the recesses of her room. And dust was getting into her nose, wafting around the rooms like an evil spirit. If Abida were not standing there like an imperious Queen Victoria, Malavika would have closed the door to the kitchen that so infuriated Siraj, so the three of them could get on with their conversation on literature and dance.

✳ ✳ ✳

Dear Haasi,

You, my dear friend, must be on a plane to London – and what a great moment it must be for you. I hope your childhood dreams of being a renowned dancer have come true. I am sure, though, you will be one of India's greatest classical dancers one day. It is only a matter of time and patience.

Remember, Siraj had told you so many years ago that you would be a great dancer whom the world would toast? You remember that day, don't you Haasini, when the curtain rod almost fell on my head, while you sat so erect and graceful listening to Siraj? I sometimes think I still have a faint pain on my head from the rod falling on me. I was so jealous that he was praising you so much, when he would chide me all the time for not reading enough or for slouching.

I wonder what he would have said to the dumbing down that has happened to me in America. These days, I read so so little, what with all the housework, television, and entertaining that I have to do. That is so strange, isn't it, considering that all I wanted to do in my childhood was to lie in bed and read, climb trees and read – and when I had a fight with you or Amma, to simply hide somewhere and read. If you had told me then that there would be a day when I wouldn't find the time to read, I would not have believed it, because I used to think my life would be wasted if I didn't try to finish one classic or the other in a week.

Remember that time in class, when Sister Ancilla asked us if we had read any books during our summer holidays, and I rattled off a dozen while everyone else had read only one or two. I even told her I had just finished Gone with the Wind, *and Sister said I was too young to understand the book! But I was already 13, and what an impression it made on me. Those were possibly the only four days of my life, when I didn't feel the need to see you, so immersed was I in the story of Scarlett and Rhett Butler.*

Only the other day I remember reading that when it comes to a man, two women can never be friends. I always thought of Siraj as mine and mine alone, and I was so angry when he seemed to choose you or when he let you sit next to him to talk about dance, about which I didn't know a thing.

I miss him so. So utterly sad that he hasn't seen us grow up and step out into the world.

I miss those long rides in his black Fiat car when I sat in the front with him. He would drive me around to his favourite places in Hyderabad. To the Nizam College, where he said the medium of instruction at one time was Urdu, and where people like Sarojini Naidu and Harindranath Chattopadhay taught. To King Kothi that was home to the richest man in the world, the Seventh Nizam, and which I hear now is crumbling – it breaks my heart everytime I read about it.

He would tell me such lovely stories of old Hyderabad, a Hyderabad he had grown up in. Of how the nawabs and zamindars moved out of the old city to build their deodis and minor palaces in and around what is Khairatabad now. He said his own grandfather had such a large deodi that they had separate rooms for men and women, the zenanas and mardanas. And rooms for children, rooms for ayahs and gardeners and some more rooms for their families. That they even had a polo ground and golf course in their compound. Imagine!

As if the mardanas were not enough, they also had rooms for men to entertain their visitors, play cards, or have a drink. He told me about the horses they owned and went hunting on, and the panthers and tigers some of the nawabi families kept as pets. The story I liked most was of the nawab who thought the Nampally station was too far to catch a train from, and so laid railway tracks to his house so the train arrived at his doorstep! This was how Begumpet station came up, he told me. Did he tell you these stories too?

All these stories will be forgotten and become, over the course of generations, mere rumours. I must write them down for a future generation, having heard it myself from someone whose family lived through such glorious days.

Already, I hear so much of the old Hyderabad has changed. Soon the older generation, in whose memories these stories survive, will die and be forgotten too. What are we without our histories, Haasini?

It's been more than two years since I last saw Siraj. When I went to his house to bid goodbye before leaving for Connecticut, he looked at me, the new bride, and smiled and blessed me when I touched his feet. And you know what he said?

"You are still not the world's most beautiful woman, Malavika my daughter, but you'll be one when you learn to love a man. No, don't protest, Malavika. I know you are a married woman now. Married to that good looking chap, too. But you will grow up when you love someone so much that you'll want to be with him so much that you'll feel you'll disintegrate into a hundred pieces if you don't see him. Like me unable to forget, Lillette."

Since I was still the new bride very much in love with Vikram, I was not sure what he meant, but felt the pain. I understand all of this much more now, though. That wanting to be loved more. That hoping Vikram and I will forge a friendship in our marriage, be able to take those long walks, sit in amicable quiet and read or have a glass of wine.

Before I took the plane from Hyderabad, I had to see Siraj one last time. I wanted to see him alone, and had to shake off Vikram who was then the just married and possessive husband. However, I am quite certain that if there was one person who knew about my journey to Siraj's house, it was you. You knew, didn't you Haasini?

I didn't have much time, but I am glad I sat with him, beside his planter's chair. As if this was just another evening between us, not that I was about to take a flight out of Hyderabad to an unknown country with a man I barely knew. He got up to fetch a book. I wondered what he would choose to read. He brought out Dylan Thomas. And read Under the Milkwood. *My Peter O' Toole with green eyes.*

He gave me a gift that I unwrapped only after I reached Connecticut. It was The Complete Works of William Shakespeare. A volume he had brought from Oxford. Maybe it was a book he and Lillette read together. I wish I had asked him. I wish I had told him how much he meant to me. He was the dictionary I opened to understand worlds and words. My love for the English language and great works of literature is because of him, surely. Somehow, we think the ones we love will be there with us, forever. In death we are so vulnerable, Haasi, aren't we? The death of those we love, and our own mortality too.

He passed away in the evening, didn't he? In his beloved Hyderabad. I hope they left the door open for him so that he could hear those footsteps from the cobbled stones of Oxford.

There's too much sadness in me today, and no one to share it with, as Vikram will never understand what Siraj meant to me. Siraj was at least 30 years older than my Vikram, but my husband will always be jealous of him and my relationship with him.

Grief shared is still grief, but it's good to share it with a sister. If this letter reaches you before London, good luck. But if you see this only on your return, do send all the rave reviews and photographs.

I miss you more than ever today!

Malavika

CHAPTER 7

When they moved to Hyderabad, Vani decided to send Haasini to the same school as Malavika. Although she was a year or two older than Malavika, Haasini was put in the same class as her for the nuns felt that after going to a Telugu medium school in Guntur, Haasini had some catching up to do.

Sister Ancilla, the Vice Principal who also took their English classes, was fond of the two girls, especially Malavika, who seemed to have read every author the Scottish nun had heard of. She had finished all the Louisa May Alcott books that girls her age were only beginning to read, and was starting on Jane Austen and the Bronte sisters. This young girl seemed to be fond even of Tolstoy – Sister had caught her reading a collection of his short stories one afternoon. She decided that she must speak to Malavika's mother during the PTA meetings about her daughter's unusual reading habits.

It always pleased Sister Ancilla that Malavika spoke correct English, and that her pronunciation was better than most, and spoken without a trace of her mother tongue. Telugu was the Italian of the East, someone had told her when she was sent to the school here, but English was English. However, she disapproved of the way the two of them jabbered in class as if they hadn't seen each other for days, when she knew they were neigbours, and met every day. There was always this hum of conversation from the backbenches, even when she was explaining some line from Wordsworth.

Looking out of the window of her class, Sister Ancilla saw Suhaasini having lunch all by herself that afternoon. Of course, Malavika had chicken pox, she remembered. Haasini herself had brought the leave letter Malavika's mother had sent. Didn't the girl have any friends other than Malavika? What! The child was throwing away half her lunch and closing her tiffin box. These girls wasted so much food! She wished they would bring less of the rice and sambar and those fiery pickles that made such a mess in the yard. She had proposed to Mother Superior that the students be given soup and sandwiches for lunch and taught to eat with forks and spoons, but the principal shot down the idea immediately.

The nun wanted to call out to Haasini in her lovely soprano-like voice and tell her not to look so forlorn. But there was no time to deal with all that now. There was afternoon mass to attend.

Haasini hadn't felt like eating the sambar and ghee rice packed to the brim in the steel dabba. She decided to go to the chapel. She liked the hush and piety of the school chapel. Kneeling down in one of the pews, she asked Jesus to make her friend better. Malavika's face was all blotchy and red and she looked so strange – even ugly. When she had said that aloud to her mother, she'd been slapped. Having chicken pox meant that a goddess was in the house, her mother told her, and if Haasini incurred her wrath, she would enter their house too.

Sure, Haasini thought. The goddess would cross the road and come to their home to inflict chicken pox on her and Dhruvi!

She folded her hands in prayer now, wishing her mother wasn't so superstitious and backward to believe that illness was caused by goddesses. She often contemplated converting to Christianity and becoming a nun. Life would be so much more peaceful then, without a superstitious mother and a nosey brother.

The only problem was, she didn't know of any nun who was also a Bharatanatyam dancer. Haasini wanted to be on stage so very much, performing to an appreciative audience. She wished Hema akka, her dance teacher, who had learnt dance from *the* Kittappa Pillai himself, would not go on with the basics of Bharata Natyam for so long. But Siraj had once made her watch a film on Hema akka on Doordarshan, and she was an astounding dancer.

"You like that, don't you?" Siraj had asked, switching off the television. "You think that comes easy? It takes years of practice to get the arm right like that, or to be able to articulate with your eyes. But you will do it, Haasini. Slender and petite as you are, you have the strength of a great dancer."

Well, she was going to practice morning and night, she told herself after that. She felt a powerful pull within her, even when she was sleeping.

Haasini chided herself now for being so distracted and not saying her prayers in a manner that god could heed them. If she didn't tell Jesus what she wanted exactly, how would he even know what to give her?

Sister Maria had told them during Assembly how the Son of God bore the cross of suffering to redeem humanity. Haasini looked up at the ivory figurine of Jesus at the altar. She often imagined that she was in love with the sad face of Jesus – more than even the blue-faced Krishna her mother went ecstatic over, especially during Janmashtami. She looked up at Jesus, feeling sorry for all the blood on his body and the crown of thorns on his head. He certainly had more troubles than playful Krishna, who only had to handle gopikas and serpents.

Haasini and Malavika had long ago got into the habit of visiting the chapel during school recess. Partly, it was to get into the good books of the nuns, especially the pretty Sister Ancilla. They would dip their hands into the holy water kept in a shell-like cup on the wall and kneel in the pews. When Sister Ancilla saw them she would nod in approval, making the girls beam with the glow of good deeds.

"The nuns are trying to convert my daughter," Vani wailed one day to her husband. "I told you not to move the children to the city, and look what has happened! Even when I take your daughter to the temple, she crosses herself like she was in a church. She always has some story about Jesus. If you were not so busy at the Secretariat you would know how Christian she has become. Do you know, last Christmas she and Malavika went around the colony singing Christmas carols?"

Vani thanked her personal gods, Kamakshi and Meenakshi of Kanchi and Madurai, that her mother had gone back to Guntur or she would have been furious with her for not teaching Haasini enough about Hinduism. Learning to speak English from these Irish and Scottish nuns was one thing, but dressing like one of them?

Vani's mother disapproved of Haasini not wearing pavadas, and of her showing her legs. Who was to tell her that in convent schools everyone had to wear a uniform, and here it was a pinafore. Vani herself didn't care for rules about what girls should wear, and when she complained to Sister Ancilla about how good Andhra families disapproved of girls showing their legs, Sister had patted her on the shoulder and said sometime next year the school hoped to let the girls wear salwars. But they had to first get approval from the school headquarters in Scotland.

Vani liked Sister Ancilla, who she thought looked like Julie Andrews in *The Sound of Music*. But how could she explain to the sweet-looking nun that even salwars weren't good enough? They would make her daughter look like a Muslim, and her orthodox mother would rather have her granddaughter display her legs than look like a Muslim. If only the school would allow girls to wear bindis on their foreheads from next year, Vani prayed. At least that would make them look less like Jane and Mary.

Sister Joanna who took the Moral Science class watched Haasini kneeling in the pew and wondered what the child was praying so hard for. A wave of sympathy filled her, making her want to stroke the girl's bent head. But she had to get her letters and classwork done. Mother Superior would call for a retreat one of these days, and then there would be no time for anything. She sighed, kissed the ivory cross on the rosary around her neck, crossed herself and got up to go to the school building.

Haasini saw Sister Joanna leave and remembered the time she and Malavika had followed one of the sisters into the nunnery. They had always been curious about the lives of nuns, wondering if they really gave up everything in the larger cause of their religion. Did leading an austere life mean they slept on the floor even in winter? Did they have mirrors in their rooms, and if they didn't, how did they dress up? Did they change into nightgowns when they slept or were they always in their white habits? Like their own mothers who never took off their saris even at night, even in summer, though they complained that saris made them feel hot.

So one day, during recess, when they thought no one was watching, they tried to walk into the convent on the pretext of carrying Sister Ancilla's books. They had just pushed the door open to the nun's private quarters when an elderly sister thundered, "Which class do you belong to? Don't you girls know you are not allowed to come in here?" Haasini and Malavika cast their eyes down, and pointing to the notebooks they were carrying said, "Sister Ancilla asked us to bring these books to the parlour."

"Sister Ancilla, so that's whose class you are in. Girls, you can leave the books on the table there. And I will have to speak to Sister. Really! Having young girls carry books for her when Jesus carried the burden of humanity on his shoulders!"

Malavika and Haasini nodded their heads in pretended sorrow, but managed a quick survey of the parlour in the brief minute that the Sister was scolding them. There was a photograph of Christ over which glowed a red electric bulb. Another photograph of mountains, in Switzerland or Scotland, they were not sure. And oh, there were cane chairs which meant the nuns didn't sit on the ground, after all.

They thought they saw a man in the parlour whispering to a young nun. They rolled their eyes, giggled and ran out. Afterwards they had much to discuss and analyse.

"Haasini, do you think that's a jilted lover come to beg Sister to leave the convent and marry him?"

"More like it's a brother come to ask her for money."

"Must be a boyfriend from adolescence who had made her pregnant and now wants to marry her!"

"Gosh, Malavika, will you shut up? What a wild theory that is. But imagine, if we became nuns we wouldn't have a man anywhere near us which would be so sad."

"The Sisters have moustaches. Which man would want to marry them, Haasini?"

A few days later, when they asked Sister Ancilla why she never married and if she was ever in love with a man, she looked at them quietly for a moment as if wanting to tell them something. Instead, she told them that all nuns were married to Jesus.

"Malavika, open your book to page 23 and read out the story of Damon and Pythias to the class," she continued. "And Suhaasini, I want you to write an essay on friendship and show it to me for my next class. No excuses, please."

My dearest Mala,

I haven't had time to eat, sleep, or even sit. But I can't resist sharing the excitement of my very first visit to London, a city Siraj told us so much about. I wish I could pick up the phone and talk to him and tell him all that I have seen and done in the last few days here. If I find the time, I shall certainly make a day trip not only to Stratford-upon-Avon, but also to his beloved Oxford.

Amma and I are staying at her cousin's house near Oxford Street, so it's basically been idli, dosa and Oxford Street. I love the fashionable clothes that everyone wears. Mala, everyone looks like so chic here, and I can't make out the difference between the madams and the mannequins!

I write such poetry at the midnight hour. I should really be sleeping but you know how increasingly I am having problems with my sleep. You will say calm down and rest, but with so much going on in my life, how do I let myself slip into sleep, that half sister of death?

While writing to you, I am wondering if this is how Keats too sat at his desk in his Hampstead home, and looking out into the garden, spied a nightingale and wrote his famous ode!

Ramya Atha lives amidst old English heritage homes. But do you think she is moved by the fact that she stays so close to where a great Romantic poet lived and wrote some of the greatest poems in the English language? Not at all. She continues to pine for Hyderabad. Especially for the chintakayalu that she cannot get here even at the Indian stores in Wembley or wherever. She makes it a point to tell us how she and her husband Ramu are deprived of good chintakai pachchadi. You would think they would find other things to desire here, the Buckingham Palace and tea with the queen, but no, they still want all the things that are from Hyderabad.

The musicians are yet to arrive, and if they don't come in the next two days, I'll have to scout for substitute musicians, sign contracts and train them. Amma is not too happy about that. She wants only the ones we work with from Madras. Anyway, the absence of the musicians has given me time off and I have decided to use it to explore London.

Amma is too tired. But you wouldn't think it is jet lag, the way she and Ramya Atha have been chatting through the day. I am sure Atha is probing into why I am not married, and telling Amma why I cannot make a career out of Bharatanatyam. Ask me something new, ladies, I want to tell them. But I hold my tongue which is getting sharper, Amma says.

I have decided to walk around London all by myself, which is really a relief in my view. Because I believe if you can't walk with someone who walks at your pace looking at the things that interest you, it is better to walk alone. Amma fears that I will get lost, but with an Underground like the one here, I would have to be extremely daft to get lost! Besides, she has to realise I am now old enough, and perfectly capable of taking care of myself.

Just this morning I went to the National Gallery, which is like going through a seven volume book on European painting. Imagine seeing Cezanne, Renoir, Monet, Manet, Degas and all the Impressionists in one breath, all in the original (not some postcard).

I would have liked to have enjoyed each painting at a more leisurely pace but there was no time for all that. Watching great art is surely a spiritual experience. At least it seemed like that when I saw the number of people gravitate towards Van Gogh's Sunflowers, as if they were in the presence of Christ himself. I bought you a poster of the Sunflowers from the museum shop, but will give it to you when we meet sometime soon – to pass on to you the awe I felt at being blessed to see such a great work of art.

Do you know of all people, it's Sister Ancilla I think of most here in England. How we wept when she was summoned back to Scotland! Do you think she is somewhere here, married to a Scotsman with lots of children? Married to Jesus indeed! Did you ever believe that Malavika? Remember how we thought if Jesus could help us not have our monthly periods, we too would offer to become nuns and serve him. How utterly mad we were those days!

But imagine having to give up all the good looking, Anglo Saxon men I see here, and be closeted in a convent. Be closeted and not be able to dance, not be able to take these walking tours of London, or have the freedom to see a Van Gogh or Matisse. Actually, not being able to do much with life but pray is sad – though I don't want to incur a Christian god's wrath by saying it's a waste of time.

Yesterday, as I was in Trafalgar Square feeding the pigeons, a stranger looked at my feet and asked why I painted them red. Did it have anything to do with my religion, he wanted to know.

Why do these people think if I pierce my nose or paint my feet with alta, it's to do with my Hindu religion? Would we ever ask these English whether colouring their hair a deep purple had anything to do with being Christian?

Although I have to admit, this stranger, somewhat middle-aged, was otherwise very kind. He looked at my feet and said they were beautiful. I've had people say that I have beautiful eyes. But my feet? Never heard that one before, I wanted to say. He sat with me for a while at Trafalgar. I told him I was a dancer. He said he was an astronomer. King's College, or elsewhere.

Would I have coffee with him? he asked.

Would I? Yes.

End of encounter. End of letter. Don't ask me too many details for now. I just got a message that the musicians have arrived at Heathrow. And I must sleep now.

Yours in London,

Haasini

CHAPTER 8

Malavika was restless that afternoon. She had been studying History in preparation for the final exams. They were already in Class 7 when their marks and grades were becoming important to their parents. In Andhra, as much as in the rest of the South, a "good education" was mandatory and parents set great store by what their children scored in exams, rewarding or punishing them according to the distinctions and marks they received.

Malavika was trying very hard to read the chapter on how the Mughals came to India to set up one of the greatest dynasties to ever rule the country. She was trying to remember all that they conquered and all that they did for the welfare of their subjects, from building roads, digging wells and laying out gardens. One of Malavika's essays on Emperor Asoka and his renunciation of violence had been lauded and read out by the History teacher some months ago, but she herself was happier in English class where they were doing *Pickwick Papers* as the detailed text. Siraj was happy that they read Dickens so extensively as he said he was one of the greatest novelists of his time.

Distracted by the March heat of Hyderabad, she wished she could go to Haasini's house. If she didn't see Haasini, she could amuse herself with Dhruv. She heard the koels crying out somewhere in the stillness of the late afternoon and decided to get up from the window sill, where she often sat to read, and go out. Her mother would find she had escaped soon enough, but at this moment what she might say didn't matter to Malavika.

Her mother had already scolded her recently for spending so much time in Haasini's house.

"Malavika, Haasini is only your neighbour and a friend, not your sister. Somehow it doesn't seem right that you should be spending so much time in their house," Rekha had said.

"Ma, I am bored. I am lonely in this house," Malavika had wanted to scream back. But the last time she'd said "bored" her mother had given her a long lecture on how she herself had grown up in small towns across the country where her civil servant father had been posted.

"There was no electricity in those places, Malavika, but did we complain? No! We were quite happy telling each other stories. And we didn't have all these fancy paintboxes and brushes that your father keeps buying you. We had to make do with chalk pieces with which we drew rangolis on the floors. Spoilt – that's what you are. We should have sent you to a boarding school where your Avva would not have been paying attention to every whim of yours."

Malavika ran quickly across to Haasini's house to look for Dhruv. She adored him and wished she had a brother like him to play and amuse herself with. She found him now playing with the maid who took care of him. Neither Haasini nor her mother was around. She carried him in her arms, sat him down on the verandah and began to tell him a story.

"There was once a naughty little boy called..." she began.

"Dhruf, but he wasn't naughty at all, Akka!" came the prompt response.

"His name was Dhruvi. But who said he was like you?"

"But Akka, I know this story is about me, and I don't want to hear this story. Tell me another one, about the boy who climbed the tree to see a giant."

"Jack and the Beanstalk? Is that the story you want to hear, you little devil. But that's too boring. Ask your Haasinakka to tell you that one..."

"Beantalk..."

"Beanstalk, not beantalk. Okay, I'll tell you one about a boy whose sister was wicked and cruel."

"Like Haasinakka?"

"No, not Haasinakka. She's the nicest sister in the world, isn't she? But this story is about a sister who troubled her brother. You know, locked him up in a cupboard, and when their mother came to look for the small boy, she would say, 'But Ma, I don't know where Dhruv is.' What's the matter now?"

"Akka I am scared of cupboards, it's dark in there."

"Okay, since you don't like this story, let me tell you another about Gloria," Malavika relented. "Do you know, Dhruv, that Gloria was under the spell of a witch?"

"Witch? Is this a witch story? I'm scared of witches, Akka!"

"You're afraid of everything, Dhruv. Not at all strong like Hanuman. Or Bheem. Maybe I should find myself another little brother. You have to listen to the story first. Witches are of two kinds. Good and bad. Now the one who cast a spell on Gloria was a bad witch. A little like the one in your storybook, but even worse. And she wore a sari, and a long black hat on her head that peaked to the sky almost."

"This is a stupid story, Akka. Which witch wears a sari?"

"But she was a funny witch, Dhruvi, even though in her heart she was wicked. Now what happened was this. She somehow captured Priti. Oh, not Priti. Gloria. And took her to her house where she made her do all her housework."

"But why couldn't she get a servant like Raji or Lakshmi?"

"Well, in Witchland..."

"Is that near Mars, Akka?"

"God, no. Somewhere a little nearer. And the witch would beat Gloria with a large stick when she didn't work properly and left dust on the windows... Dhruvi! What's the matter with you? Why are you crying like that? This story is not about you or your sister, is it? It's about someone else. Some other boy's sister. If you're going to cry then I'm not going to finish the story. And then Haasinakka can't even finish this story because it is *my* story... Come on. Let's see what my mother has been making since morning. I think it's the murukus you like so much. We'll take some and go to the park."

She picked Dhruv up and put him on her waist as she had seen his mother do, and carried him to her house. Post lunch and cleaning up, there was no one in the kitchen save the silence that sat there along the railings listening to them. Malavika opened the steel dabbas that were stacked one against the other, lifting each one of them and listening for the rattling sound that a half-filled tin of murukus would make.

But she couldn't find them anywhere, though she was sure her mother had been making them the whole morning with Vijaya's help. In fact, if the smell of murukus frying had not been so overpowering she would still have been studying.

Malavika put Dhruv on the stool, stopped to wonder if he would topple over, then put her own two legs on one corner of the stool, even as he screamed, holding her leg, "Akka, Akka, be careful! Don't fall down! I don't want you to die!"

"No one dies, Dhruvi, from falling off a stool," she reassured him. She located the dabba in which the murukus were stored and jumped down triumphantly, the sound of murukus in the steel tin rattling behind her, like the church bells that echoed over and over again long after the hour of prayer.

Malavika put her hand into the tin and extricated a muruku, one coil entangled in another, and slid it down Dhruv's little finger.

"Ha, a Vishnu chakra on Dhruv's little finger!" she cried out triumphantly. "Now you can chop off all your enemies' heads and see them fly in the air, just like in the Telugu films that your akka likes to watch," she added laughing. If only she had a brother like little Dhruv she wouldn't have to play with her dolls, which was getting tiring as they would not talk back to her.

When she was younger, she used to like dressing up the dolls in bits of cloth that she pretended were saris and blouses. Sometimes, along with Lakshmi, she played at finding a bridegroom for the doll she called Nimmi. When they imagined they'd found one, they would cook in the small steel vessels. Lakshmi would be a guest and eat broken bits of biscuits and pieces of chocolate that they pretended was wedding food.

But she tired of these dolls very soon, for when she scolded them they just smiled vacantly. Especially the English doll her father had brought for her from London – Natalie, with brown hair and blue eyes, whose arm kept coming out. Malavika had to fix it back in the armhole through the puff-sleeves of her frock.

Malavika now prised open Dhruv's eyes, and gave him a little poke. He began to cry, unlike Natalie, and she smiled happily. But then his wails became so loud that she was sure her mother would hear them and come into the kitchen, and then she would have to confess every crime she had committed in her life. And how would she explain how Dhruv was here and not in his own house?

She lifted the child, stuffed a few murukus into the two heart-shaped pockets of her dress and stepped out of the back door into the yard to take him to the park. Once outside, the boy was dazzled by the light. He blinked his eyes and stopped crying. He was growing heavy, Malavika thought, and put him down on the steps for some respite. She wondered, just for a fleeting moment, if she should be taking the boy to the park without his maid or at least Haasini. But Haasini was prone to closing the door to her room and practicing her dance or singing, and there was no way she could call her without banging on the door.

Or was Haasini in Siraj's house? She was there often these days, talking about Rukmini Devi Arundale or Kalakshetra, subjects that she herself didn't know much about.

"Akka, let's go to the park," Dhruv pleaded.

Malavika carried him across the road because of the traffic, but walked him the rest of the way to the park in the neighbouring street.

Dear Haasi,

You know I enjoy writing letters to you. At times I've written so many that I've kept them away to post together. But these days I have been feeling so listless that I have begun many letters to you and to Amma and left them incomplete. One or two must be lying somewhere by my bedside even now, if I have not torn and thrown them away.

It's winter again and cold in New Haven. This morning, as I saw Vikram taking the car out in the snow and rain, I asked myself, why do we struggle this way in an alien country, so far away from our homes and from all those we love? Yesterday was a horrid day, and in the television news (we are so governed by the weather reports here, and unlike in India, they always turn out so true so that there is no hope of the report being wrong) they predicted today will be another day of heavy snowfall. Do you know what that means? It will be cold, dark, grey the whole day, and I have to wear all the woollens in the world even if I have to go down the street.

What's more, when I think of the elderly lady, Patricia something, who lives in the same neighbourhood, going out in the snow, holding onto a dog on a leash with one hand and groceries with the other, I feel my heart going out to her. To her loneliness. I feel like taking her shopping with me, carrying her bags and dropping her back home. Pat is just as old my Avva was when she came to live with us in Hyderabad. But you should see the way the lady dresses! Her clothes are from Fifth Avenue in New York City, and I must say she has the fanciest minks and boots. I just wonder why she can't get someone to be with her. But then people here place so much premium on being independent. Well, good luck to their independence and the loneliness it can bring.

In the last few years that I've been in the neighbourhood I have never seen her with anyone except the poodle – Pipi – as she calls her. And you won't believe this, Haasini, but Pipi leads the most luxurious life of haircuts and shampoos at the fanciest hairdressers in town! To think how our own grandmothers thought it was blasphemy to wear matching blouses or flowers in their hair after their husbands passed away! This is a different world out here, where they don't think you are old even when you are 70.

Why is it that among the many women we know, who marry and come away to America, no one talks of how difficult life can be here. Of the snow that has to be shovelled, the yard that has to be cleaned, and the bathrooms... Yes, the bathrooms. Even a spoilt girl like me has to go down on her knees and scrub the bathtubs and pots. Heavens! Instead, all that we have from these women is pretty pictures of the country – the Statue of Liberty and the Empire State Building. Fifth Avenue shopping. As if they go to Ellis Island every day and dine at the restaurant atop the Empire State building every other week.

My God! How bitter I sound. Do I sound like a shrew, Haasini? Do you want to know the reason? Amma, I think, hasn't guessed anything as yet. In fact, I'm trusting you to break the news to her. I lost the baby I was carrying. A son, Haasini. Five months old, and I saw him as a blotch of blood in the bathroom. What did I do, or did I not do, Haasini, that I lost the baby, a child I had wanted so much, someone whose soft hair I wanted to touch in this country where I long for the tactile, sometimes even wanting to run and touch Pat's poodle.

Was this some sort of karma working itself out? If I had to be punished, why couldn't it have been me under a motorcar? Me, instead of him who would have grown up to be another little Dhruv. Someone I would have made up stories for. Someone who would have helped me face the world here.

When I'm better I'll call Amma myself. Don't worry. I'll be all right.

I remain even in sadness, your friend, Malavika

CHAPTER 9

Their exams were over, and it was that time of the year that children loved the most. Not only because it was summer when days would stretch endlessly, but also because classes and school were a few weeks of worry away and they could enjoy the long summer break.

Both Malavika and Haasini knew that they had not done well in a few subjects – Malavika in Telugu, and Haasini in Science, and they knew they would have to pay for it by way of extra classes and tuitions whenever the results came. But in the meanwhile, they had planned on doing things together, including a visit to Haasini's mother's hometown in Rajahmundry.

For the moment, Malavika was not only writing a play but planned to have it enacted and call parents, neighbours and school friends to watch it. She would talk to Haasini about how much they should charge as entry fee. That money they could use to buy books at AA Husain, she told herself, not realising that Haasini might not want to invest in books even if it was the only thing Malavika wanted.

The play was about three friends who would unravel clues to find a treasure that had been buried under a hill for centuries. She was halfway through it, when she decided to show it to Siraj. She was sure he would praise her for it. The thought made her smile as she raced to complete the script, sitting on her bed, hunched over a notebook.

But when she took it to to him, Siraj didn't seem happy at all. He sat down with a black Mont Blanc pen to correct a few sentences here and there, only to give up the task in exasperation.

"Malavika..." he said gently.

"Siraj?" she answered becoming stiff like a reed in anticipation of his remarks.

"You can write better than this, girl. Three friends looking for a treasure?"

"Yes, Siraj. I will be John, Haasini will be Nancy, Dhruvi will be...."

"Why, why, Malavika, this half-hearted attempt at writing? You can do better than this imitation of a mystery story from Enid Blyton. Even the names are so Anglicised."

"But..."

"Forget writing your own play, charming as the idea is. Shakespeare – why don't you stage *King Lear,* instead of some dimwitted play that you have written? At least that would sharpen all you childrens' memories, and I can help you with the lines."

"King Lear? It's a tragedy, Siraj."

"So what, girl?

'Pray do not mock me

I am very foolish fond old man,

Fourscore and upward, not an hour more or less, to deal plainly

I fear I am not in my perfect mind,

Methinks I should know and know this man;

Yet I am doubtful: for I am mainly ignorant

What place this is, and all the skill I have

Remembers not these garments, nor I know not

Where I did lodge last night. Do not laugh at me;

For as I am a man, I think this lady

To be my child...' "

Siraj quoted, oblivious of Malavika's expression.

"Nothing, Malavika, there is nothing in the whole of English literature to describe the complex act of recognising a human face as these beautiful lines."

"But Siraj –"

"Don't interrupt me. Let me finish."

Later, after a one-hour lecture from Siraj about *King Lear*, Globe Theatre and Stratford-upon-Avon, Malavika came home to lie sprawled on her bed, crying. Siraj never seemed to like anything she wrote these days. When she was younger he was more appreciative of the little poems she made up and pinned some of them on his notice board, where he put up invitations for talks and weddings.

Once he had even made her read out her poem called *The Mango Tree*, in the presence of his friends who were part of the Hyderabad Poetry Circle that met once a month in his house. Sarojini Naidu was once a member of this poetry circle, he had told her. It was *that* old.

She wondered why Siraj had been behaving so strangely in the recent past. Leave alone chatting with her, he was impatient when she hung around his study longer than necessary. Despite the heat, she decided she was better off sitting on the branches of the mango tree to read these days than in his house.

Malavika had overheard some gossip from her parents recently. A woman had been coming to Siraj's house, her mother was telling her father, and he had been quarreling with her.

Malavika had known about the woman from Oxford who she imagined was his girlfriend or wife. But this Indian woman? She wanted to ask her mother if she was Siraj's wife. Once, when she knew Siraj had a visitor other than his friends from the bridge club and poetry circle, she wanted to drop in to see who it was. But when she saw her mother sitting in the backyard reading *The Illustrated Weekly of India,* she decided against it. There would be too much explaining to do,

It struck Malavika that it was this woman who must be making her genial and wise Siraj so bad-tempered. If he didn't like her, why had he married her in the first place, she wondered. She would have to grow up some more to understand the world of adults, she thought. If only she were older, she would not have minded marrying Siraj herself. He looked so like a Mughal prince, Akbar or someone, albeit ageing.

But Haasini seemed to know more about Siraj. She told her that Lillette whose photograph they had seen hidden in the pages of his *Faber Book of Poetry,* was his girlfriend.

He could not marry her, as his conservative Hyderabadi Muslim family wouldn't allow it. Siraj's mother didn't look the kind who would prevent him from doing anything, from what Malavika could make of the photographs of her in a khada dupatta and large gold and pearl nose ring, which hung in the living room. Haasini said it was rumoured his mother threatened to commit suicide if he married Lillette. He had later married Zehrabibi and had a son.

"But Haasini, how do you know Siraj never liked his wife? My God, how did you even find out his wife's name was Zehra?"

"He told me one day."

"Told you what, Haasini?"

"That he had a wife who walked out one day taking their only child with her. He said he hasn't seen her in a decade."

"A child? Why is it that in all the years I've known him, he never told me anything about his marriage or his son?"

"As if you understand everything."

"Yes. I do."

"Maybe the marriage was not important to him. Only Lillette was. Now, are you or are you not coming to Rajahmundry with us?"

"I want to, Haasini, but my mother..."

"Ask her, talk to her and convince her. Don't be such a namby pamby. "

Malavika was angry with the way things were not going right for her. There was Siraj who no longer seemed to think anything she did was worth his while. There was Haasini who teased her saying she was a baby. And worst of all was her mother, with whom she could not talk to reasonably about a trip to Rajahmundry with Haasini and her family.

"But Amma, Haasini is hardly just a friend. She is like a sister, and you were the one who told me to call her mother Atha."

"That's the problem. We have allowed you to spend too much time in their house. And you know they didn't like you taking Dhruv to the park by yourself."

"But Amma, I have never been to a small town and I want to go. Haasini says Rajahmundry is really lovely, so close to the Godavari. We want to go to the river bank every evening."

"Rajahmundry is just a small Andhra town. What is there for you to see, Malavika? These are old fashioned Andhra homes, and there won't be cots to sleep on, no fridges, or fans, no bathrooms, and the other fancy things you are so used to here."

"Ma, that's okay. I don't always need a cot. I can sleep on the floor with Haasini and Dhruv."

"Sleep on the floor? Let me see you sleep one day on the floor here without a mattress! The amount of fuss you make if Lakshmi doesn't make your bed one day. She even has to put back the clothes you pull out from the cupboards and drop all over your room. I haven't seen anyone so irresponsible as you. God alone knows who will marry you and who will take care of you," Rekha went on in frustration.

"Ma, please don't be angry with me like that. It's alright, I won't go on this holiday. I will stay here with you and Pa, while all my friends have a good time. Never mind if I don't have anyone to play with when Haasini and Dhurv are gone."

"Malavika, that's no way to talk to your mother. For that you'll stay in your room and work on your Telugu reading. At least read the Telugu *Chandamama* and not the English one."

Malavika was so upset with her mother's harshness that she stayed in her room, and went to bed earlier than usual. It was at times such as these that she missed her Avva most.

If she were still alive, she would not have let her cry. She would have entertained her with stories till she forgot why she was crying. But she was gone now. Her dearest, dearest Avva passed away just like that one evening some months ago, collapsing in the bathroom. Her mother and father told her then that Avva was no more, she had gone to meet her Thatha. And Malavika had no one else in the world who would love her ever again in her life as her Avva had.

Amma had told her she would give her Avva's diamond earrings and nose ring when she got married, but all that Malavika wanted was to hear her grandmother's voice as she raised it to tell Vijaya how to make crisp dosas, and the smells she brought with her in the evenings, of tinctures and balms that she used for her joint pains.

In the morning, her father came into the room to find her eyes swollen and red.

"Child, what makes you so sad and weepy? Your pillow is all wet. What is that you want so badly that makes you cry so much?" he asked, hugging her.

"Pa!" she sobbed into the pillow refusing to look at him. Her anxious father was bewildered. What could the matter be with his young daughter who was, he imagined, mature for her age with all the books she constantly read?

"Pa…" said Malavika, still talking into the pillow.

"Yes, child." He waited for her to continue.

"Haasini and Dhruv are going to their family home in Rajahmundry. Amma won't let me go with them. She thinks I can't take care of myself. I've never been to a small town, Pa. I want to go with them. It's only for a few days. Besides, I don't know what to do here without Haasini. It is so boring here without her. Or at least if they left Dhruv behind it wouldn't be so bad, Pa," she continued from deep inside her pillow.

"We could go to the zoo together. Or you could hike up to Golconda with me. You know your mother is not a great one for outdoors, but we could go and I could tell you about the Qutb Shahi kings," her father offered.

"'Pa, please, I don't want to go hiking with you. Or hear about the Golconda kings."

"Oh, let's see you smile. Then we will talk to Amma!"

"You talk to her."

Malavika never got to know what charm her Pa used, but her mother reluctantly agreed to let her go on the holiday.

When the time came for departure, her father wanted to drop her off at the Secunderabad station, and Rekha decided to go with them. Malavika couldn't contain the excitement that ran through her, jolting her like their ageing car did now – APU 478, which needed to go for repairs very soon.

She looked at her mother, leaned to the front of the car, and touched her on the shoulder lightly.

Her mother looked back startled. "Malavika! You!" she smiled. "Be careful with the suitcase in the train. You already forgot about it in your room as if you had nothing to do with that piece of baggage. I don't know when you will learn some responsibility."

"Amma, sorry. I won't forget anything, and I promise to be careful."

"What was the need to see Haasini again in the morning, when the next few days anyway you are going to be with her? Don't trouble Vani Atha. Eat well. And this is most important..."

"Yes, Ma?"

"Comb your hair twice daily. If you can't do it yourself, take Haasini's help. How well she plaits her hair. And if I hear from Dhruv that you've been sitting in your room and reading, not helping around the house, I will be very angry. You know that."

"Let her be, Rekha..." murmured her father. Don't be hard on the child, he wanted to say. Remember how hard we prayed to have a child when we didn't have one even after three years of our marriage? She's a gift from the goddess Meenakshi, Rekha. So, like my sister who passed away. I even wanted to name her after her. Lalitha. But you named her after Kalidasa's heroine in *Malavikagnimitra*. Now I can't even think of her as anything else. Look how our little girl has grown. How long before she gets married and goes off, and whom will you scold then, Rekha?

"Ram, what are you thinking? Do keep an eye on the traffic. Hyderabad traffic is growing and is not at all what it was earlier," Rekha jerked him back to reality.

"Nothing, Rekha. I was just thinking about Malavika and how much we will miss her."

"But she's going only for a few days. She will be back soon, Ram." Rekha touched his shoulder gently.

"Pa.........! Oh God! I've forgotten..."

"What have you forgotten? Not the water bottle, I hope..."

"No, Amma, that's right here. Siraj told me to keep a diary about my journey. He said all great travellers keep a diary. Herodotus, Tavernier, Ibn Batuta. He bought me a lovely one too with an embossed leather cover. I don't know where I left it in the room. But at least I've taken the Tolkien."

"Never mind the diary, Malavika. You have money. Buy a notebook in Rajahmundry."

"But the diary..."

"Forget the diary now. It's too late to go back. We are at the station already. You get off from the left side of the car and hold Amma's hand..."

By the time Ram found a parking space for the car and came to the platform looking for them, Malavika was already seated in the train with Haasini's family, bouncing on the cushioned seats of the First Class compartment and quite oblivious that her parents were standing at the window.

Ram amd Rekha were sad to see her go. Only the other day she had held their hands tightly so she wouldn't lose balance and fall on the ground. And now here she was, waiting to fly away from them. When did children stop being children, they wondered.

Ram got onto the train to see his daughter once again. He was surprised at the way Malavika sat with her legs crossed, her skirt below her knees like a young lady. Who had been teaching her all these things, he thought, amused. Must be Rekha, such a graceful woman herself, whom he had not stopping loving even for a day. Malavika would acquire her mother's poise some day, he was sure.

When Malavika opened her eyes in the moving train she saw it was already morning and they had left Hyderabad far behind them. The jostling of the train must have put her to sleep, she couldn't remember when. She pressed her face against the window to see one small station after another pass by. As the train picked up speed it would go dhadak, dhadak, dhadak, beating to the rhythms of her own heart. The sounds became louder as they passed small cactus shrubs. Dhadak, dhadak, dhadak.

"These are paddy fields, where rice grows," Haasini's father explained to her and Dhruv. "When the paddy is harvested, they sow a second crop."

Haasini had woken up too but was practising mudras with her mother. It was always nice to hear Vani Atha hum a raaga, and see Haasini dance to her mother's rendering of a kriti. But Malavika wished Haasini would spend time with her too, playing cards or just chatting.

She was soon distracted by the little boys and girls by the tracks waving to passengers on the train. She waved back to them envying them their freedom.

But what was it they were doing near the railway lines? Surely not...

"Uncle!" She turned towards Haasini's father. "Don't they have toilets in their houses?"

Haasini squealed from the other berth. "Bathrooms, Malavika? You mean I never told you before that in my Maama's house, too, there will be no bathrooms?"

"No bathrooms?"

"And guess where you and I are going to have a bath. In the yard, in a small space partitioned by bamboo twigs!"

Bathe in the open? She would not have a bath at all, then, even if it was for a week. She was so shy that she locked the bathroom door even in her own home when she was taking a shower.

"Haasini is teasing you, Malavika," Haasini's mother told her. "We have more than one bathroom. And wait until you meet Haasini's Ammamma. She's waiting to give you two girls oil massages. She'll make you sit in the sun in the yard, give you a nice oil massage, and then scrub you with pesarapindi mixed with with pasupu that will make your skin glow. That's what a beauty routine is, not going to those parlours that have caught everyone's fancy in Hyderabad these days."

"Please, Amma, I don't want to have those oil massages this time. But since Mala has never had them, let her have one every day."

"Actually, Vani Atha, I'm allergic to turmeric. I don't even like it in my food," Malavika mumbled.

"This is the first time I've heard of that, Mala," Haasini teased.

"Oh, shut up, Haasi. Are you my friend or not?"

"Girls, let's not have any fights now. If all of you get washed up, I'll get all of us some idlis at the next station," Haasini's father stepped in.

"Idlis? No, Pa. I don't want any," Haasini said.

"And I haven't even brushed my teeth," Malavika added.

"Or brushed your hair," Haasini said, looking at her.

Venu bought idlis and coffee for all of them. Even if the children didn't like the idlis smeared with spicy chutney, they enjoyed the watery coffee that they were allowed to drink.

For the rest of the journey, they amused themselves playing cards. Then, as it gew time to reach Rajahmundry, Venu and Vani got all the luggage together in preparation for disembarking.

"Maama!" squealed Haasini, even before the train screeched to a halt, waving to an elderly man waiting with his son on the platform.

That must be her uncle and her cousin Ravi, thought Malavika, jumping off the steps of the train onto the platform.

"Haasini, this must be your friend, Malavika. What a pretty girl!" remarked Haasini's Maama after giving Haasini a hug.

Malavika took one look at Ravi, and cursed herself. Why had she not changed from the blue bathroom slippers she had on for the train to the lovely pink sandals her mother had bought for her just before she left?

She smoothed her hair. At least she had on the American barette clip that her aunt from Houston had brought for her last time round. She looked slyly at Ravi, and found him looking at her.

Malavika smiled. Already Haasini was holding her Maama's hand and skipping around. Just like her to do that – abandon her who didn't know a soul in this Andhra town, she thought. A coolie in a red shirt and a lungi hitched up to his thighs, pushed her, shouting "Paapa, jarugumma!" and almost dropped the huge steel trunk he was balancing on his head onto her feet.

Paapa? Did she look like a baby? Malavika wondered. She was even carrying her own suitcase with her clothes all packed neatly for this trip. Surely this made her grown up!

Ravi and his father had come to the station in their small Herald car. So while Haasini, Dhruv and their father got into that, she had to climb into the autorickshaw with Vani Atha and Ravi. The auto rattled through the crowded streets for a while, turning onto what was once a road, and then stopped because it became too narrow a lane for it to enter.

Malavika looked at a small house, with open sewage and pigs around it. A typical Andhra town, her mother would have said triumphantly.

"No, that's not the house. You have to walk inside the lane some more," said Ravi who seemed a nice, polite boy even if his English had a Telugu accent.

They arrived at a house with a red-tiled roof and large granite pillars in the verandah, around which Dhruv was swinging madly to make himself dizzy.

"Malavika," Haasini said, "at what snail's pace has your auto travelled? We have all not only washed up, but eaten pesarattu made by Ammama. And your mother has called twice already wanting to know if you were alright. I don't know what she thinks would happen to her baby girl," Haasini teased.

A wave of homesickness washed over Malavika. She suddenly yearned for her mother even if all she did was scold her for not combing her hair.

In fact, that night when she was speaking to her mother over the phone, she began to cry. Silly tears of children who don't know what they want. Salty tears that she licked over and above the din of a pillow fight. Alongside, some adult had turned on the radio for Wednesday night's Binaca Geetmala, though the hit film songs as well as host Ameen Sayani's baritone were drowned by static in this distant Andhra town.

Mattresses had already been spread on the floor of the large room. Malavika stepped over them to sleep next to Haasini, and was about to lie down when she saw a figure quivering underneath a checked sheet on the other side of her. It was little Dhruv, shaking with fear. Haasini and Ravi were deep into ghost stories and seemed to exclude her completely, so she lay down quietly. But she too began to get frightened by Ravi's talk of the ghost that he said haunted the pond near their house, where he promised to take them the following evening. She moved towards Dhruv and hugged him tight, muttering the Hanuman Chalisa that her Avva had taught her to recite whenever she was afraid.

Soon all of them had frightened themselves stiff but continued until midnight, fascinated by the ghosts and ghouls, till they fell asleep exhausted with fear and hugging each other. Ravi too, though he was the oldest among them, and he decided to go and sleep with his grandmother.

Ravi paid unusual attention to Malavika the next day during a special lunch the family had organised for all of them. They were all sitting in a row on the floor eating off banana leaves, and when he saw that Malavika wasn't able to handle the majjigapulusu that kept slipping off the leaf, he got up to get her a silver plate.

Knowing that the plate was kept exclusively for him, Haasini raised her eyebrows.

Her friend did look pretty in the pattu pavada and odhni that her Ammama had insisted they both wear. Malavika was in a green pavada and pink blouse, with little gold jhumkies in her ears that Haasini's mother had persuaded her to wear for the lunch.

Everyone kept telling Haasini that she had such a beautiful friend.

Haasini looked away trying not to show her emotions. She looked at the ghee rice and pappu rice on her leaf, and suddenly decided she had eaten enough and wanted to get up.

My dear Mala,

I wonder if you got my last letter that I wrote to you from London. I haven't heard from you in a long time. Or maybe your letters are waiting for me at home in Hyderabad.

I am now in Paris and so looking forward to performing in this city of eternal light. And dare I say, city of eternal love? I went to the Louvre two days ago and it was quite an exhausting experience, I have to admit. What can I say of the Mona Lisa except that she was enigmatic, and like any beautiful woman always surrounded by an army of admirers! I liked the Rodin and Monet museums so much better. I could have sat for hours together before Monet's Water Lilies, looking at the light playing on the lily pools much the same way that he did.

I met a young man at the gardens there, Pierre, who guessed I was an Indian classical dancer. I didn't ask him how he knew that, but he later told me over coffee at a patisserie in Montmarte that he studied Carnatic flute with Lalgudi. We had a most interesting conversation as he walked with me all over Montmarte where the likes of Renoir and Dali had their ateliers. Mala, if you and I could do a trip to Paris one day, what fun it would be. I do miss you, especially when I have something exciting to share with you. News such as Pierre, that I know you're now curious about.

He wanted to stay in touch with me. I told him to come for my performance the following day. He may have, but didn't come backstage to see me. He wanted to know if he could call me when he was next in Madras for the music season. I told him yes. But somehow, I have learnt to let these friendships be what they are. Why look for anything more? I know Amma is anxious for me to get married, but I will find the man I want one day. For all you know, here in Paris.

I forgot tell you that while I was in London, I met your admirer, Ravi. Remember him? My cousin Ravi, whom you met when you came with us on that summer sojourn to Rajahmundry. You must have been hardly 13 but looked so lovely that you had all the boys in town lusting after you, especially Ravi.

Well, he went on to study medicine in Hyderabad and went to London where he did his residency and stayed back. Did I ever tell you all this? I can't remember. He married a pretty little (or large, I don't know) English girl who now wants a separation. We don't have an opinion on her, as she didn't even think it important for her to come along when Ravi took us out for dinner.

I wonder why marriages crumble and crackle halfway through, when the commitment has been made for a lifetime. Is it that people change their minds along the way or that their expectation of this institution itself changes in between? Or maybe marriage cannot take the burden of a lifelong commitment, for we grow and change as human beings. I don't know what it is that we are looking for in marriage finally – the excitement of a soulmate as a lover, or the comfort of always having someone you care about, sharing dinner with you and helping you clear the dishes after that?

I do hope marriage and Vikram are all that you wanted them to be. Your mother was in fact telling me that you would soon announce that you are pregnant, but she told me not to discuss this with you. Me and my big mouth! I am not sure if it's Rekha Atha's fantasy or that you are really pregnant because I can't believe you wouldn't have told me about a baby.

I am in a train going to the South of France as I'm writing now. (I couldn't finish it in Paris.) Everything is so clean and quiet on the train here, and everyone so well behaved. It's quite unlike the train journeys we used to make when we were young, when we would be covered with soot from head to toe. And so, we'd wear the oldest clothes in the cupboard for travelling, and the ugly, if useful, Bata chappals. Here they are so well dressed, and look so chic even on trains. Of course, I must not forget I am going to the South of

France where all the rich and famous live, and they are bound to be tres chic! I almost died when the train stopped at Monaco, Grace Kelly country. But I have to go further. I am performing in Nice, in an old cathedral, which will be inspiring.

I feel so far away from home suddenly, Mala. Images of my grandma flash before me. You were there that evening. We were all sitting in the large central courtyard of my uncle's house in Rajahmundry, and when she began to sing 'Krishna nee begane, baro', the Purandaradasa Kirtane, I got up and began to dance. I know none of you were paying attention to my dance. Maybe I was still not that good. I don't know what it was, but I continued to dance. I have yet to recapture the magic of the moment but here in Nice, I shall attempt to do so.

I realise only now, how Amma and Ammama were such die-hard lovers of classical music and dance, even with their very traditional upbringing. Were it not for them, I would not have imbibed this love, or the discipline that classical dance requires. Do you remember how I did not have a life after school? While you went to college in Hyderabad, I was sent off to Madras to study at Kalakshetra. You talk of missing home now – I have not been home since I was 17 years old!

I am convinced dance is a calling, and that it requires the same kind of dedication as any other profession. Who is to say that Balamma's passion for dance was any less than Ramanujam's devotion to numbers? Or that Martha Graham was not as great as Einstein? I still am not sure why I was chosen to dance, but I have begun to think of it as a sacred calling. Only the French would understand the sanctity of the arts. Otherwise, why would they organise a performance in an old church?

Ravi sends his love. I told him you were happily married. I know that was unnecessary, but I do believe way back then he was completely besotted with you.

I am joking! He actually said, somewhat sadly, "If your friend Malavika remembers me still, tell her that I enquired about her, and said hello." Aha!

From a speeding train to Nice,

Yours,

Haasini

CHAPTER 10

There were little seeds of red pomegranate on a porcelain plate, made all the more red by the fading light of the evening which came far too quickly during these winter months. The girls were sitting in Siraj's house reading Malavika's favourite book, *Gone with the Wind*. In their colourful clothes – one wearing a pink sweater over black bell-bottomed trousers, and the other in a green and yellow salwar kurta – they looked as if they too would dissolve into the painting of the evening.

Though they were leaning against the pillars of the verandah of the old Hyderabad house, in their mind's eye they were looking through a window into the large house called Tara, where well-dressed folk were descending from their carriages and walking into a grand house for a party. They could hear the music and laughter around them. They weren't in Hyderabad at all, but far away, deep in America's South, in Georgia, a century ago.

Malavika was wishing that the elastic of her bell-bottoms didn't hurt so around her stomach and she pulled it a little below the navel for comfortable breathing. She crouched forward, for these were her favourite pages when Rhett Butler met Scarlett for the first time. She had read the book once by herself, but now she wanted Haasini to move more rapidly with her reading.

The pomegranates that they were picking up with their hands and dropping by fistfuls into their mouth were almost over. Only a few were left when some of them slipped from Malavika's hands and rolled out onto the ground. She absent-mindedly followed the movement of the ruby red pomegranate so closely, it seemed as if the progress of the evening depended on the journey of those seeds.

Malavika, all of a sudden, was jerked back into the world of an adolescent girl with its many fears. Fear, in particular, of the death of a loved one.

Siraj had suddenly been taken to the hospital three days ago due to breathlessness. The doctors said it happened because his lungs were weak from smoking. When Malavika went to visit him with her mother, he had tubes that went from the veins of his hands and ended in a mask on his face. He looked like a Martian who was about to take off into space, she thought. She had brought a bunch of chrysanthemums with her, but the nurse wouldn't let her carry them into the room.

"Why can't I give Siraj these flowers? Is he going to die, Ma?" Malavika asked.

"Shhh, don't say such inauspicious things. Just go up to him and say hello. And try to speak softly, be gentle," her mother said.

Malavika had not wanted to say hello but sit by his side and read Yeats that sounded so magical when he read it out to her.

'Had I the heavens' embroidered cloths,

Enwrought with golden and silver light,

The blue and the dim and the dark cloths

Of night and light and the half-light,

I would spread the cloths under your feet:

But I, being poor, have only my dreams;

I have spread my dreams under your feet;

Tread softly because you tread on my dreams.'

Remembering that evening, Malavika's eyes brimmed with tears. She wanted to tell Haasini that she was not going to let Siraj die. Already she had seen her beloved Avva pass away, though at that time it had seemed that she had merely gone to visit her brother in Calcutta. Only, she never returned to her room and her mother had called Lakshmi to pack her things and give them away to the poor. Wanting to believe that Avva would return one day, Malavika had hidden her reading glasses and the small photo album that she'd always kept by her side, which had photographs of Thatha, her mother and her uncle as children. There was one photograph of Malavika as a baby that was never pasted but stayed loose amidst the pages.

She wanted to talk to Siraj about Govindaiah, Lakshmi's husband. She felt uncomfortable about the way he looked at her and smiled. He had a thick moustache that he curled like a Telugu film villain, and a dark body that she could see through the holes of his banian. Recently, in the morning when she had dropped the towel after a bath and was getting into her uniform, she saw him by the window peering into her room – two eyes upon her naked body.

Malavika's breasts had begun to grow. She was becoming conscious of their taking shape, especially since her mother had brought her her first Maidenform bra.

Malavika had caught him looking at her from the window whose bars he had held on to tightly for a better view of the room. She didn't know if this fear and shame she felt when she caught him looking at her had anything to do with what her mother kept telling her these days. That she now was a young woman, she should make sure she drew the curtains when she dressed, not wear tight clothes, or let any man touch her.

Though she felt uncomfortable, she imagined all that Govindaiah wanted to do was to break into her room and take away her small radio. She had heard Lakshmi telling her mother that he couldn't hold a gardener's job for long, that he often came home drunk and beat her up if she did not give him money.

He was a thief, that's what he was, though she was not clear why he was not looking into her parents' room that had both money and jewellery. She would certainly keep an eye on his movements.

She wanted to tell Siraj all of this so he would sort it all out, her fears, her dreams. She yearned to sit with him and look at old maps, tracing countries that she knew existed somewhere. He would tell her about how indigo dyed cloth was sacred in Africa, where they used it for rituals associated with birth and death. It was called the cloth of sorrow there, he said. He told her of how valued kalamkaris, or chintz as they were called in the West, had been at one time in the salons of London and

Paris, and how traders actually stayed in port towns like Machilipatnam to have them printed. He would show her rare telia rumals, in squares of black and red, that were dipped in seasame oil, which he said were common in Hyderabad. He had promised to gift her a telia sari when she graduated.

"These are precious not because they are expensive. In fact, telias are not expensive at all – they're worn by gardeners around their waist or over their saris in the Public Gardens. But they will be precious, my love, because in time there will be no one to to weave this complicated double ikats, such as these," he had told her.

There was comfort in the world of knowledge. In books and especially in poetry. And in his voice. If only he would get better and come home.

Haasini, tired of reading, was now painting Malavika's toenails with a bottle of nail polish that she had carried with her. It was becoming dark, and Govindaiah came to fetch them from Siraj's house. He was walking over the dry leaves shed by the big trees, towards Malavika.

"Baby, come home now, let's go," he said, staring at her.

"Govindaiah, you go. I will walk home with Haasini," she said, wishing he would just go away and leave them alone. But he stood, waiting.

All of a sudden it was dark. There was no one in Siraj's house. Not even Abida, who had taken the opportunity of Siraj's absence to visit her son in the Old City.

Haasini, Malavika wanted to say, he is not a good man. I am scared of him.

But would Haasini understand her fears? It was better that she discuss Govindaiah with Siraj. She prayed again that he come home soon.

"Siraj," she would say, sitting by him on the mora in his room. "I am afraid of Govindaiah."

He would pat her gently and tell her that there was nothing in the world that she should be afraid of, now or later. That she should look the person in the eye and tell him that she was not afraid of anything in the whole world. Even, and especially, during the moments she was scared or worried. With these thoughts she fell asleep only to feel someone on her bed.

"Siraj, I thought you were dead," she wanted to scream, opening her eyes as she felt someone's touch on her body. But it was not Siraj who was stroking her hand. It was Govindaiah sitting on the bed by her feet, his other hand on her thigh, and his lungi riding up high.

But the scream choked inside her throat, and was buried in the dark of the early morning, as she saw Govindaiah hurry out of her room.

She would never know what else he had done. But that touch on her exposed thigh sat in the deep recesses of her psyche for years, and revolted her.

She would never be able to talk about it, this shame.

Not with Haasini. Most certainly not with her mother.

This shame of childhood, of having seen a grown man's penis in that early morning hour.

✳ ✳ ✳

My dear Haasi,

Guess what, Haasi? I have now enrolled myself for a workshop on Ritual Hinduism at one of the studios in New York City. Amma was shocked when I told her about the class and what I was paying for it ($1000 for about 10 classes). But she doesn't realise, nor can I tell her, that I am doing it more to meet people and make friends. Dr Derek, our professor who has studied with yoga teachers in Madurai, says that Hinduism is not a religion but a way of life. He looked at me and said that the class was lucky to have an Indian Hindu. Indian Hindu?

I was hoping he wouldn't make me stand up and speak about our rituals or gods, and thank god he didn't. I know for one of the classes he will want me to wear a sari and speak about some birth or death ritual, but until then I am happy wearing these skirts that I bought at at Macy's. But on sale. The good thing about this country is that everything comes up for sale, and one day, I imagine, you should be able to buy the Kohinoor diamond too, only you must have patience and bide your time.

My humour has returned as you can gather. Yes, I am happy to step out of the silence of my home in New Haven. You don't know what joy it is to be out in the summer months walking the streets of Manhattan, watching the young women in their so-so-short dresses and stillettos, to watch children in strollers in Central Park with their mommies, to pick up a sandwich and sit at the Lincoln Center listening to musicians playing Beatles' songs that leave me humming and happy...

'It's been a hard day's night, and I been working like a dog

It's been a hard day's night, I should be sleeping like a log

But when I get home to you I'll find the things that you do

Will make me feel alright....'

I take the subway to Manhattan, and people have warned me to be careful. But to me, when I enter a subway station it's a challenge to come out unhurt. I enter one, refusing to meet the drunk and the

derelict in the eye, half-expecting to be attacked. When I emerge in another street unscathed, it's a relief whose sigh I'm sure you'll hear in another part of the country. The excitement is in the fear as much as in the relief of not being attacked. Do you get what I am saying? But anyway, they're not all that bad, our New York subways.

But how we live burdened with these subliminal fears that are imprinted deep on our psyche. You know, like my constant fear in childhood that a parent will die by the time I come back from school in the afternoon, and the relief to find Amma standing, smiling at the gate.

Or the oppressive dreams at night in which you think you will be stifled or drowned, only to wake up to another ordinary morning when you have to go to school. I always feared the dwarf who appeared standing by my window staring at me. What a relief it was after that to get up and realise that the dwarf couldn't get to me in this world, though I don't know which world he was part of. Even you, Haasini. How many times I feared that I would lose you. That you would move out of my life. Get married, go away and forget me. Silly me.

Now there are mornings when I wish I was in a dream where the baby was still inside me, safe.

It's so strange that Vikram doesn't seem to be as affected by the loss of the baby as I am. I admit, though, I have become moody and difficult. Nothing he says pleases me and I am secretly delighted that he finally reacts to something – my stubbornness!

I eat little, which upsets Vikram, and sleep even less, happy to be reading through the night. I sometimes wish life was about moving from one page of a book to another, living someone else's story, not mine. I wouldn't have to face reality. The reality of my life, of having to do laundry, cooking and the dishes, and more dishes and laundry the next day.

I know I am sounding disgruntled, but last weekend we had a party and I spent a whole week cooking, and another whole week cleaning up the mess. The Indian migrants here run such perfect homes with not a spot of dust anywhere, or a single cushion out of place. Don't their children jump on sofas like we did at home, loving that bouncy-bouncy feeling? But then the children here are so angelic too. Such high achievers, everyone studying to be a doctor or working at getting a PhD.

Whenever I vist their fancy homes in Long Island or Westchester, they make me feel so inadequate about not keeping a proper home, that I come back and scrub my kitchen, and arrange flowers and light incense sticks all over the house.

And they make such lavish spreads for their dinner guests. I have eaten the best rasmalai and paneer here. Wonder what the secret is, though I know that even if they told me, I wouldn't be able to do it. I cannot ever aspire to be that perfect NRI wife though I know my NRI husband could do with fancy entertaining with our silver and fine china that will help his career. If only one of them had read a book, I would be willing to cook them a good pulao. Vikram says books are not everything. I guess for most they are not.

Another thing I need to tell you, though I don't know how you will react...

One image from my childhood has been bothering me recently. Of Govindaiah. The thought of his dark body fills me with dread even now. I am not sure why. I am not entirely clear if I had seen him naked making love to Lakshmi or if he made a lewd gesture at me. But throughout my growing up years, I was afraid of being assaulted by him sexually. The same feeling of nausea and dread rises in me when Vikram touches me these days. I wish he would be a little more kind. Who would want to have sex now when my heart is grieving?

That's the reason I insisted on taking the class on Ritual Hinduism – ask me one day what it is. Vikram went into a rage because these classes cost almost $100. He said that if I went to the Ramakrishna Mission in Hyderabad, I could have received enlightenment for free. He does have a sense of humour, my Vikram. If only he were a little more patient with me, and not so obsessed *with the stock market and or baseball, we might have got along. Unfortunately, I have little interest in either.*

When will you get married, my Haasini? Is it that you are busy and have no time to fall in love with anyone? As they say, when the time comes and you are ready for it, the man will walk into your life.

But I was thinking too, except for the fact that we women can't make love to each other (thought they do even that in America, and a same sex partner is becoming an accepted thing), we could happily live with each other. To begin with, we wouldn't have to bother with this letter writing and constant need (mine) to be connected. We could sit together and watch Audrey Hepburn and Gregory Peck in Roman Holiday *any number of times. And we could banish football, baseball, cricket forever.*

A woman would hold your hand and let you weep on her shoulder if you told her about a stillborn child. Not say, it's going to be bearish this morning on Wall Street, and I have to hurry, when you want to have coffee and chat with him. Men!

I have to end this letter now. I have to put my mind to a paper on Adi Shankara's life that I have to write. I have tentatively titled it, 'Shivoham, Shivoham'.

My mother would be so proud of me!

Love,

Malavika

CHAPTER 11

Though Haasini and Malavika found it difficult to wake up early to walk to the bus stop at the end of the street, they loved to take the double-decker bus to school. Now that they were old enough to go on their own, their parents felt it would teach them to be independent and tough.

It was a green coloured bus, run by the local bus service, going to different schools at Gunfoundry meant especially for older children. It was a tumultuous ride of adolescents either happy imagining they were in love, or unhappy that they were not.

As the girls waited at the bus stop in their pink pinafores and white blouses, pockets filled with leaking fountain pens and chocolates, schoolbags full of secrets and notebooks, the bus would rumble up spewing diesel fumes. The smell of this in their noses mingled with the faint aftertaste of Protinex or Ovaltine that they were made to drink in the morning, so that whenever the girls smelt diesel in later life, they associated it with these early morning rides in the double-decker bus and Protinex in the pits of their stomachs.

They would clamber onto the upper deck, and Haasini was happy that Dhruv who insisted on going with them, much to her annoyance, liked to sit with Malavika, so she could take the window seat and sit by herself. She would put her chin on the bars of the window, press her nose against the lower half of the window and look at the cyclists and rickshaws that whizzed past below as in a Charlie Chaplin film. She wanted to wave at other schoolchildren bundled together in a cyclerickshaw or stick her tongue at young men on scooters who would wink at her.

Malavika, who sat behind her, frowned at Haasini's behaviour. Frivolous young girl, the frown would imply, disconcerting Haasini even if she was the older of the two.

Haasini knew that Malavika was watching her disapprovingly when a good looking young boy, almost effeminate in his looks, a senior from their school, began to take the seat next to hers, at least whenever he found it empty. Haasini liked that nearness of a male presence. That unfamiliar smell of another. Not the smell of her father or Siraj, but the very male smell of men's colognes that she inhaled in magazines from abroad that Siraj subscribed to.

Although she smiled at him whenever she caught his eye, she didn't know what to say to him or how to begin a conversation. If Malavika were not breathing down her back from behind, she would have liked to lean against his shoulder like romantic heroines of the Georgette Heyer novels that she was beginning to get addicted to.

Recently, she had realised that he was the prefect of Blue House, called Golconda. She was in Red House, Charminar, and she wished all of a sudden that she was in Blue House. Maybe she would ask Sister Ancilla to change her house. After all, she was good at classical dancing and singing, and could win medals for Blue House, which usually did badly in competitions.

She sighed, looking out of the window, not even noticing that they had just passed the Lakdi-ka-Pul bridge, where once again someone had committed suicide by jumping off from the bridge onto the train tracks. Once, she and Malavika had seen the head of man roll outside the rail track as the body was crushed under a train. The bus went past too quickly, so they couldn't remember if they had seen blood too.

In all the reverie and daydreaming, Haasini suddenly sensed an outstretched hand offering her a Chiclet. Chewing gum was forbidden in school, but there was nothing to prevent her from accepting it during a bus ride. She was never going to open the yellow cover in which were ensconced the Chiclets that had just made their entry into the country. In fact, till she died she would not chew on them, she thought, as she slipped them into the pocket of her school tunic that was getting tighter by the day around the chest.

"Thank you," she said softly, and smiled at Blue House. One of these days she would ask him his name, not today. This much was enough from someone she had such a severe crush on, she told herself.

Her daydreaming was shattered by screams behind her, as if the bus was on fire and they would all have to rush down the narrow steps and out of the bus.

"Akka! Akka!" Dhruv was shrieking.

"Shhh! Dhruv, can you not scream like that?" she glared at him.

"Akka, can I have some gum?" he asked.

She was of course reluctant to give him her precious gum, but Blue House took out another packet of Chiclets from his school bag and gave it to Dhruv. Did the boy's father own a chewing gum factory, Haasini wondered.

Dhruv opened the packet, threw the paper out of the window, put the gum into his mouth, and spat it out into a piece of paper, all in a jiffy.

Haasini was embarrassed. Why did she have a brother who called her Akka so loudly in a public bus? Besides, he was littering the streets! Why didn't Malavika stop him and tell him to behave himself? She hoped Blue House wouldn't think she came from an uncivilised family. Actually, why did she have to have a brother at all?

But Blue House didn't seem to mind Dhruv. He was shaking his hands as if he were a gentleman, not a brat. She even heard him ask Dhruv if he was already in middle school.

Dhruv for some reason was tongue-tied. It was Malavika who answered for him. Haasini hoped that Blue House thought Dhruv was Malavika's brother, not hers.

Sure enough, he was telling Malavika that her brother was such a cute little fellow.

Haasini had an impulse to tell him yes, he's cute just like me. See, I have straight hair like him. She has curly hair. Say I am more beautiful, please. At least you.

That evening, when Malavika came over with her books and pens to work on the physics problems she found overwhelming, Haasini decided to ignore her. Malavika was sure to ask for help but Haasini continued scribbling in her secret diary, not saying a word.

"Haasi, you like that boy don't you? That boy in the bus who looks like Archie in the Archie comics?" ventured Malavika.

"Who says I like him?" Haasini asked petulantly, not sure why she was angry with Malavika, when all that Malavika wanted was to be her friend.

Realising her folly, she let anger bounce off like a tennis ball from one to another, and then out of the room. They both burst out laughing, relieved that all was well, and wondered what to do the rest of the evening as it was a Friday with no school for the next two days.

Haasini decided that they would have fun dressing up. She took out a bottle of red nail polish that she had bought with her pocket money a month ago but kept hidden along with her underclothes in the chest of drawers. Her mother did not like the girls to use nail polish or lipstick. Or to tweeze their eyebrows. Haasini wanted to tell her that almost everyone in their class was going to Begum's, the only decent beauty parlour in the city, to tweeze their eyebrows and upper lip, or to cut and style their hair.

She decided to be defiant that evening. She shaped her nails painted them with the nail polish. She then passed on the bottle to Malavika and asked her too to paint her nails too. She would bring out the one lipstick she owned and show Malavika how to rub it on to her lips.

The strong smell of nail polish drew Dhruv into the room soon enough. He wanted his nails painted too, and when they refused saying boys didn't colour their nails, he began to scream and threatened to sneak to their mothers.

"Boys, especially strong boys, don't paint their nails, Dhruvi," Haasini said.

"No, Akka. See – when Ammama came from Rajahmundry, she put gorintaku on my hands. See…"

The girls held his little hands and laughed, telling him how red his hands were from the gorintaku.

Dhruv rolled into a ball of delight. He was relieved they were in a good mood that evening. Of late, he had noticed they had become moody, and weren't playing with him or teasing him that much.

His own sister was so rude to him these days that he wished Malavika were his sister. She was always nice to him, and told him stories and taught him to fly kites on the terrace.

Haasini had been locking the room that they shared, from the inside. What did she do there by herself, he wondered. Once when she hadn't locked it properly, he burst in and saw her half-naked without a blouse. She hit him so hard that his face went red with pain, and he howled with the shock of a sister gone hysterical.

Haasini had always been impatient with him as far back as he could remember, but he couldn't understand why Malavika too had become irritable. He looked up at her now painting his nails and smiled at her.

He liked the camaraderie and friendship between the girls. But it puzzled him that they spent so much time these days trying out shirts and skirts, plaiting or twisting their hair. Once he had even caught Haasini wearing lipstick. He promised himself this was something that their mother would get to know at an appropriate time, when he needed to blackmail his sister for some favour.

"Akka, you look smart in the floral shirt," he said to Malavika. But he didn't like the way Haasini had knotted her hair up like Andal, the saint poetess whose pictures he saw in the puja room. The next time she was sleeping he would tie her hair to the four poster bed, he thought.

Sitting by herself in the drawing room, sipping her evening tumbler of coffee and reading the popular Telugu weekly *Andhra Jyothi,* Vani wondered why the children were so quiet in Haasini's room. She had not even seen Dhruv for some time. At moments like these, when she was free, he liked to come and sit in her lap.

She hoped Haasini was behaving herself. These days she was snapping everyone's head off at home, including hers.

Only the other day when she had asked her to demonstrate the alaripu that Hemamalini was teaching her, Haasini had leapt in the air like a ballet dancer. She clicked her tongue, wishing that Haasini would pay attention to her dance and body movements. These classes were costing the family a lot. Hema, who knew the family, initially refused to take any fee but Vani would not let her give classes without the gurudakshina. This Diwali she would buy Hema a nice Gadwal sari. But she wished Haasini would get more serious about her dancing. Hema too had remarked that the girl had a natural talent for dance, a remark that pleased Vani.

Her husband wanted Haasini to study and be a doctor. He said he had lost his mother when she was barely in her forties because there was no hospital or doctor near their home. Well, someone else from his family could be a doctor and save lives, Vani decided. She wasn't going to have Haasini become a doctor, keep late hours delivering babies and performing Caesareans, and neglect her own family and children.

If she became a dancer, of course, Vani herself would take care of the children. In fact, the children could come to live with her – with this grandmother who so loved classical dance.

Just as she was planning to get up, cursing that she hardly had any time to herself with two children and a home to look after, she saw Malavika and Haasini walk out of the room holding Dhruv's hands.

"Haasini, what is that nail polish on your fingers? How many times have I told you not to paint your nails? And you too, Malavika! I don't know what your mother will say to all this!"

"But Ma, it was all Mala's idea..."

"Mala...?"

"But Haasini, you were the one who said we should paint our nails and dress up..."

"Ma, look at my nails! Red like when Ammama put gorintaku..."

"You too, Dhruvi? Haasini, throw away that nail polish or give it to Lakshmi. And go to your room and take it off now. You don't have a remover? Well, use kerosene and remove it!"

"And what was Dhruv telling me about you trying on sleeveless shirts?" Vani continued, outraged. "Malavika, you too? I thought you would set an example to your friend who is getting more rebellious by the week. Oh, have you girls been tweezing your eyebrows? *Please save these girls, dear god in heaven..."*

Dear Mala,

I haven't seen any letters from you, though I am sure there must be some waiting for me at home. We barely came back from London, and here I am in Delhi having to perform again. Not that I am complaining, as there is so little patronage these days for classical dance. Besides, we South Indian dancers are second class citizens in this great capital that is as imperial as it was during the British Raj. Where there is privilege and honour for the North Indian musicians and dancers, there are only third class fares for the South Indian artistes. You should hear about this sitar player who throws tantrums demanding plane tickets not only for himself but also for his wife, daughter and possibly his dogs! We lowly dancers from Hyderabad and Madras have to be happy with train fares and government guest houses that come only with cockroaches if we are lucky.

Let me not complain, because I am happy with my life as a dancer. What else did I have the talent for anyway? Pa imagined and hoped I would become a doctor (who knows, then maybe I would have been able to afford a fancy bungalow) but that was not to be. Can you imagine me as a doctor? Frail as I am myself, people would have asked me to have a spoonful of Feradol before prescribing it to their kids! (Am assuming, of course, that I would have become a paediatrician.)

In any case, Amma had decided I would be a dancer and when Amma decides, where is the choice? You know what a strong woman she was. Remember how one time, she yelled and scolded us for tweezing our eyebrows and painting our nails, as if we had committed a cardinal sin! But Andhras from Rajahmundry were like that – old fashioned. Their idea of beauty was buxom women in lovely Venkatagiri saris decked in gold jewellery. Which reminds me, I wonder where those lovely Venkatagiri saris are that Amma had? I must look through her cupboards one of these days when I have the time.

I wish I could feel that joy now in dressing up, because I am all the time in make-up and finery for my dance. People take a holiday from their work, I want to take a holiday from wearing this excessive make-up. Because even when I am not performing, I have to be at functions where they expect me to look like, well, Haasini the glamorous dancer.

But I have to tell you what a sacred time it is for me, when I sit in the green room before the performance. It's a contemplative moment when I gather all of myself into a sacred space within me. It is that moment of meditation that Frida Kahlo or Picasso must have retreated into, waiting for their hand and imagination to move into a fine dance.

I like to be quiet in my dressing room backstage, when I don't let anyone enter, save Amma. She too knows that she mustn't make a noise or speak loudly, and even apologises when she has to move to get herself a cup of coffee! I make her so tense that both of us jump out of our skins even if one jasmine bud falls out of the bunch in my hair. It's a moment of tension that every creative artist feels I am sure.

Anyway, yesterday when I was sitting in the green room, doing my eyes with kajal and mascara, applying the tilakam on my forehead, clasping flowers into my hair, and placing the sun and moon on the two sides of my head, I saw myself in the mirror.

Who was that woman, I wondered, leaning forward to touch the reflection in the mirror. My mind revolted at the split in my person that I myself had caused. I wanted to wipe off the make-up, the kajal and the tilakam from my face and appear before the audience exactly as I was. NAKED. Not with this special face I had for my dance. I wanted to dance simply and honestly, like those pure notes in an MS raaga. At least then I would know that when the audience applauded, it would be entirely for Haasini and the beauty of her abhinaya rather than for being a good-looking dancer. That's the thing about dance, Mala – a good looking dancer can lull an ignorant audience into appreciating her dance however crude it is. In that sense, music is so much more pure. Who cares how the musician looks? What matters is the voice that rises into the air and fills the hearts of the listeners, lifting them above the mundane.

I think part of the anger with the made-up face was that all my life I wanted to be good looking like you. I wanted, not your curly hair (not that for sure!!), but those large, light eyes and lovely ears that my grandmother said were made to wear glittering diamond earrings. And that well defined nose. You should have been the nayika, not me. Everyone in school liked you because you were pretty. Even Siraj. He loved you more – yes, I know that. I know you will deny this, but wasn't it you who spent hours with him listening to poetry and poring over books? Not to say eating those platefuls of badaam ki jaalis, which surprisingly didn't make you any fatter.

I was small built, and even the saris for dance had to be cut so that I wouldn't trip and fall. I was told I had lovely eyes, but I don't know about that. No one even thought I would have stamina for dance. I tweezed my eyebrows, wore lipstick and sleeveless shirts, imagining I would sculpt myself into a beautiful person. But you didn't love me because I wore sleeveless clothes and wore lipstick, did you Mala? I know you loved me anyway. I know Siraj was fond of me too. And maybe Thatha. But I know Amma wished I was better looking because dancers had to be attractive. Like a Sonal Mansingh or a Yamini Krishnamurthy.

But we all grow and change. Like cities that will, grow, flourish and decay.

I can't believe that Dhruv, that bane of my life who would talk loudly on the school bus, and who ruined my budding romances now heads a marketing firm in Bombay. And has a five-year-old daughter himself. Everyone thinks she looks like me, her Atha! Arundhati they call her. I call her my little pumpernickel.

Love,

Haasini

CHAPTER 12

Rekha rarely saw her daughter in her puja room and so she was surprised one morning to see her sitting before a photo of Hanuman which had him carrying the mountain with the magic herb Sanjeevani. A Raja Ravi Varma print that her mother-in-law had given her when she had got married – of Rama, Sita and Lakshmana, with Hanuman at their feet – also sat in the room along with a silver idol of Devi, a painting of Shiva and Parvati, and a black and white picture of Ramana Maharishi that had been with the family for ages, all adding to the piety of the room. But these Malavika didn't seem to be interested in. Everyone in the house knew it was with Hanuman that she had a special relationship.

It was some time before exams, so Rekha wasn't sure what Malavika was praying for, reading the Hanuman Chalisa in that soft voice she was so fond of. It was Rekha's mother who had taught Malavika the Chalisa, and she was happy that Malavika still read from the little book that she had got bound for her.

Maybe it was Siraj's health she was praying for. The girl was so attached to him though she didn't even call him 'Uncle' or any of the things that children usually called an older person. Many times, Rekha had wondered what the special bond was between the two, despite the difference in ages. But she was wise enough to understand that many relationships in life could not be defined or understood. They could only be accepted.

Rekha herself felt sorry for this man who was refined and cultured like many of the well-known old Muslims in the city. She would telephone him often to see if he needed anything. If human beings were not kind to each other, who would be nice to them? Rekha often asked herself.

Helping Vijaya in the kitchen with the day's lunch, she wanted to go into the puja room to see what the matter was with her daughter, but she decided to sit quietly, and have the dialogue with her favourite god. Who knows what goes on in the minds of teenage children, what catastrophes they think will befall them, Rekha mused, as she told Vijaya not to put that much oil into the guttivankaya kura, the family's favourite brinjal curry.

They were not a conservative family and would encourage Malavika to go to a good college after she finished high school, maybe even continue to a Masters degree. But even so, they would have to get her married by the time she was 21 or 22, for sure. Rekha was seized with a sudden panic about how fast Malavika was growing up, and how soon that day would come.

She now moved out of the kitchen into the verandah adjoining her bedroom. Here she sat on the swing with her sewing, wanting to finish the embroidery on her organdie sari. But as she crinkled her eyes working at the satin stitch buttercups on the sari, she wondered what it was about Malavika that had changed. Her daughter was growing to be a beautiful young woman, certainly. But Rekha was sad, nevertheless, that she had grown up so fast that she felt she had not fully enjoyed the joy of having a young girl in the house – that smell of powder and puff and the girlish laughter at nothing.

Malavika's body had begun to acquire contours and she had developed a grace. She was even walking differently. She was going to be a tall girl, her Malavika, and they would have to find a tall husband for her, Rekha thought. Tall and good-looking, yes, but her husband would have to be qualified too. These days so many Andhras were looking for bridegrooms from the US, but she wasn't sure if she wanted to let their only daughter live that far from home. How was she to know though what was written for Malavika? She just hoped that the marriage would be a good one, just like hers had been.

Malavika was indeed tall for her age. She had such long and firm legs that her father thought she should become an athlete, and Malavika had excelled in sport in junior school. Since then, however, she had not so much as seen a playground, sitting on trees and window sills reading or writing. When she was winning medals for her school, Ram had thought athletics would be a good career for his daughter, but his wife argued that high jump or tennis would be no use to her when she was 30 or 40 years old, when younger sportswomen would take over. She wanted Malavika to learn music because she believed music would give her solace when she was lonely with children in school and husband at work. It was music that had given her, at least, comfort. Rekha had to only hear an old Geeta Dutt song or a Thyagaraja kriti by MS Subbulakshmi for her spirits to lift up. She needed to only pick up the shrutipetti to feel an unexplicable joy of being. But Malavika had not shown any inclination for Carnatic music even if she sometimes sat by her mother on the cotton dhurrie, and sang Thyagaraja's *Bantureeti koluvu, iyyavayya Rama,* joining her shy voice with her mother's.

Today, Rekha was troubled. How was she going to talk to Malavika about the changes taking place in her body? The menstrual period she would have soon – was it cause for worry that she hadn't as yet? – and the woman she would become, healthy and mature, to have children of her own. Had she and Haasini discussed periods? Maybe she should talk to Vani about what they should tell the girls.

She looked around for Malavika who, having left the puja room was now lying on her mother's bed and was immersed in a Charlie Brown omnibus. Rekha called to her to come out and sit on the swing with her, and get some fresh air. At this time of the year the seetaphal trees were in bloom in the rocky garden outside her window and she loved the fragrance they threw even as far back as into her room.

Malavika came to sit on the long wooden swing, and began to push the two of them faster than what Rekha was comfortable with.

"Slowly, Mala, don't take me so high, darling," Rekha said.

She remembered when, as a child Malavika had once swung so high and so furiously that she had fallen off and hurt her ear. That had left a deep scar on one of her ears which she tried to hide with her hair.

Malavika slowed down to a gentle back and forth, back and forth. The momentum created a different kind of bond between mother and daughter, and they held hands and laughed in easy companionship.

Malavika sensed that her mother wanted to speak to her about something. She had noticed that Amma had been anxious since morning. Her mother too realised that in Malavika there was an anticipation, of the little secrets and confidences that bond a mother to her daughter.

This was a moment beyond the present, a moment that belonged to the future, in fact, that both would recall many years later.

But Rekha was hesitant suddenly. She wanted to postpone talking to her, not just about the period, but about many things the child should know – the happiness of a loving husband and unruly children, but also possibly the anxiety, children coming down with measles, husband wanting his way... Rekha felt an unbearable anguish about what the future would hold for her daughter, and leaned on her bony young shoulders for comfort.

"Amma, are you alright? Shall I ask Vijaya to get you a cup of Bournvita? Shall I read out a Peanuts strip? This one is really funny, of Charlie Brown saying there is no problem in life you can't get away from!" Malavika said anxiously.

She stroked her mother's hair and saw the diamond earrings that she always associated with her Amma. She had never asked, nor was she told, if the earrings were a gift from her father. Malavika was aware how much her parents loved each other, but she concluded that was how things were supposed to be between parents.

"Haasini, I've never seen Amma and Pa even argue. Do you think they are a perfect couple that those cigarette companies are giving away prizes to?" she'd asked Haasini one evening.

"My parents argue all the time. Especially when it comes to Dhruvi and me. But it's really irritating that they spend so much time together in their bedroom. They even lock it. Uggh!"

"Haasini, do you they lock the doors because our fathers want to beat our mothers? In which case how are they any better than Govindaiah?"

"Mala, my dear, they lock the doors because they make love. You are such a dumb idiot," Haasini had told her.

Malavika now pushed aside her mother's hair, and touching the earrings wondered if her father gifted them to her mother after they made love.

'Making love' didn't sound nice to her. Although at least it proved that her parents still got along, which was so much better than what had happened to Preeti, whose parents had separated. It was whispered that her father was having an affair with a colleague at office, and Preeti had to stay with her mother in her grandparents' house. She saw her father only occasionally, when he would come to the school to pick Preeti up and take her out for a movie or to the park. He bought her lots of gifts. The girls all peeped from their class windows when Preeti's father came to pick her up, as none of them knew what a man who was having an affair looked like.

They were jealous of the clothes and books he bought her, but Malavika had decided right then that it was better to forego some books than have a father whom you saw only sometimes. She loved her Pa and Ma so much, and she was glad they still stayed together even if they excluded her so many times from their special bonding that seemed magical.

Malavika tried to imagine what it would be like when she herself got married, though she did dream sometimes that she would become a nun like Maria in *The Sound of Music* and be a governess to children. She couldn't sing all that well, but she could do the 'do re me fa'. She began to sing, *Far, a long, long way to run...* and her mother looked at her wondering what had brought on *The Sound of Music* all of a sudden.

Malavika stopped abruptly. She wanted to tell her mother that she didn't want to get married until she knew what men and women did behind closed doors and what making love was all about. She had asked Lakshmi, in fact, but she too had smiled coyly and told her that she would know when the time came. Malavika wished she wouldn't act coy, and that when the doors to their quarters were closed it was Lakshmi who beat up Govindaiah.

She hoped her father, her near-perfect father who had travelled all over the world and looked so dashing when he smoked his pipe, was kind to her mother. She would never get married but be a support to her beautiful mother, she decided then and there.

Rekha was surprised by her daughter's sudden tenderness. She was still a child, but there was already a womanly compassion about her. Well, she would know about menstruation, husbands and babies soon enough, she thought and postponed broaching the subject for the moment.

Malavika was trying to tell her something. The child was such an introvert that it delighted her mother to hear her talk.

"Amma, you know Haasi…"

"Haasini? What about her, Mala?"

"I don't know if Haasi will be angry with me for telling you all this, especially if you went and told Vani Atha."

"Mala, I promise I won't go to Vani's house for a whole week. And least of all, talk about you girls," Rekha responded, laughing but nervous about what the girls had been up to, for they were growing up and the world was not what it used to be during her time.

"Amma, I think… This prefect boy, he is really cute, came and sat next to her. Actually, he sat next to her because Dhruv was sitting next to me. And Haasini instead of getting up and changing seats with Dhruv encouraged Blue to come and sit next to her…"

"Prefect? Blue?"

"Yes, Ma, of Blue House, not mine or Haasini's house."

"Don't you girls even know his name? So what happened, Mala? Do you girls like him? You? Haasini?"

"How can I like him, Ma? Actually, I think he's cute too. But Haasini likes him more. I am not sure, but I think she may even be in love with him. What will we all do, if he wants to marry her? Haasini is behaving like a Georgette Heyer heroine. He's from Goa. We don't even know if he can speak Telugu."

"Goan? But what makes you think, Mala, that they want to get married? Has Haasini told you anything?"

"No, Ma, because she sat next to him, I thought..."

"Just because a boy sits next to Haasini, it doesn't mean they want to get married or that they are in love. Do you know, she and you will have to have so many crushes like this before you fall in love with someone and decide you want to get married to that man?"

"You mean, Ma, you fell in love with Pa? Did you fall in love with others too?"

"No, my darling. My parents chose your father for me, and I am glad he was the one for me. Just as I am glad you were chosen to be born into our family. We will choose a husband for you, too, when the time comes."

"But were you in love, Ma?"

"What a question?" Rekha said, pushing the hair off Malavika's ear to see if the gash had disappeared with time. But of course, it was still there and was in fact, growing proportionally with the ear, unfortunately.

Laughing, Rekha got up to look for her husband, to tell him about their daughter and her fears.

A Goan! She hoped Ram would find the story as amusing as she had.

Dear Haasi,

Finally, a letter from you! I had not heard from you after that one letter from London. Where on earth are you? Back in Hyderabad? And I, after the baby hardly have time for anything. I feel like a cow sometimes with the constant feeding I have to do. Where are those maternal feelings in me? Sometimes for nothing at all I'd burst into tears, but didn't let Ma see it of course.

And I feel exhausted and alone with the baby, especially now that Amma has left after a six-month long stay. Thank you for the silk sari you sent with Amma. My favourite colour too, the double shade of pink and orange! But when will I wear those gorgeous Kanjeevarams again, as I'm mostly in maternity gowns these days. Yuk!

It was nice having Ma with me, but I think she was lonely in this country without Pa. I should have asked them both, but he is always so busy, especially now that he so senior at the bank. Erudite and informed as Ma always is, I was surprised that even a trip to New York City didn't excite her as much as I imagined it would.

I took her to the Metropolitan Museum (before the baby of course) which has some of the earliest Satavahana jewellery from Andhra, but there she merely raised an eyebrow and said, wonder how these jewels came this far! She saw Picassos, (his exhibition, Woman, is currently showing at the Metropolitan) and she was neither amused nor moved by the beauty and the grotesqueness of the Cubist woman. Vikram had bought tickets for Cats, *much before she even boarded the plane from Hyderabad and being an admirer of Eliot, I thought she would love this. She didn't say it, but I know she couldn't take the cacophony of this Andrew Lloyd Webber production.*

She was happiest when we went to the Battery Park. Not because she could get to see the old French lady whom we call the Lady Liberty, but mostly because she ran into a Bengali couple visiting their children too. All of us sat together at the restaurant sipping Coca Cola and eating French fries (completely unhealthy I know), and you should have seen the way they bonded discussing all that ailed America. The way children were brought up here, the television commercials that sold everything from soaps to cornflakes. They were discussing their life back home in India. Those people were talking of Calcutta, and she of Hyderabad, but somehow it didn't matter whether they were discussing the Kalighat temple or the Meenakshi temple, Darjeeling tea or filter coffee, because what mattered to Mrs Chatterjee and my mother was that they were talking India.They couldn't be separated until they exchanged phone numbers and promised to visit each other. As if it were a street in Secunderabad that she would ask me to take her to, and not Philadelphia where those Bengalis lived.

But I really did feel sorry for Amma that she had to come to the US where there is little activity during the best of seasons. Why do Indian children think they are doing their parents a favour by sending them tickets to come to America? At least I was not working, but do you see how awful we are to uproot our parents from all that sunshine, neighbours and local temples to live in a country where there is more snow and sleet than sunshine, and where you have to call your daughter before you go to visit her and see your grandkids. Ugh.

After the trauma of the first miscarriage, she did nothing but worry about my every movement during her stay here. I told her not to spoil me so much, but that's a mother, especially my dear Ma.

One day out of the blue, while she was on the rocking chair by herself and reading a book, she asked, "Mala, what happened to Haasini's Goan?"

For a moment I didnt realise what she was talking about. I am sure you too have forgotten. It's that effeminate first boyfriend of yours who sat with you on the bus to school.

I told her, I'm not sure Ma, what's happened to him, but Haasini never married him or anyone else. I am not sure why, but we both laughed for a bit over you!

The next day late in the afternoon, we sat on one of the many cotton dhurries from Hyderabad, and we began to sing a Thyagaraja kriti, your favourite – Marugela ra, o Raghava... anni neevuanuchu, antaragamuna – almost in perfect consonance, though she wished she had the shrutipetti to keep tune.

I realised living with Amma in such proximity that I knew so little about her. We in fact, know so little about our parents, don't you think Haasini? Why is this relationship that is closest to us left unexplored until there is no time, or is too late? Is this why children are surprised at the many things they find in their parents' cupboards when they die? Pa always wears this one set of tiny gold buttons on his kurtas. I wonder if it was my mother who gave them to him that he treasured them so much. Once when I helped myself to them for my kurta he went into such a rage that I had to go and hide in Siraj's house. I wish I could ask him now who gave them to him. I should ask Amma ideally, but I felt diffident.

Then, I always see these pressed flowers in Amma's books. I imagine she keeps them in memory of another day when they were in bloom, these orange and yellow flowers. Was it a time when my mother and father sat in some garden in Coonoor, talking to each other, and he picked those flowers for her?

Really, it's so strange how we never see our parents as people who could have their own stories independent of their children. But we don't see them as anything more than parents who have little to do except bring us up. Even now, Since I was pregnant, she wanted to do so much: cooking and cleaning, apart from making not only my favourite dishes but Vikram's too!

Sorry, but I couldn't finish this missive for quite a few weeks now. Babies are exhausting, I haven't slept well like say in the last 100 years. Today I have got a nanny to take care of Avantika, and am able to finish the letter so I can give it to Vikram to mail it. I'm going to get her more often, as it's tough having a baby and managing a house and cooking. Amma wanted me to come to India with her, but Vikram wouldn't hear of it. So here I am...

Love, and write soon.

Malavika feeling like Madonna

CHAPTER 13

It was the hour of dusk when neither had the day concluded nor had the night begun. It was inauspicious to sleep at this time, but Vani had to keep her superstitions aside for once. Haasini had high fever and Vani had sat up the whole of the previous night, applying cold compresses on her fevered brow, with a concerned Dhruv running to the fridge to get ice cubes.

Removing a strand of fine hair that was stuck on Haasini's forehead, Vani sent silent prayers to all the gods and goddesses she knew to make her daughter well.

She had received a fright the night before. Malavika's father had taken the children to the circus. Vani had not cooked dinner and was cleaning her cupboard instead, not expecting the children to be back until late at night.

But it was not even eight o'clock when they were back, escorted by Ram and Rekha.

"Ma, there was a fire in the circus, and we all ran out. Some people got hurt and died," Dhruv was screaming in his loud voice.

"Died? What! What happened, Ram bavagaru?"

"There was an electrical short circuit somewhere at the back. I had to literally carry Dhruv. Rekha had to hold onto the girls and drag them out."

"Well, tomorrow in the newspapers we will know if anyone died. But at least our children are safe, Vani, even if little Dhruvi was afraid and we had to carry him out in our arms," Rekha was saying.

Vani was first concerned for Dhruv but he seemed alright. It was Haasini who came down with shivering and high fever, delirious through the night.

There was one recurring image in Haasini's mind. The fire. They had all been laughing at the clowns who were swinging on the trapeze and tumbling down when a cry went up from somewhere, "Fire! Fire! Run, run...!"

At the back of the tent, Haasini saw the fire. Malavika's father lifted Dhruv in his arms and told Rekha to hold the girls and run out of the tent which was in chaos. Malavika had been clutching her hand, but somewhere Haasini got disconnected from the chain that was her immediate family. She kept trying to wake herself from that horror, screaming in her delirium, "Malavika! Ram Uncle! Don't leave me here! Please, I don't want to die. These people will trample me to death. Please...."

Vani reached out to stroke her head and calm her. She touched her forehead.

"Child, you are alright. You are back home, you are safe. See, here is Dhruvi, who is alright too."

But Haasini was in another world where she could only hear screams, fire and people running everywhere in what seemed like inferno itself. She was being knocked back into the chair as her hand broke away from Mala's, and someone was trampling and crushing her, hurting her so much. She was too exhausted to tell her mother anything.

She felt she was on fire.

"Ma, water," she was saying. She wanted her mother to quench the fire that was consuming her body, to pour so much water that her body would cool down.

She was a little better in the morning, but still delirious, when she felt a cool hand on her brow that she knew was neither her mother's or Dhruv's. Or her Pa's.

"Who's this? It feels nice and cool."

Vani told her that Malavika was now sitting by her side.

"Malavika, Ma? I thought she died in the circus fire. I think the animals, the lions and monkeys all got burnt in the fire. Did the baby elephant cry because its mother was lost? Did the lions roar in pain, Mala? Tell me it's all a nightmare, Ma!" Haasini cried.

Malavika was frightened by Haasini's delirium. Vani reassured her that Haasini would feel better once the fever came down.

"All of you had a scare last night. Haasini more than others. You didn't go to school either, did you Mala?"

"No, Vani Atha. I didn't. I couldn't sleep very well and had to ask Amma to sleep with me."

"You must go to school tomorrow. It's not nice to miss school now that your pre-finals are approaching. To think all of you went to keep Dhruvi company in the circus."

"No, Atha, both Haasini and I wanted to go to the circus too. There are not that many circuses which come to Hyderabad nowadays."

"Dhruvi seems okay. Where is he? Will you sit with Haasini while I go look for him? And let me get some soup or curd rice for Haasini to eat. Will you also have something, Mala? Shall I make you a nice crisp dosa?"

"No, Atha. I will just sit and here and talk to Haasini. Later maybe... And Vani Atha, Haasini looks so ill. Is she dying? I am so scared."

"She will be alright. Talk to her, but not about the circus or the fire."

Malavika was upset that Haasini was so ill that she couldn't even talk to her. The circus had been for Dhruv's entertainment, and he insisted that that his "two sisters" go with him. She and Haasini had wanted go for *Anne of a Thousand Days*. They were studying British history and had been told to watch the film. She had already asked Siraj to go with them, and they could have gone on Sunday evening if only Haasini had not been so ill.

She had seen posters of the film on the way to school. It had Richard Burton and a new young actress called Genevieve Bujold. Malavika desperately wanted to see who this young woman was who so enticed King Henry that he had wanted to split the Church of England so he could marry her. And Siraj had spoken so much about Richard Burton and his forays into theatre. He even had records of Sir Laurence Olivier and Richard Burton in Shakespearean plays. Sometimes she wondered what Siraj was doing in Hyderabad when he should have stayed back in Oxford. He would have been so much happier with Lillette around him, and all those British pubs and cricket and theatre.

"Haasini, you know Anne Boleyn…"

But Haasini was screaming that Malavika had been trampled in the circus and died. That she now had to make new friends.

Malavika wanted to run out of the room. How could her friend say she was dead when she was sitting right before her, trying to talk to her? Vani came quickly into the room hearing Haasini's screams and saw Malavika on the verge of tears.

"Mala, don't take anything she says so seriously. Haasini has no idea what she is saying."

"But Atha, how can she wish me dead?"

"She is not wishing you dead. She just thinks you are dead. It's because of the fever," Vani said soothingly.

The girls had remained friends so long, she thought. Haasini would soon be leaving for Madras to study dance. Vani hoped the two would continue this friendship. Her Haasini was outgoing, but found it hard to make close friends. And good friends come so rarely in a lifetime, Vani thought wisely. She was happy these two young women – yes, they were no longer children now – had each other.

Malavika left the Jane Austen she had brought with her to read out to Haasini, on the table, and decided to go home. She was not only hungry, but if she didn't go soon, Govindaiah would come to fetch her and she didn't want that too, in all this turmoil.

She glanced at Haasini one last time before leaving the room and wondered if her friend had a secret that she was not telling her. She certainly looked as if there was something she was hiding. But she would ask her another time. It still didn't feel good to be thought dead by someone in whose memory and mind you wanted to live forever.

Malavika stayed away from that house the next few days, and though Haasini sent Dhruv to call her, she sent word that she was busy studying for a Hindi test.

When Malavika did go to see Haasini some days later she found her standing at the window, preoccupied. Her thick straight hair hung about her shoulders, unbrushed. Dhruv had told Malavika that his sister had not been eating well, adding, "Akka, maybe she is dying. So many of our aunts and uncles have come from Rajahmundry suddenly."

Even their grandmother had come from Rajahmundry, laden with laddoos and putarekulu. Dhruv couldn't understand why everyone was converging in the house with sweets if his sister was sick.

Malavika wasn't sure if Haasini was angry with her. She also couldn't still forget that she thought she was dead. Unsure where their friendship stood at the moment, or where it would proceed from this day onwards, she decided to say something to Haasini. She stretched out a hand and tapped her on the shoulder, then moving closer and combed her hair as Haasini stood motionless. Malavika heaved a sigh of relief. At least she wasn't angry with her, she told herself as Haasini turned to look at her.

"Ouch, you're hurting me, Mala. Don't run your hand through my hair like that."

"Your hair is all in tangles, Haasi. Haven't you brushed it the past few days?" said Malavika, afraid to use the word 'illness'.

Haasini was not her usual effusive self. She was becoming moody, Malavika thought. She so wanted to tell her about *Anne of Thousand Days* that she and Siraj had gone to watch in Tivoli. She did feel guilty about going without her friend, but even in good friendships there are moments of selfishness.

Malavika did want to tell her so much about how Anne insisted that her daughter Elizabeth should be the queen of England, rather how she went to the guillotine holding her neck saying, "And I have such a short neck." She had held Siraj's hand and wept in the theatre. Wept so much, in fact, that he took her to the Taj Mahal Hotel nearby after that so she could calm down over tutti-frutti ice-cream.

"Mala, why did all of you abandon me at the circus that night of the fire? I was so afraid. All those men stamping and walking over me…"

"But Haasini, it was you who let go of my hand. I was holding Ma's and Pa was carrying Dhruvi…"

"And all of you left me weeping on the chair and went home. I could hate you forever for that!"

"Don't say that, Haasi! Don't! We waited for you in the car while Pa went into the circus tent once again to look for you. He found you sitting on a chair and weeping. You were so dazed, you refused to get up and walk…"

"I don't remember any of that. But I was terrified I'd been left alone in that stampede. I've never felt so alone. Mala, don't ever give up on me…"

"Shhhh, don't cry again. You know I'll never leave you. Not in this lifetime, or in another. For sure."

The girls had never been so sentimental with each other before. The trauma of that night of the circus fire and Haasini's subsequent illness had disturbed both of them equally and made them each realise how precious they were to one another, and how integral to each other's life they were.

Malavika combed Haasini's long, soft hair and plaited it up. Not finding the hairbands with which Haasini usually secured her hair, she turned the ends together to keep them in place, only to have the silken braid untangling itself like a restless anaconda.

Aware that Malavika was being playful, Haasini turned and tried to pull her hair back, but not being able to fight Malavika's firm grip, she let go. A sudden tiredness seeped through her bones, and she went and lay down in her bed.

"This has happened to you already, hasn't it? Amma said you'd already begun having yours," said Haasini.

"Is that what the matter is with you? You've got your first period? Uggh! Even the word sounds disgusting," said Malavika.

"It's so messy, isn't it?"

"It's messy. But your mother, grandmother, aunts, will all be nice to you. You'll get a lot of gifts."

"You got a lot of gifts, did you? Was that the commotion in your house last month when so many of your relatives turned up? Why didn't you tell me about it?"

"I don't know. I was shy, I guess."

"Think of this, Mala, we'll have blood coming out of our vaginas for the next hundred years."

"No, Haasini! It'll stop after about 50 years. Anyway, by then it'll be too late to care about anything."

"Mala, this has everything to do with getting married and having babies."

"True. That's what Amma says. But these grown-ups are so unclear. They'll tell us a little and not explain the rest. Amma will go to the extent of warning me to be careful when I go out, not to let anyone touch me. But she won't tell me what will happen if a man touches me."

"You can't become pregnant, of course. For that someone has to have sex with us."

"Maybe... Anyway I don't think I want a man or a woman to touch me when I'm bleeding. And I wish Lakshmi and Vijaya wouldn't get so excited when they see me these days."

"Look at the number of relatives who have been summoned by Amma. Making a public announcement of my biological functions. She might as well announce it on All India Radio or put an ad in the *Deccan Chronicle*. For tomorrow's big lunch they want me to wear a sari."

"At least, look at it this way, Haasini. When we wear blouses, we won't look flat-chested anymore."

"But I want to be flat-chested."

"You're going to become a famous dancer. You don't want critics to call you 'that flat-chested dancer', do you? Kalpana told me the other day, that if we eat badams soaked in milk, it will give us large, round breasts."

"I've got a lovely new sari from Amma, another from my Atha in Rajahmundry. You're going to gift me something too, Mala, aren't you?"

"Maybe not. Considering you wished me..."

"Wished you what, Mala?"

"Nothing. Of course, I'll give my sweet sister who is going to become a world famous dancer, a big gift!"

Dearest Mala,

My apologies for letting your lovely, long letters remain unanswered. I find your letters so touching these days, it's almost better than speaking to you in person! Somehow you are more articulate in letters, as I think I am with my dance. Dancing or writing is a way of discovering and describing our worlds even to ourselves, isn't it?

I notice that you are writing from the depth of your being, the core where I believe we hide our pain. You're not hiding anything from me there, are you? You never say much about Vikram and the things you do together. Or when you do, it's only to complain! Of course baby Avanti must occupy all your time.

It's not that I have not wanted to write to you but just that there are times when the mind and heart want to shut themselves off from the world and stay put in a healing silence. Grief shared is still grief, you wrote once. I agree. The intensity of our sadness is no less because we have shared it with someone because it's a cross whose burden we have to carry on our own shoulders finally.

Where do I begin, Mala? Amma has been falling ill frequently and become quite weak after a recent bout of pneumonia. She has been having severe headaches and nausea and generally feeling run down. After a series of tests its turned out that she has breast cancer.

Cancer, and my mother? How can that be, Mala? But then why do we imagine we are personally immune to life's tragedies? Somehow we imagine these happen to people who have not been good, or who have cheated, lied or raped. But as someone said, bad things happen to good people too. People like Ma who left grains in the backyard for the sparrows in the mornings. Who generously supported the education of girls, (even if it was only of Brahmin girls).

Even the word 'cancer' has such a finality to it. The doctor says she is not in any emergency situation and she should respond well to the chemo and get better. But my heart skips a beat, skips several in fact, every time I think of her in the hospital, which is where she's been the last few months, in and out.

There will be Dhruv and his family who will stand by me, but they're so busy with their own lives. There is still my father. But who will now order Complan for me in the hotels and scold the waiters for not bringing it at the right temperature or with the right amount of sugar? Or who will now sit a little behind the nattuvangam while I perform, watching every movement of my hands and eyes to discover a new interpretation to an age old piece that she has been watching me perform since I was a little girl? Only Amma detects the subtle nuances I might have introduced in the evening's performance. Haasi, she will call me. Why that exuberance in the tillana, as if you were playing with Malavika? And she will ask me about the quiver while performing an allarippu, and remark, "Tired? Too many performances? Shall we go to Ooty for a holiday?"

Sweet, caring Amma. What would my life be without her hovering over me, cleaning my room at home and at hotels all the time?

The other night when she was feverish, she was talking of you and me as young girls. She said, after a circus or something, when I lay delirious, I had thought you were dead, and hearing that you were angry with me. I can't imagine I would wish that on anyone, especially you, my sister of many lives.

She even confided that she wished she had not insisted on taking me to dance classes, because she now believes if I hadn't become a dancer and become so obsessed with it, I would at least have led a normal life with a doctor or engineer husband and two children.

She wanted to know how she could atone for it, as if it was a sin to let you discover what made you happy. If she had not scolded me, pushed me to Hema Akka's house and later to Kalakshetra, making those trips to Madras every fortnight, how would I have discovered this language to express myself? This is my space. My métier. Each time I make a gesture with my finger or move my eyes, I'm trying to find meaning in the chaos, and bring harmony to the world around me. You know, everyone can't be a dancer. For this you need to be graced, you have to do penance for many years to be given this gift. It is Amma who is doing the penance for me!

I have begun to go to the Ramakrishna Math here to listen to talks on Hinduism. There are no answers any swamiji can give, really, but it gives me a sense of peace to go there in the evenings or whenever I can.

Guess what, I lost a few months ago – the ruby earrings you and Rekha Atha gave me as a gift. I was in a panic when I could not find them among the jewellery that I keep in boxes. I couldn't remember having worn them since my trip to Paris. I really need to sort them out one of these days – keep away the ones I wear for dance, separate from the little pieces of gold and silver that I have been buying over the years.

Right now, being in a superstitious mood I was afraid some disaster would strike me if I didn't find these mango shaped red earrings you gave me. But thank heavens, I found them amidst some other trinkets in a box. I now wear them all the time, in case I misplace them again if I take them off. Ma noticed them, smiled and remarked, "I didn't know you still had them, considering you are always losing your earrings."

Mala, I've always been touched by your ability to give gifts. Sharing your jewellery and clothes when I wanted them. Giving, too, is a metaphor for the boundless affection you have for someone. I have noticed those who are miserly with their feelings also refuse to give gifts.

I'm sorry for the depressing letter. PMS blues, and other things.

Pray for Amma. Pray for me. Pray for this family.

Love,

Haasini

CHAPTER 14

Malavika was excited that she would soon be going to college to study her favourite subject, English Literature. Her banker father was urging her to study economics but she had no head for numbers. She would talk to Siraj one more time before she filled in her college applications, she said to herself, lounging lazily in bed.

At the end of summer, Haasini would be leaving for Madras to study dance full-time at Kalakshetra. She would miss her once she was gone. But for now there was still their friendship, and the magpie-robins in the garden outside. They were chattering like old women in the vegetable market. Malavika wondered if the scarecrow she had made with Dhruv in the vegetable patch, where they were trying to cultivate tomatoes and cabbages, would keep the birds away.

"It doesn't look like a scarecrow at all. More like clowns," Govindaiah had told her contemptuously.

"That's okay, Govindaiah. We are not asking for your opinion, in any case," she had replied tartly though she knew her mother would admonish her if she knew she was being rude to him.

"And it really will not scare anyone away from your vegetable patch, least of all the crows," he continued. "I can teach you how we paint fierce faces and stick them in chilli fields in our village."

Malavika was angry with him for making fun of her coconut shell scarecrow and had told him rudely, "Actually, Govindaiah, I should tie you to the stick and keep you as the scarecrow. I have not seen anyone uglier looking than you," she said, regretting her words even as she uttered them.

Rekha did not like it when Malavika was rude to the staff and when she overheard this argument she called Malavika inside and told her not to have any conversation with Govindaiah, good or bad.

Malavika heard him sniggering outside her room after that, until Lakshmi told him to be to be quiet, and not tease her. She wanted to complain to her mother about the leaves and papers that were gathering in the garden because he didn't seem to have swept the yard in what seemed like ages. All that uncleared rubbish made their garden a home for rat-snakes and vipers.

Mostly, Rekha let Govindaiah be without taking him to task as she was fond of Lakshmi who was an indispensable member of the household. Aware that no one in this house would really get rid of him, Govindaiah spent time smoking cheap beedis whose stubs he threw all over, or spat frequently making an awful gargling sound in his throat.

Malavika got out of bed to go the window to spot the magpie-robin. Siraj had shown her how to distinguish between magpie-robins and tree pies.

Instead of the magpie-robin, which must have flown away, she heard the commotion, chatter and laughter of women and their babies.

Was this the prelude to some festival, she wondered. Why were dozens of women arriving through the front gate into their house? Maybe Lakshmi and Govindaiah had a tiff again the previous night, and her relatives had come from the village.

She wanted to run out to see what the commotion was, but decided to have a shower first and wear something light and summery. Her mother had told her to wear dupattas with her kurtas, but she much preferred wearing skirts with short, sleeveless blouses as the summer in Hyderabad was unbearable.

When she went out to the backyard in a skirt and a short blouse, she was arrested by the sight of at least half a dozen women whom she recognised as coming to her house for years now, from the time she could remember. How could she have forgotten this was the time of the year when her mother made avakai for the whole year? The typical Andhra pickle would be stored for the whole year to be brought out at mealtimes, even distributed to other families.

This used to be a grand ritual when her grandmother was alive, when she morphed into a queen of a minor fiefdom ordering people around. The avakai itself would be made on the day of Rohini Kartika when the sun was the sharpest in these parts. But a day or two before that, her Avva would take Lakshmi and go in the family's Fiat to Sultan Bazaar to choose firm raw mangoes with kernels. She would convince the hapless woman at the bazaar into giving her a few mangoes for free, which they would use to make the avakai's less fiery sister, magai. She would then get Lakshmi to wipe each of the 100 or 200 green mangoes with a wet cloth before having Vijaya cut them into perfect pieces that would be left in the puja room so no one meddled with them.

To her, as to many Andhras, making the yearly avakai was a sacred ritual.

Rekha too followed her mother's method of making avakai though she was not so meticulous, leaving most of the finer details to Vijaya, or having Vani over, too, to supervise the help. Ram was still particular about the pickles and pachchadi he ate, otherwise Rekha would have long given up making the avakai and opted instead for the readymade pickles by companies like Priya and Ruchi that were making inroads into many Andhra homes.

If there was one image Malavika associated with a Hyderabad summer, it was this ritual of pickle making, when so many of these colourfully dressed women came to their house, laughing and chattering, to pound chillies and mustard, singing songs that were common in Telangana.

The Hyderabad summers were so bad that the heat would seep into the house by mid morning. That's when the older people would retreat into cooler rooms to rest under the swirling fans. The children, of course, would pour water on their clothes and look for shade under a tree to conjure up another imaginary game.

Malavika, like most youngsters, was unmindful of the heat, though she did wish she could wear minimum clothes, like those English friends of Siraj's.

The women walking into the backyard seemed to be cool despite the coarsely woven handloom saris that they wore. Whoever said you stayed cool in white clothes had not met these women from Telangana, who liked to wear bright colours. Orange and green saris with yellow and purple blouses on which they had sewn, on idle afternoons, mirrors and badla that made their clothes glitter.

They wore no slippers to cover the erotic nakedness of their dark feet, and you wondered how the heat did not scorch their tanned, calloused feet. Some walked barefoot, and those who wore thick leather slippers were made to take them off before they entered the house, as Lakshmi would have no muddy footwear spoiling her clean floors. There was something sacred about the space where the pickle was to be made, and it was Vasantha, Malavika's Avva, who had invested this space with sanctity.

Rekha was exhorting them to keep their children away when they were sorting out the dried red chillies that would be soon pounded. The fine powder would then be mixed with mustard and gingelly oil that would be poured onto the cut mangoes. Rekha was in a flutter as the chillies had to be pounded soon. She was already wondering if the pounding should have been done the day before with the help of Vijaya and Lakshmi. Even if these women added colour to the summer morning, they seemed in no hurry to accomplish anything, unmindful of the time or task at hand. They were more absorbed with throwing the colourful ends of their sari pallavs elegantly over their heads, exposing their waists seductively in the process, and chattering among themselves. Govindaiah was at hand to fetch and carry things, but his eyes constantly roved to the women and their breasts.

Rajeshwari, a buxom woman, who had been seeing Malavika every summer since she was a child almost, rolled her eyes looking at Malavika.

"This child has grown up into a woman. Lakshmi, you never told us," she said.

"What is there to tell, you wicked woman, Rajeshwari? To us she is still a child."

"She looks filled out in the right places. She should be wearing an odhni. Why doesn't her mother insist?" another asked.

"Abba," Lakshmi said. "Get on with your work. You'll all get a good meal if we finish this by evening."

The chillies were making Malavika sneeze and she wished the women, fond of them as she was, wouldn't look at her with such open amusement. Each one of them was appraising her separately as if she had grown extensions to her body, when all that she now had was round breasts that she tried to hide by wearing loose, ill-fitting clothes.

Malavika in turn stared at Rajeshwari, who was Lakshmi's cousin, and who'd brought the women from her basti to their house that morning.

Lakshmi had confided to her that Rajeshwari had left her husband to run away with a younger man, a driver who was doing well for himself. The woman didn't look as if she was capable of finding one man for herself – how did she have two, thought Malavika. Was it all something to do with the sexual prowess that she was reading about in DH Lawrence's novels?

Soon, Haasini and Dhruv arrived with their mother. Lakshmi urged the youngsters to sit in a corner of the verandah so they wouldn't get chilli powder in their eyes. She wanted to serve them the curd rice with fried potatoes that

Vijaya had made for the household. But seeing they were not hungry but excited, she decided not to force them. Instead she got them each the mango juice that Dhruv especially liked, made from Andhra's famous Chinna Rasalu.

Malavika wanted to complain to Haasini about the women staring at her, but with Dhruv around she did not even want to say the word 'breasts'.

The women were grinding the chillies to a powder in the stone mortar with a wooden stick that they threw into the air this way and that way in some premeditated rhythm.

They hummed softly to themselves until it reached a crescendo.

"What is it you want husband, I asked. And he said, I want to eat that betel leaf into which you have folded a supari nut."

"And I want to kiss your full mouth with my betel stained lips," sang another, hitting the stone with the stick in an erotic gesture.

By afternoon the chillies had been ground and the whole backyard glowed with the dust from the chillies like a Matisse painting, only his blue was replaced by red. The women moved to the garden near Lakshmi's house to eat their lunch that they brought with them. Those who didn't come with lunch were given something to eat by Vijaya who was prepared for such a contingency.

Rekha urged Malavika and Haasini to finish eating.

"I know you children like to eat nothing but mangoes at this time of year. You especially, Dhruv. But you have to have plenty of curd rice, too, to keep yourselves cool," she told them.

"I am dying to eat the avakai, Ma. When will this be ready?" Malavika asked her mother.

"Malavika, today we will mix the chillies, mustard and oil, and soak the mangoes. You know how particular your grandmother was about storing the avakai carefully in jaadis for a week at least. So patience, child!"

"Yes, I remember Ma. She wouldn't even let me go near them. Siraj was telling me how they make wine in France. This almost sounds like that."

"Wine and Andhra pickle? That would make a great combination. Sure to hit the spot!" Haasini whispered to Malavika as she ate her curd rice with a curd-soaked dried chilli known as urumerapakai in Telugu.

Some of the women retired to Lakshmi's room for a quick nap while others sat under the mango tree chewing betel nuts and gossiping. On days like this, Lakshmi too would forget about the chores in the house, enjoying herself with her friends.

Malavika and Haasini let Dhruv go to sleep in Malavika's room, left the fans on, and slipped out into the garden. They walked to Lakshmi's room on the pretext of looking for her, but in reality wanted to hear what the women were gossiping about.

They had often wondered why these women laughed so much. They had never seen grown women laugh and chatter this way, not even their own mothers, who they imagined were not unhappy in any way.

That afternoon, it seemed Lakshmi was the cynosure of all eyes. The women were feeling her sari and asking her how much it had cost, and she was telling them it was a Narayanpet sari that her mistress had bought for Diwali.

"It must be a 1000 rupees at least. Rekhamma won't give me anything inexpensive," Lakshmi said.

"And these bangles that are shining so much with all those stones, did she give them to you too?" Rajeshwari asked.

"Umm, when I went to the Numaish with Govindaiah he chose them. I had to pay for them, of course. He hardly has money."

"Wah! What a nice husband you have! But tell me why have we not seen a child?" Rajeshwari asked. It was a typical question that older women asked the younger ones.

"Is there something we need to worry about? Why don't you ask Rekhamma to take you to the doctor?" another told her.

"Does he make love to you at all? He seems drunk all the time!" Rajeshwari remarked, which threw the women in a fit of laughter, while Malavika and Haasini blushed a beetroot red.

By then Rekha was calling Lakshmi to fetch the women, as they had to finish mixing the oil and the mangoes before sunset when this ritual would have to conclude.

The women would pick the cut manoges from steel trays in which they had been placed a day or two ago and wiping them with a clean cloth hand them over to Vijaya who had already mixed the chilli powder, salt and mustard powder with gingelly oil into which she would place the mangoes. The whole mixture would be thrust into long jaadis, and oil poured over. The more the oil, the happier the mixture looked, bubbling in its effervesence like a little betal.

White flakes of garlic would be removed from the pod, meanwhile, by some of the younger women who were not yet experts at pickle making. The chunky cloves of garlic would be mixed with the pickle, and the jar tightly sealed with white pieces of cloth and kept in the dark, out of reach of everyone.

But the garlic peels, some of them now free floating objects would cling to the roof of the backyard for a week after that, the dry ones falling off at inopportune moments on a page of a book lying open.

A few days – sometimes even a week – later, Rekha or Vani would go to the store room in the kitchen to untie the knot of the muslin cloth tied to one of the jaadis, and put a wooden ladel to pick out the first few pieces of the new avakai.

The memory of the day-long ritual would have Malavika, especially, yearning for a first taste of the avakai, but she knew there was no way her mother would open the jaadi that soon. The same night, never. She would offer to let her taste a 'temporary' avakai that was made as a prelude, so called because it was not expected to stay year long like the 'permanent' avakai.

Much depended on the time the mangoes were plucked. Pluck them too early and they would never see the year end, Malavika's Avva had told her. To save the pickle, oil or salt could be added, but Vasantha would announce like a sphinx the fate of the avakai if the mangoes were not of the right firmness.

By evening, Lakshmi and Rajeshwari led their friends out of the courtyard into Lakshmi's house. On the way out, Rajeshwari pinched Malavika's cheeks making them red.

"This one will be quite buxom," she said and sniggered.

Malavika and Haasini laughed in embarrassment.

"And you, you are tiny, but well filled out too. Look at those hips. You will bear many children," she said to Haasini.

The May evenings being long, the women retreated to Lakshmi's house to have some sweets, and count their money. If babies had to be fed, they opened their blouses unabashedly to breastfeed them. By night, most women had left the house.

Only Rajeshwari stayed back with Lakshmi, who was like her sister now that her own family had abandoned her. She stayed on there for a few days, and Malavika would see her sometimes in the garden chatting with Lakshmi or Govindaiah.

That night, when Malavika was unable to rest, her eyes burning from the heat and body feverish from the chilli powder, she went to the bathroom and noticed a speck of blood on her panties. It was that time of the month again.

She walked towards the window and saw Lakshmi and Rajeshwari lying side by side on the cool yard outside Lakshmi's house that had been smeared with cowdung.

Only an oil lamp threw a glow on their dark bodies, their faces turned toward each other talking of this and that.

✳ ✳ ✳

Dear Haasi,

It has been years since I went to Queens and to the Indian stores there. They don't call it Little India for nothing, with its unique smells and sounds of India. When I got married and came to America years ago, I used to go there almost every month. I guess I loved going to Queens because it made me feel I was back in some obscure gully in Sultan Bazaar or Chikkadpally in Hyderabad where we used to buy bangles, hairclips and slippers, and eat samosas and mirchi bhajjis.

Well, last Sunday, Vikram, Avanti and I went to Queens. With another baby inside me I yearn more than ever for the taste and smells of India. We had a nice South Indian thali at a restaurant. The sambar left much to be desired, but I wasn't going to complain. Plus I have to be a good example to this young miss who is my life now. She ate only the jalebi – or sweet pretzel as she called it – from my plate.

More than the food, what I loved was talking in Telugu to the waiter who said he was from Vijayawada. You should have seen the way Avanti looked at me when I was talking in a language she didn't understand and asked me to talk American!

It was so delightful to smell home when I went to the grocery store run by a Gujarati couple – the smells of sambar powder (555 brand), talcum powder (Ponds) and soap (Mysore Sandal and Lux). For a few hours that afternoon I forgot I was in Manhattan and instead imagined I was in Begum Bazaar in Hyderabad. Only the ubiquitious cow that would absently chew our dupattas or sari ends on those streets in Hyderabad was absent. But heavens, you can even have a paan here!

There are these little kiosks selling paan and playing loud Hindi music much like that paan guy near Nanking in Hyderabad who was a cult figure. I was not sure if this guy I was buying my paan from was a cult, but he had half a dozen rings on his fingers and an array of photographs of Indian gods who stood along with Nutan and Hema Malini. He insisted on speaking to me in Hindi and gave me a discount of 10 cents because I was from India. But I hated the fact that he kept calling me "sister" in that Indian fashion of being overly familiar.

He was the typical Indian immigrant who had made it in this land of opportunity. Actually, even I need to complain less about my life here and see it as a fantastic opportunity to learn and grow. At least there is the New York Public Library, there is the New York Times, New Yorker which redeems everything about my life here!

What was nice was to see groups of Indian women go from one store to another, from sari to grocery shops, with a look of unadulterated joy on their faces. They become animated here as they argue with shopkeepers in Gujarati or Hindi that the rice they were selling was inferior quality basmati, or telling the jeweller that the price of gold in New York was more than in Bombay. As if it made any difference to him! They even confided in him that if the prices of gold went up any further, they would not be able to get their daughters married!

It's amazing how the shy, introverted women I have seen elsewhere come alive in Little India.They tend to spend a whole day here eating and shopping and even catching a Hindi film if they have the time, and I'm sure they feel safer here than anywhere else. They are no longer the frightened and intimidated women brought to an alien land by their doctor or engineer or trader husbands.

I myself know the relief of being attended to in stores by middle aged Indian men or women with whom I can have a conversation about things I am familiar with. It's such a relief from the high school kids at check-out counters at the malls. I hate telling these gum chewing white kids preoccupied with music blasting into their ears from their Walkmans that their math is all wrong, and that I need to get more change back for my 20 dollars.

There is something about the tactile feeling of holding the very Indian fruit, the mango. And how much you remember home when it passes from one hand to another – from the grocer's to yours! It makes the fruit warm and your homesick heart, warmer.

Nothing brought home the fact of how far from Hyderabad I was until I saw row upon row of Andhra pickles in the grocery stores. I remembered the time – I think of the mind as some sort of screen where images flash in a continous manner as in a film – when Lakshmi would bring her relatives and their friends to help us in the yearly ritual of making pickle.

Do you remember those summers? Do you remember those women? Can you imagine, I can still recall some of their names when I can't remember any of the names of the people we met at a party four weeks ago. Well, do you recall how the women laughed and teased each other, and cast knowing glances at us, as if to say, now that you are menstruating you will soon have unlimited sex. Such lusty women they were.

And the song they used to sing about betel leaves and arecanuts, which were vulgar to say the least. It still plays in my ears. How we sang their songs even if we didn't fully understand the underlying meaning – and one day when we found Dhruv humming them, we stopped singing them abruptly!

It's this bellyful of laughter, that makes a woman's bones rattle, that makes her breasts jiggle and brings tears to her eyes, that keeps Indian women sane. It's this maddening loneliness, the absence of community that drives women neurotic here. We don't need to visit psychoanalysts in India or lie on couches to talk about our suffering. We have sisters and sisters-in-law and mothers and aunts to talk and laugh with. Even in an in-law's house we have that sister-in-law to sit with in verandahs and talk about your husband or children. Or your childhood. Anything and everything.

Or we have women in the neighbourhood who are always willing for a chat provided you give them a cup of good coffee. What pleasure in reviling a daughter-in-law who wears too much make-up or worrying about a daughter who has gone into the IAS for whom it would be difficult to find a husband!

How our own mothers stood at the gate of their houses, promising to come over and have lunch with each other, but quite happy to stand at the same spot for hours, chatting away. How we would laugh when we heard them saying that they had to be going because they had a lot of work in the kitchen – because we knew even after they said this, they would continue standing there and talking for another hour.

Here in America, especially in these posh suburbs, they say your neighbour could be murdered or screaming with pain and no one would know about it. In New Haven, our neighbourhood is so exclusive that we just don't stand at the door and talk to the woman next door about what we are cooking for dinner. My neighbour is an oncologist, divorced and single, so probably she opens a can of tuna for dinner, and eats it in front of the television. Maybe one of these days I should send her idlis and sambar. But such familiarity would be misconstrued by Dr Margaret, and I'm sure Vikram would be angry with me too.

Avanti, child as she is, already thinks India is dirty. The poor child thinks Little India is India. But what would she know about the smell of mangoes and red chillies and the pungency of fresh garlic in the air, that is India for me? How would she know what summer was – the sounds of the koels and magpie-robins on our fruit trees, and such happiness in our lives because we didn't have to go school and could sit under the mango tree reading a Gerald Durrell or Salinger. Or the summer smells of jasmine flowers that threw such a fragrance all around our mothers as they walked around with these flowers tucked in their hair.

Guess what? Avanti, who was at her cranky best by the time we reached home, wanted for dinner? Spaghetti and meatballs!

Love from the mother of a brat.

Malavika

CHAPTER 15

Haasini sat in front of the dressing table combing her long straight hair, trying to twist it into a fashionable French knot, quite oblivious to her surroundings. All of a sudden, she heard someone tapping on the door that she had closed. She hoped it was not her mother who wanted her always to plait her hair, and secure it with clips like traditional Andhra girls.

She wished she could chop off the long hair and wear it till her shoulders, the current fashion among girls her age. On an impulse, scissors in hand, she chopped off a strand in the front letting a fringe fall on her forehead in what was called the 'Sadhana cut' after a popular Hindi film actress.

Someone continued to knock persistently at the door.

Haasini was sure it was Dhruv. These days he was not only playing with her lipsticks and nail polishes that were on the dressing table, but sneaking to their mother about the Rajesh Khanna posters she had stuck inside her cupboard. She had just seen the film *Anand,* and like many young girls of her generation, was smitten with this hero who wore guru kurtas and crinkled his eyes so endearingly.

"Ma, Akka has a poster of the pimply Rajesh Khanna. She actually bought it for five rupees, Ma," she had heard him telling her mother.

"Rajesh Khanna? Haasini? What is this hero worship, when you know your final exams are coming up! And soon you will be off to Kalakshetra. You have to get serious about dance, you know," Vani said looking up from the newspaper that she had time to read only in the afternoons.

Haasini wished she didn't have to share her room with Dhruv. She wished she had a room to herself like Malavika did.

In Malavika's long rectangular room there was a dressing table in one corner, and on the other side was a study table with her books. She had large windows too, on whose sills they both often sat talking. But then, Malavika was an only child and she could afford to have a room to herself, she sighed.

Waking up from her reverie she realised to her surprise that she was in fact in Malavika's house. This was not her room!

She recalled now, twisting the hair firmly into a snake-like coil at the nape of her neck, that she and Malavika were going out with their friends for a film and then to Lavanya's house for dinner. Her mother, her conservative mother, had as usual protested. But Malavika's mother convinced her that the girls were old enough to stay out late, and promised she would have Ram pick them up by midnight.

Haasini was after all 17 years old, Malavika just a tad younger, and the girls should be given a little freedom Rekha had argued.

It was Malavika at the door. She pushed it open when Haasini unlocked it and came into the room in a lemon green dress secured at the waist with a leather belt.

Haasini gave her own clothes a long and hard look. She looked so old fashioned in the maroon salwar kurta her mother had made her wear. Not cool or chic at all. She felt envious that Malavika looked so nice in the clothes her father had brought for her from a trip to London. In an act of defiance, she flung the white dupatta on the bed, pulled off her kurta and looked in Malavika's cupboard for clothes she could borrow.

"I think I'll wear this white sleeveless shirt with my jeans. Do you mind, Mala, if I wear your clothes?"

"Hmmm... it's not really my best shirt, but take it if you want to! Wait, let me look for a scarf..." Malavika said, rummaging through her chest of drawers.

"Ha, now I look like a fashionable *Femina* model, instead of someone who has just arrived from a small Andhra town," Haasini said.

She turned towards Malavika, an eyeliner bottle in hand. She wanted Malavika to help her contour her eyes with it. That, and dab a little rouge to add a flush to her cheeks.

Malavika looked at Haasini and thought she looked radiant already. Different, with hair coiled at the neck and those high-heeled shoes that made her small friend look so tall. She smiled and took the bottle of brown eyeliner from Haasini's hands. Dipping the brush into the liquid, she drew smooth, unfaltering lines around the almond shaped eyes that had a life of their own, dancing even when her friend wasn't. Haasini's face came alive. She was working with the expressive eyes of a dancer, Malavika realised and she touched that face with affection.

Haasini smiled. She is my friend, my dear, dear friend – but why do I feel jealous of her sometimes, of her looks and her confidence, she wondered.

She turned toward the mirror and on an impulse, picked up a lipstick and painted her lips a bright red. She looked at Malavika. Make-up made Malavika more beautiful. Why did the lipstick and tight shirt make herself look like a painted doll?

Haasini tried to still her mind, telling herself to banish jealousy from her mind, from her heart and from the room itself. Should she rub off the lipstick, after all?

"Mala...."

"Haasini, now what? You look gorgeous, and can we go now? I can hear Lavanya's car honking!"

Malavika was all of sudden a girl in a hurry. She had been excited the whole week about this Saturday evening, her first adult evening out.

"Haasini, come on. We have to go, look at the way Lavanya is honking, as if the car's on fire...."

"Malavika, just a minute, I don't know if..."

"Hurry, Haasini, we have to pick up the others. And I don't want to miss a single frame of *The Graduate*."

"*The Graduate*? I hope you haven't whispered a word about the film to Amma..."

Malavika grabbed Haasini's hand and both ran out of the room, past Malavika's mother, who stood stunned like a policeman in Hyderabad amidst speeding traffic.

Rekha shook her head in amusement. But she was beginning to have her moment of doubt. The girls looked as if they were up to a lot of mischief and it was she who had persuaded Vani to let them go out with their friends. Had she been too liberal?

But let the girls have fun, she thought. All too soon they would marry, have children and be burdened with responsibilities. She herself had been married by the time she was 20 years. Let them enjoy being on the threshold of womanhood, she told herself, walking into the kitchen to set the table for dinner.

She smiled thinking of the two young girls who had rushed past her in such excitement. How quickly they had grown up and how pretty they looked! It seemed only yesterday that Malavika had crept out of her lap to crawl in the courtyard, and now she was ready to explore the world. And that child, Haasini – how graceful the small gawky girl had grown up to be. How transformed she was on stage, dancing like the great Yamini Krishnamurthy herself. Her arangetram had been nothing short of spectacular, at least she and Ram thought so. The critics were complaining about this and that, saying the dancer was too young to be doing those love soaked varnams. Well, somebody should first tell them a thing or two about their own grammar!

She turned on the gas to heat dinner of phulkas, dal and potatoes that Ram liked, and prayed to her favourite goddess, Meenakshi, that the two girls would have long and happy married lives.

Once the movie was done, the girls got into Lavanya's car to go to her house. Her parents were not at home so they would have the house to themselves.

The film had moved them, and Malavika could hear Haasini humming Simon and Garfunkel's *Sounds of Silence*. She wanted to talk about how Mrs Robinson seduced the young boy, but she couldn't get Haasini to herself all of that evening.

Malavika sat on the floor cushions in Lavanya's room and looked around the room bursting with clothes, posters and LPs. There were pants, shirts, belts and shoes all around, and it looked as if Lavanya never ever folded her clothes and put them away in a cupboard. Even her bras. They hung sadly from a hook like a saint martyred.

Malavika quickly averted her eyes hoping no one has seen her looking at the bras and thongs, and turned to the bookshelves. Except the high school texts, Shakespeare's tragedies, *Tess of the d'Urbervilles*, and Basham's *The Wonder that was India,* she couldn't find any other reading matter. She looked closer, confident that she wouldn't find anything that would embarrass her there. But what was that? She spotted a book by Erica Jong called *Fear of Flying* which had a picture of a woman's lips shaped like a clitoris. Malavika had been afraid to read even Wodehouses's *Mating Season* lest her mother think she was reading pornography. Clearly, Lavanya was already reading adult books. Maybe, as was rumoured in school, Lavanya really had boyfriends. The gossip was that she had even become pregnant, and gone for an abortion during school hours. But surely, thought Malavika, being their good friend, Lavanya would have told her and Haasini about it. So this must be only a rumour.

On the other hand, that seemed a stupid idea. What would she tell them –"Girls, I'm pregnant, shall I keep the baby or have the foetus aborted?"

Malavika stepped out of her dreams, and looked around for Haasini. She had hardly had her at all the whole of that evening. The room was being darkened now as if it were one of those new discos, with Bob Dylan playing full blast on the on the gramophone. She saw Haasini sitting in a corner with Lavanya, smoking.

Smoking? Her best friend, smoking? No, it couldn't be! Haasini and Lavanya beckoned to her to sit with them by the music system and listen to *Tambourine Man*, her favourite Dylan song. If Haasini's mother knew what she was doing here, she would be angry not only with Haasini but with her too, Malavika wanted to scream.

She refused to catch Haasini's eye, feeling guilty instead at the way the evening was turning out. It was as if it was she who had gone astray, not Haasini.

There was a discussion of some sort going on in a dark corner of the room. Malavika moved towards that, hoping to be a part of the animated group. It was late, but it looked as if no one was planning to eat any dinner. Was Lavanya giving them any dinner at all? They had eaten something after the film, but chaat was hardly dinner!

Lavanya got up to bring something from the fridge. A bottle of white wine. Her aunt from America had given it for her 18th birthday, she announced, as one of the other girls got up to bring the small gold-rimmed glasses laid out on the study table. Lavanya seemed to know that white wine had to be chilled before serving. The wine was passed around.

Malavika protested, but no one else paid any heed to her disapproving looks. Not even Haasini. She was already stretching out her glass for more that Lavanya, quite high herself, was pouring.

Malavika picked up a glass and sipped a little wine. Her throat burned, but after a few more sips, she began to like the bitter sweet taste.

"My aunt also wanted to give me a bottle of champagne, but said she couldn't carry it all the way from America as she had so many gifts for people that she had to bring," Lavanya was confiding to her friends.

"Not that I haven't had champagne already. Lovely... bubbles hitting you on the nose..."

"This is great! I love the taste," Haasini was saying, taking a deep puff of her cigarette.

Malavika looked at her awestruck. When had Haasini learnt to blow rings like that in the air? And she was giving her judgement on the quality of wine as if she was born in France, not Guntur!

Although in a daze, Malavika still felt obliged to be part of the conversation.

"Dustin Hoffman was soooo sexy. I wouldn't say no if he asked me to sleep with him," gushed Lavanya.

"Neither would I," giggled Haasini.

"Boys are so immature, you know. Why do they have to make these silly comments and stare at your breasts when they see you on the streets? These Hyderabad boys are frustrated, take it from me," Lavanya continued. "There is this 25-year-old hunk I know. His idea of after-dinner entertainment is driving in his father's Fiat on Tank Bund."

"So how many men have you stayed with after having dinner?" someone asked.

"Wouldn't you like to know?" Lavanya retorted. "Only the other weekend Rahul called to ask if I'd go with him to Goa for two days."

"And did you, Lavanya?" Haasini asked, agog.

"If I liked him enough, I would have. But then, this guy is a first class creep. Forget Rahul. Malavika, why are you so quiet? C'mon, tell us about the love of your life?"

"Love of my life? Honest. I don't have any boyfriends. And Haasini knows about it."

"But your best friend Haasini has one. We know that. That guy, what's his name."

Haasini smiled enigmatically. A boyfriend! Malavika now believed the girl would do anything.

"You don't know about it, Malavika? Poor, poor Malavika. Naturally she hasn't told you about it. When it comes to a man there are no friends. It's a woman who will hurt another woman the most."

"Lavanya, no. A man will hurt you. But a woman can never hurt another, especially if she's a friend. I'd never hurt Haasini. Not in this lifetime, at least."

"You are welcome to your opinion, Mala.... I'll get the Ouija board out."

"Is there anyone we want to conjure up and talk to? Haasini? Malavika?"

"Yeah, Rhett Butler," Malavika said retreating to a corner. Her head hurt and her stomach churned. She wanted to throw up. She felt betrayed by the girls around her. Especially Haasini. She moved away from the smoke and the noise to a bed where she laid her head on a small pillow on which was cross-stitched 'Sweet Dreams'. She clutched the pillow, hoping to fall asleep and wake up only the next morning. Or even a year later.

"Abortion? It's a most painful experience."

"Better to be on contraception. You know that Kiran in the Commerce class? She got pregnant. The principal, Mrs Ruby Thomas, called her parents...."

Malavika wanted to ask who had become pregnant. Not Scarlett, she hoped. "Clark Gable wouldn't do such a thing, especially before getting married," she whispered, wondering who would be her Rhett.

Dear Malavika,

I'm being featured in a magazine for Indian dance and music and I think I am their cover story. I find this publicity a little distressing, though I am happy too at all the attention I get nowadays. If I didn't confess to that, I would be lying to you.

A journalist, a young writer who is charming and intelligent, has been coming home to speak to me on behalf of her magazine. Every time she has come home, she has found me in one of my kaftans, hair oiled and rolled up into a bun, which seems to surprise her.

After we got over the initial formalities, she asked me, "Akka, why do you never dress up when you are at home?" Which must have been a polite way of saying you look like a hag! She herself is so young, so eager, so full of enthusiasm. In the polite celebrity laugh that I have now cultivated, I told her that when I was young like her, I loved dressing up and spent an enormous amount of time looking at myself in the mirror.

She didn't believe there was ever a Haasini unlike the one sitting before her, who loved dressing up. For that matter, even I can't believe that I could be so obsessed with beauty, or the lack of it, all those growing years. But you will vouch for that Malavika. You, with the deft make-up hands, whom I think of often when I have to do my eyes up for a performance. Mala, I have to dress up so much for performances, and I have to do it so often in a month – all the rich Kanchi silk saris and gold jewellery, bangles and nose studs, the hair ornaments – that I revolt at the thought of dressing up even at home.

These kaftans will do. I no longer feel the need to be someone else. Do you think, Malavika, as the inner life gets richer, you accept yourself for who you are, and dispense with unnecessary ornaments and baubles? Or do you think the external austerity is a reflection of the inner restraint I've developed?

The wildness has gone out of me. Many years ago, I know you were shocked that I smoked and danced and drank like all those other girls, on our first evening out at Lavanya's. That was a phase, Malavika. If I'd not gone through that I wouldn't have reached where I'm today. At that time, I had to defy Amma, do everything that she hated, to prove that I could be my own person. Why does a daughter feel the need to rebel against her mother the most, when she is one person who will love her unconditionally?

You write that Avantika is growing, but you worry about her growing up in America. You wonder if they'll date American boys. But Malavika, how can you protect them, prevent them from finding out what hurts? Tweezing the eyebrows hurts. Waxing hurts. Tell her that. Tell her, her Atha from Hyderabad wants her to know these painful truths, and asks her to find things that will make her happy. A bag of hot popcorn still does it for me. And songs from the film Guide still move me. We never listened to our mothers. Why do you expect your daughter to pay any attention to what you say?

Don't impose your ill-gotten wisdom of middle age on the girl. At 17, I thought Amma was old fashioned because she told me not to use make-up. But now I find painting my face is the most unnatural thing to do. What we know at 35, we don't know at when we are 16 or 17. To know, to understand that, we have to live each day.

That benediction of the elderly (I avoid using the word 'old') – "Child, bless you with a long and happy life"– would be a curse. Eternal happiness, like eternal youth, would be painful. I'm actually beginning to like the furrows and lines I'm developing on my face. The lines are for all the roads I've travelled and all the experience I have gained. I even think with the insolence of a woman in her thirties, that if I were to meet the Haasini of 15 years ago, I would find her extremely frivolous and empty-headed.

Why was it so important for me to wear high-heeled shoes to parties? How I used to hide them in your house, wear them when we went out and put them back in your cupboard! I'm angry with that silly girl for wanting to prove a point to her mother. Your daughter will begin to question everything you tell her. Have you noticed how life moves in such concentric circles?

As I grow older, I realise happiness is neither desirable nor one prolonged state of being. But happiness is in the arbitrary moments – when I know my abhinaya in the long piece has been particularly good, which only one or two in the audience may have noticed.

It was a moment of pure happiness when I was at the ashram recently for some meditation classes. I saw a young girl sitting by her mother or aunt, I am not sure, who couldn't keep her eyes closed and let them wander around the hall to see me looking at her eyes so wide open.

A more shocked smile I have still to see!

Happiness is sitting by the window to listen to the koels sing on the trees, and wonder if it's some male crying for his mate, Koo-Kooooo. How he makes those mating calls.

These isolated moments of happiness are enough for me now, Mala. I've stopped looking for the highs. Or for enlightenment.

I'm discovering who I am. I know I'm going through an important phase of my life.

Little plants, tiny saplings, are sweet and endearing. But don't you think of them as being silly, too playful, swaying this way and that way with every wind? I much prefer the giant trees for their maturity and wisdom. They are like grandmothers and grandfathers in their strength.

And I thank the mother goddess who brought us together many years ago – sisters born in separate houses to different mothers, but sisters nonetheless!

Love to your daughter, my goddaughter. And you, my sister, stay well.

Yours as always,

Haasini

CHAPTER 16

Shoulders tensed and back arched, Malavika's slender body was taut with anticipation. She was sitting on the edge of her seat in Ramakrishna 35mm, wondering if the director would allow the hero and the heroine to kiss, or if two birds would fly across the screen symbolically as they usually did in Hindi films.

But this was one of the new wave films which had won several awards in East European cities like Karlovy Vary, where such festivals were held. And indeed the hero took the heroine's face in his two hands and kissed her right and proper on the lips.

Malavika sighed with satisfaction, collapsing back into her chair. She extended her arm to reach for the popcorn that Haasini was holding, took a handful and stuffed it into her mouth knowing it wasn't ladylike at all. Once she stuffed the popcorn into her mouth, she became aware of her surroundings and of Vikram. In the excitement of the film she had forgotten about him, the young man from America who, if she said yes, would turn into a husband with whom she would have to live forever. Vikram's parents were in a hurry to get him married for they believed, with his qualifications in finance and marketing, he was quite a catch.

She looked at him, sitting next to her, handsome even by a Rhett Butler standard. He had lived without a wife for 26 years of his life and quite happily, she told herself. He could live without her or any other girl for a few more months, by when she hoped she could make up her mind about marrying him.

Vikram had been staring mesmerised at the arched back of the young woman sitting next to him. It reminded him of the rainbow that had so fascinated him during his childhood in Calcutta.

He was seized by the desire to run his fingers down that back, and tickle her through the sari the he guessed rightly she was not used to wearing, for the pallav had fallen off again, revealing her blouse and through them her full breasts. He turned his eyes away quickly. Her parents didn't seem conservative, so why had the girl worn a sari? Surely, it was not done to impress him? Would she be comfortable in pants, dresses and snowboots? It was going to be a tough life in Connecticut where he lived – would she be able to cope, be a wife and friend to him? She had a strong back, he could tell, looking at it one more time.

Malavika had become involved in the movie once again. But that was her. When she watched a film, she became so engrossed in it that she would imagine that she too was a character in the story, even if only a minor one. Often, she would imagine she was a friend of the heroine, especially if she was someone as beautiful as Deepti in the film. If she liked the hero, she would follow him to his room, wanting to be his girlfriend and listen to him sing a song for her as Rajesh Khanna had done for Sharmila Tagore in *Aradhana.*.

Suddenly, she was weary of the drama of the film, and asked herself why she was becoming so involved with the heroine's life when she had her own issues to sort out. She had to make the most important decision of her life, and soon.

In the meanwhile, the heroine, Deepti had run into the hero, Partha, who began singing a song for her. New wave or old, every Indian movie had to have songs, and this one was no exception. The song had a nice lilt and was based on a classical raaga. It gave her the opportunity to move away from the story and contemplate her life.

Haasini was nudging her and whispering, which made Malavika irritable. Why did Haasini want to talk to her in the middle of the song? For a dancer, Haasini was pretty insensitive.

"Mala, do you like him?"

"Like who? The hero? He's a little effeminate, no...?"

"No silly, not him. Vikram. Are you going to marry him?"

"Oh, him? Nice of him to bring us to the movie, and that too in his father's car, no?"

"He has been looking at you from the time we came to the theatre. I think he wants to marry you."

"Oh, shut up, Haasi. But why does he have to speak so softly? Can't hear a damn thing he says."

"Ssh... he's looking at you. Don't shout. I think he's nice. If you don't marry him, I will."

"Will you? Do you think he has read *Wuthering Heights*? Or *Gone with the Wind,* my favourite?"

"*Wuthering Heights*? Chheee, but I know you have your opinion on that. Why don't you ask him yourself, Mala? He's staring at you."

Vikram couldn't understand why the girls were talking so much during the film. Did women always talk so much? His mother didn't, and he didn't have any sisters. The girls he knew at college when he was doing engineering were a different lot, somewhat studious. He returned his gaze on Malavika, and was pleased with what he saw.

There was a lovely light streaming onto her face making it glow. He decided he wanted her in his life.

This film was interesting but he wanted to take Malavika out of the darkness of the theatre into sunlight. She seemed to be a girl who would flourish in sunlight.

The film was Malavika's idea, and her friend Haasini's. He knew Malavika's parents wanted Haasini to accompany them to the theatre, but he wished she had dropped out and left them alone. However, she had not only chosen to come to the film but talked to Malavika incessantly. She had bought popcorn and chips enroute as if they were on a long journey to a place where they would be deprived of food.

He began to get restless because the heroine, a beautiful lady with a lovely smile, no doubt, had begun to sing another song. This sounded like a sad song and Malavika had whispered to him the heroine was pregnant without having got married first When had the heroine become pregnant – he had not even seen them go beyond a kiss? He wished women wouldn't want to watch such mushy movies and wondered if he'd have to do this for the rest of his life. He had been warned by his friends in America, but his mother was determined to see him married now that he had settled into a good job.

If this beautiful girl agreed to marry him, he would be saved the bother of seeing other girls his mother and his aunts had lined up for him.

He wanted to take Malavika out somewhere where he could look at her beautiful face, hear her laughter, decide the colour of her eyes. But she seemed so engrossed in the film, and it would not be polite to ask them to leave. He got up, and walked across the aisle to go outside to have a smoke.

Malavika was surprised to see Vikram going out of the theatre in the middle of the film. Was he bored? She prayed to Hanuman that he liked going for Indian films. She herself was addicted to the make-believe worlds of movies and books.

She liked being in someone else's stories. And dreams.

But what were her dreams, she asked herself. She wanted to write, maybe to teach. Travel around the world with a man she loved. More than anything, she definitely was going to love the man she'd marry.

She was not sure if she loved Vikram as yet. She loved Amma, Appa, Haasini and Dhruv, but then she had known them forever. And she adored and looked up to Siraj. She was supposed to feel ecstatic in the presence of Vikram, wasn't she? Feel some magic? She didn't know for sure if love existed. But all the great books of the world spoke about it. Elizabeth Barrett Browning wrote beautiful poems on her love for her husband. Even with their conventional upbringing, Jane Austen's heroines fell in love. And what about Audrey Hepburn in *A Roman Holiday*? If all these characters with whom she lived with in her imagination felt love and passion, she was sure she was going to feel it too.

But when was she going to fall in love with Vikram? After she went with him to America? But what if she married, went with him to America, and then discovered she did not love him at all?

She noticed from the corner of her eye that Vikram walking back to his seat next to her. As he sat, his hands brushed her elbow. She liked that, this intimacy. She sniffed the air, her nose like a radar. What was that smell? Vikram didn't smoke, did he? Well, if he did he would have to give all that up once they married, and vodka and whisky or whatever he drank too, if he drank. But then, if she decided not to marry him, none of this would be her concern at all. She relaxed, deciding to concentrate on the movie.

After the film they walked to Havmor in Basheerbagh to have ice-cream. Suddenly Vikram felt happy as there was music he was familiar with playing from the juke box and he wanted to dance.

"Will you dance?" he was about to ask Malavika but changed his mind. What would Haasini do if they danced?

The girls had started talking once again.

"Malavika, say something to him. Talk."

"Umm...."

"Anything. Tell him the music is nice. That you like the *Lovely Rita, Meter Maid* by the Beatles that they are playing. I think he's itching to dance with you."

"Why can't he ask me? Why are you smiling coyly like that?"

"Because he is looking at me. If you'll excuse me, I'll go to the bathroom to touch up my lipstick."

Vikram was relieved that Haasini had decided to leave them alone. But he'd better be quick with whatever he had to say. That girl would probably come back soon.

"Is your friend going to come with us to America when we get married, Malavika?"

Malavika, what a lovely name... he thought.

Malavika... It sounded nice when he said it that way, softly. Eh, what was he saying. Marry him?

"Vikram, Haasini is my friend from childhood and except for brief periods in our lives we've never lived apart from each other. Marry? Is this a proposal?"

"Yes, Malavika will you marry me?" he asked, placing his hand on hers and engulfing not just her small hands but her life.

She opened out her hands and he traced the curving lines of her palm and said, "You have a long life..."

"A long life, and a happy marriage?"

He looked at her. "Yes, most definitely so."

"Do you like to dance, Vikram? Do you like music?"

"Yes. Yes to both. And I would ask you to dance with me except your friend the chatterbox is coming back. I'm sure you've much to tell her." And he leaned forward and kissed her on the lips.

"In love you have loosed yourself like sea water, I can scarcely measure the sky's most precious eyes and I lean down to your mouth to kiss the earth..."

The lines from Neruda's poem came to Malavika's mind. That's all she could think of at the moment when the sky and the ocean met at a point in the horizon. The precise moment when he touched her lips.

Dear Haasi,

We are separated by such distances, such illogicality of time and space that we have to depend on the letters to keep in touch. I do wish this irrational distance between us was somehow closed, and we would be able to see and talk to each other more often. Calling you would be so expensive! But my problem is, if I don't talk to you, I feel out of touch with some part of me that is me.

I just celebrated another birthday and the years do roll by somehow. Vikram was out of town at Baltimore. At this stage in our marriage, it does not matter much that a husband is not there to help you cut the cake and blow the candles. It was just the girls and me doing their favourite thing – eating at a lovely eatery near our home, a pizza place. I haven't got a card from you – have you been travelling again? Because I can't imagine you forgetting 1st November.

I have to confess, I am in a state of shock at hurtling towards middle age so rapidly, so swiftly, so quickly. I mean before you and I know it, we'll hurtle towards the forties and fifties, an age we thought belonged to our mothers, aunts and their friends. Forty, in fact, was an age reserved for people like Rani Pinni, Amma's sister. Recently, however, she herself turned 60, as her daughter told me recently. Her daughter, my cousin Vidya, delivered a girl recently and so Rani Atha is a grandmother now. People in America talk of gender becoming obiliterated in the modern world. I think what is getting diffused is the difference between generations. We are our mothers, and our mothers, their mothers. And our daughters will be like us sooner than we want them to.

Anyway, do you remember Rani Pinni? How she was always one of us, helping us to drape our saris and getting us to wear low-necked blouses, even if our mothers didn't approve of that? Well, she was visiting the East Coast last fortnight and came to visit us. And of course we played Scrabble for old time's sake. Vikram joined us, but not Avanti and Anisha. "Aww Mom, we've got lots of homework," they said, when I asked them to play.

Fortunately, in this country they don't address me as Aunty, so I can forever be Malavika here. But recently, I did ask myself whether I should still be buying pink lace bras or wear those large hoop earrings that my daughters too love. Especially Avanti. I may be too old for lacy pink bras and dangling earrings but inside I still feel 17 or 18. When people who meet me after a long time and say, "Malavika, you're still the same," I want to say, "Yes, I am. Why should I be any different?" I still feel the excitement of the young woman who sat in a corner of her room, and read one classic after another.

Haasini, inside us, do we age at all? By the same logic, think of this. As babies, we have our mothers to take care of us. But when we are old, too weak to move, when we dribble from our mouths, when our memory fails us, who will take care of us? Our mothers would have if they were alive. But do you think our children will hold our hands and take us for medical check-ups and to our friends' homes? Just as we did for them when they were young, and I presume, we would if they had children.

There is still in me the same capacity to laugh, to cry, to dream and to question. I am still as vulnerable to hurt and pain. Why do people think as we get older we are better able to cope with pain and sorrow? The same things still hurt me, Haasi. Lies and callousness still hurt. Though I have to admit, I am more capable of forgiving and letting go now. Which is what I think age and maturity are about...To have that compassion to forgive. Even if you cannot forget. We will still grieve the betrayals, but with age, we learn to accept.

This is my birthday revelation: Haasini, in life we must never ever become world weary. Though I think optimism is a matter of hormones. There are those days before those dreaded days when I feel so gloomy that I don't want to get out of bed. At other times I'm so euphoric I want to wear my purple dresses, dangle outlandish earrings, slip into my stilettos, smear a shade of bright red lipstick, run out to the pavement and embrace the world.

My wedding anniversary is coming up too shortly. Wonder if Vikram will remember the day.

Yours in age, as in youth,

Mala

PS: I believe we carry the child within us through out our life. To me at least, she is like a third daughter to me, my favourite daughter whom I want to protect and nourish for a long time to come. While my two other daughters have each other, this little girl was a lonely child, happy only when she was with you.

CHAPTER 17

Haasini was trying to wake up, but was so sleepy that she could barely open her eyes. It was dark outside. The moon and the stars were still glittering in the night sky, and she decided to turn her face towards the wall and continue sleeping for a few more hours. In the periphery of her mind she knew that the room was not her own, but in its familiarity seemed comfortable enough. There was the fragrance of jasmines and roses even in her dreams, and she tossed in her bed. There was an indescribeable excitement inside her that made her want to get up and dance. In her sleep.

She realised with a start that it was the morning of Malavika's wedding. She opened her eyes and noticed the light was already switched on near the dressing table, and Malavika was having her hair plaited by her mother who was trying to press down those wayward curls so they wouldn't break out of the bobpins. Into the hair from where jada gantelu with gold bells on them would dangle, would be plaited jasmine flowers that were specially ordered for the bride. Amidst the fragrance of jasmines, roses and sandal in the room, Haasini sat up with a jerk and rubbed her eyes. She glanced affectionately at her friend. They had talked so late into the night that she had no idea how Malavika had even woken up, and looked so completely beautiful that early in the morning.

The previous night, hearing the chatter of the girls, Rekha had come into the room and switched off the lights.

"You should go to sleep. I am exhausted. You need to feel fresh tomorrow, Mala."

But when Rekha shut the door and left, they continued to talk. This, after all, was going to be their last night together sharing girlish secrets. From the next day, Malavika's life would take a different turn. At some point in the night Malavika had fallen asleep, but Haasini unable to sleep, prayed to Jesus, Krishna and assorted goddesses for Malavika's happiness.

Malavika caught Haasini looking at her now, and gave her a faint smile. She did not say anything, and she didn't have to. She knew her friend was muttering a prayer for her, for this day and for others after this.

"Haasi, look at Malavika, how beautiful she looks!" Rekha's energy and enthusiasm radiated through the room like the fragrance of sandal. She was wearing a maroon silk sari with a green border, and Haasini remembered the sari she herself wanted to wear.

She turned to her mother who was also in the room. In fact, not just her mother but there were so many women there that Haasini was surprised she had slept through the commotion.

"Ma, have you brought the orange silk Gadwal...."

"The Gadwal? I thought you were wearing the Kanchi pattu sari, the parrot green one with a pink border. I've also brought the matching emerald bangles and earrings for you to wear."

"No, Ma. I want to wear the Gadwal Rekha Atha has given for Malavika's wedding," Haasini said Rekha had told her while gifting the sari, "You're like a sister to Mala. More than a sister."

"But Haasi…"

"Yes. Ma. I've changed my mind. Must we argue in the morning? Let Dhruv go home to bring the other sari, Ma please…"

"Yes, Haasi. Let's not argue on an auspicious day like this. But do you know, Mala, when your friend Haasini decides to get married, we won't know who she will marry until the last minute because she will keep changing her mind. And to think you made up your mind so quickly. Vikram, of course, is such a good looking boy. Handsome like a Telugu movie actor!"

Haasini decided to have a shower and get ready. She couldn't usually keep her eyes open without her morning cup of filter coffee. But she decided to have a bath first that day, wanting to be by Malavika's side the rest of the time. There was something else she decided at that moment – she was not going to have any of these early morning weddings that were so precious to South Indian brahmins. She would have a church wedding at an appropriate time in the evening. Or a Punjabi wedding at a nice hotel on a convenient Sunday.

She draped on the Gadwal sari, the pallav with gold peacocks falling over her shoulders. Her mother plaited her hair, tucked some jasmines into them, cracked her knuckles to ward off the evil eye, and said, "Haasini, next year by this time we will have to find a bridegroom for you."

"Ma!"

"Malavika, now you have to look for a good looking boy for your friend. Just like Vikram. "

Haasini turned away coyly, which was not like her at all.

Weddings made most women sentimental. Rekha had had a tear hovering around her eyes permanently the last couple of days. And to think she was the one in a hurry to get Malavika married, for she believed when the right man came, a girl shouldn't wait.

Vikram was an eligible bachelor with good qualifications as everyone was whispering, but Haasini felt they could have waited for a year or two before getting married. If Malavika were just getting engaged, and not going away the next month, she would have been less miserable. In fact, she should have waited for another two years and done her Master's in English Literature, Haasini felt.

She looked at Malavika in the mirror, and saw the face of a pixie-looking girl she had loved all her life, and that face seemed even more beautiful today. She sighed. Where was the question of completing a Master's degree? In the current mood her friend was in, she didn't even want to wait for the BA results! She had not been paying attention to anything Haasini said.

Malavika had begun to daydream even more than usual. It would frustrate Haasini that she could withdraw and drop out of the conversation so easily. If there was one person who knew Malavika well, it was Haasini. Yet there were aspects about each that the other did not comprehend.

"Haasini, child, why is it that you have become so preoccupied. I thought that was Mala's privilege."

"No Rekha Atha, I was just thinking...."

"Don't think too much today. You have to take care of your friend. From tomorrow she won't need you or me..."

"Amma, why do you say things like that? Just because I'm getting married how can I not need you or Haasini?" Malavika said, adjusting the addiga chain her grandmother had left for her to wear at her wedding. She missed her Avva. She had wanted to see Siraj too that morning, but she had not had the the time to see him at all in the last few days, with all the shopping and last minute things she and Ma had to do. He at least would understand that strange feeling she had begun to have in the pit of her stomach when she was not near Vikram.

"I didn't mean it that way. But you'll see... Haasini, will you tell the cook to send all of us hot cups of coffee, especially for Mala. See if you can get some breakfast for us," Rekha said.

Haasini looked around for Dhruv or one of Malavika's young cousins to get them some coffee. But there was no one. At weddings, everyone seemed so busy making food, serving it or eating it. So much excitement and commotion, Haasini thought, unwilling to pretend at anything. There – there was Dhruvi in his new kurta pyjama and mojris. Were these the mojris Malavika and she had bought at the Numaish in January?

"Dhruvi, be a dear and tell those young girls you've been trying to talk to for the past few days to have the cook send coffee and pongal for the bride."

Haasini hurried back into the room. She was more concerned with getting Malavika ready for the muhurtam. She was in charge of the bride's make-up. Since Rekha Atha had insisted that she do the elaborate bridal tilakam on Malavika's forehead, she took a toothpick and began to draw the kalyana tilakam with affection. She drew the pattern easily, for Malavika had the ability to sit still.

"Akka...." Dhruvi interrupted, cutting into the stillness of the moment. The two had fallen silent for they knew the moment of parting would soon come. Sooner than they would have ever imagined.

"The cook wouldn't send coffee through me. He was lying, saying that coffee wouldn't be ready until 6.30. Of course, I told him it was for the bride and after that, he was all smiles. He then gave me the pongal with nice piping hot sambar. Just like the way Malavika Akka likes it...."

On the brink of adolescence, his voice was beginning to crack and made him sound like a frog. Malavika gave him a smile.

"Akka..." Dhruv said, ready to fall in love with Malavika himself. "You look so beautiful. Be careful, don't let Haasi Akka smudge and spoil your face."

Haasini glared at him but ignored his remarks.

It was time for Malavika to be taken to the mandap that had been built in the large garden of the house. Ram did not want any hotel wedding that was becoming the vogue in a newly rich Hyderabad. The nadaswaram and the mridangam players were involved in the complexities of a raaga.

Seetha Kalyana Vaibogame... is what they are playing, for sure," thought Malavika, as she held Haasini's hand

and walked out of her room as demurely as a modern girl brought up in Hyderabad could.

Vikram was already sitting in the mandap unable to tolerate either the cacophony of the mridangam beats, or the smoke billowing into his face. The priests' sonorous chants made him even more uneasy, and he wondered if the handsome young boy, Dhruv, would be able to smuggle another glass of coffee for him. He wanted to halt the proceedings and go out for a smoke. But he was hedged in by his parents on either side, his mother having woken him up even before sunrise, which he had rarely seen in his life. At least they let him wear a silk kurta over his dhoti. Otherwise his wedding photographs could never be circulated among his friends in America if, as he'd originally been told, he was bare-chested.

"Vikram sir, repeat after me, *Mamah*...." The priests were prolonging the proceedings so much that Vikram was sure he would choke with the fumes. That was when he saw Malavika walking towards him escorted by Haasini.

He stopped himself from letting out a gasp of admiration. Malavika sat next to him, and smiled as she said something to him. At that moment Haasini realised how deeply in love they were – and to think that Malavika had not breathed a word about it to her! Anyone would fall in love with her friend, she thought, fiercely loyal – she was that good looking, and had read all the books in the world, it seemed to her sometimes. Why, if she were a man, she would be in love with her too, though what she already felt was nothing less.

Her legs ached from standing steadfastly behind Malavika, and her jaws ached even more from smiling at the steady stream of guests who were throwing akshintalu at the couple. She decided to sit down for a while behind Malavika and Vikram, smoothening the folds of the sari that had become crushed. She wanted Dhruv to bring her a napkin or a tissue to wipe Malavika's back that was damp with sweat in the humid morning that had settled over Hyderabad.

"Malavika, your friend doesn't seem very happy about your marrying me. See how possessively she's holding on to your sari. Are you sure you've asked her permission to marry me?"

"Sssh... she's got very sharp ears. When we were kids she could hear the smallest sound that was made even in the front benches of the class."

For a moment, Haasini became jealous of the growing bond between her friend and her soon-to-be husband. She decided to get up and supervise the lunch towards which most of the guests were heading.

She wanted to look for Siraj who she knew would be looking at the proceedings with interest. Maybe she could sit with him for the lunch and not feel so lost.

Dear Malavika,

Happy birthday! I know these greetings are late, and I'm sorry. Please put it down to my hectic dance schedule (partly) and my inability to sit still and write to you (mostly).

The easiest and simplest thing for me would have been to go to a shop and buy you a birthday card that will tell you how much I miss you. But that would be sending you someone else's cleverness.

I find the commercialisation of emotions that is occurring way too vulgar. We seem to have an appropriate card for every occasion these days. Even a painful experience like grief is neatly packaged into a few words, so all we need to do is to buy one of these cards, sign on it, mail it to the person, and be content believing that we have expressed sympathy.

But where in the card is that empathy you feel for a friend who has lost a mother or a husband? How can a card express the numbness you feel for that friend? Such helplessness, in fact, that you can do little else than hold the hand of the person going through the pain. There is nothing of that mutual silence in these cleverly worded cards.

Why can't we learn to communicate our feelings directly? Which is why I'm sending a card, however naïve it looks, that I drew and painted it myself – can you believe it?

I was reading somewhere (I have begun to read a lot of feminist literature) that all of us are born gifted, but that as we become older we become conscious of being judged and shy away from our creativity. I find that so true. Do you recall as children how we painted greeting cards or sang the songs we composed? And the monumental adventure stories that you wrote which we put up during our summer holidays? We didn't care a whit what the adults thought of what we did (except Siraj's opinion – he of course ripped the plays apart, which I am sure you have not forgotten). We expressed ourselves because we wanted to, because we were young, because it gave us happiness. Where have we misplaced all that innocence, Mala?

Why is that I am so diffident when someone asks me to sing now? Yes, even I, the trained Carnatic vocalist choke when I realise someone is listening to me. Why is it that I become so afraid of the apashrutis, why am I not able to set my soul free, feel for a few seconds at least the same joy that I have seen on the faces of great musicians. Why great musicians? I see the joy even in the faces of men and women who sing simple folk songs, and dance with such abandon.

Even the birds sing with such abandon in our gardens during summer. Even in the creative arts, why must we feel competitive and sing to be the best and to be better than the others or receive applause? Why can't I dance or paint only because I want to, not because I want to win an award?

I like to think of dance as a way of exploring my innermost self, a way of listening to its longings and secrets, not as something that will get me the Padma Shri. But you won't believe how commercial dance has become these days, all that bitching and politicking for favours. The one-upmanship that goes on among my peers about which dancer is performing at which festival, or speculation of how she got that far and who her godfather could be. Yes, as you've probably heard even there, some do sleep their way up. All this makes me weary.

Then there is the constant talk in the media as to who the number one dancer is, as if it's a matter of mathematics. Spiritual experience and creativity? Forget it! We are no longer even aware of the spiritual element in dance or music.

"I sing, I celebrate myself," I say, if you will forgive my paraphrasing of the Walt Whitman quote.

I hope you like the painting I have done on your card. I like it quite a bit myself. As a dancer, I've made some attempt at singing, but never at drawing and painting. As I work with this box of crayons – Staedtler, for your information, that I picked up in London – I feel I am visiting some primal gardens of childhood..

With Amma not being her usual self, and feeling the need for my presence more, I have been thinking of cutting down on my travels. This will allow me to spend more time with her as well as give me the freedom to do all the things I have wanted to do in life. Find time to read some of the great literature that you and Siraj read together.

You wrote in your last letter asking if Amma's illness has made me religious. Yes. Though I would say, not religious so much as spritual. The harmony of certain places affects me deeply now.

The piety that hangs inside the Notre Dame Church, the coolness of stone walls under my foot at the Meenakshi temple in Madurai, and circumambulating the Bodhi tree in Bodh Gaya where Buddha attained enlightenment. These places not only take my breath away, but anchor my wayward mind.

The one question that still plagues me – plagues you too no doubt – is, who am I? What is the purpose of my life? But at least in the few hours I'm at these temples and churches, ancient as they are, I'm lulled into calmness. An inner peace descends.

My love to Vikram. To little Anisha and my own favourite, Avantika. The other day I was looking at your wedding album and thought how young, how immature, and how hopeful we three looked. Such naivete on our faces, so unsure of ourselves that we didn't even know whether we should stand or sit for the photograph. Everybody told you and me how gorgeous we looked in our silk saris and jhumkies. How as the bride you looked radiant and how I, as your friend, was also beautiful, so beautiful they said that I would be married soon.

But did we know who we were then? I doubt it. We had to arrive at middle age to discover that.

Let me sign off now. I wish you well on this, and every coming birthday, dear Mala.

Love,

Haasini

PS: Have you heard of the great film and theatre director, David Abraham? I hear he is looking for me. And here I am, wanting to cut down on my dance. Is anything about our destiny that is ever in our hands? I doubt it.

CHAPTER 18

A stillness, similar to the hush that settles in convents when the nuns have prayed and retired to their rooms, had descended on Seshagiri Rao's home. The cook and the maid had left for the day, and there was the faint sound of a tap leaking somewhere in the house. Tip, tip, drop by drop it dripped. Maybe in the kitchen. Or in the bathroom. Or somewhere else. It was a sound that occurred in the periphery, so it bothered no one.

Haasini locked the front door and went into her room. Her mother and father would be resting and there was still time before she left for the dance classes she taught.

It had been around a year or more since Malavika had left for America, and Haasini continued to miss her. She thought she could get over the void that seemed to have settled deep within her by writing to her often. But today was one of those days when she wanted to see her.

Haasini wanted to sit with Malavika in the verandah of Siraj's house, their legs entangled, talking about school and their future, or simply reading together. Malavika loved to read stories out to her. So if anyone were to ask Haasini if she had read the great works of literature she would have to tell them, she'd *heard* great literature!

She walked towards her bookshelf and took out one of Jiddu Krishnamurthy's books. She sat on her bed leaning against a pillow, and opened the book to a random page for she liked reading him from wherever she pleased. But then she decided to make herself some coffee before immersing herself in the book, and got up and went to the kitchen. She liked her coffee just the way it was traditionally drunk in South India – in steel tumblers that sat in steel cups instead of saucers, in which the milky coffee was poured back and forth, down and up till bubbles from the froth travelled into the air, along with the aroma of the Arabica.

She heated the milk in a saucepan, poured the decoction that was kept through the day in a large brass filter by the stove, and looked for the Horlicks bottle in which now sugar was stored. It wasn't in the cupboard where her mother usually arranged her bottles neatly according to size. And certainly, without sugar she could not drink the coffee. She did not want to wake up her mother, so she renewed her search, looking in the corners of the cupboard and all around the kitchen, even in the dining room.

Haasini wondered if her mother had hidden it away from her father who had begun to sneak around eating sweets. No one would have minded that except that he'd been recently diagnosed with diabetes. If her mother didn't make any sweets, he would wander into the kitchen to eat lumps of jaggery or palm sugar. Once when her mother had opened the Horlicks bottle for sugar, she had been very upset to find it empty.

Since then she had taken to hiding the sugar, though Haasini wasn't sure if her father had perhaps found the bottle and left it elsewhere. She was sure one parent was trying to outwit the other but the result was that she did not have sugar for her coffee. She debated if she should give up on the coffee and go read her book. Maybe even write a letter to Malavika. But the commotion had meanwhile woken Haasini's mother, who came into the kitchen sure it was her husband hunting for sugar.

"Amma? I thought you were asleep."

"Asleep? You think your father will let me sleep? Fidgeting all the time, opening cupboards, opening files, looking for punching machines and stamps. Or calling up that lawyer, Mohan. I heard the sounds in the kitchen. I thought it was your father and had to literally sprint here. Is it already time for your class, Haasi?"

"No, Ma. I was just trying to make coffee. Shall I make you some? But I can't find the sugar anywhere."

"Oh, that. Because of Nanna, I've hidden it inside the sack of rice where he can't find it. The other day, I found sugar all over his easy chair near the radio. He listens to news all the time as if our lives depend on who wins the elections. There are ants all over the house because of the things he drops everywhere."

"Amma, I'll look for the sugar. Don't strain yourself."

"Strain? With him in the house where's the rest for me? Have you found the sugar?"

"Ma, but the sugar isn't here. Are you sure you kept it here in the sack of rice?"

"Not there? Where could it have disappeared? There's the thief – let's ask him what he's done with the sugar."

"Vani! Looks like Haasi and you are about to have some coffee. Can I have some too? And put an extra spoon of sugar for me, Haasi?"

"Coffee? Why do you want coffee now when you know you have to have a glass of Horlicks in the afternoon? Forget that now. What have you done with the sugar?"

"Sugar? I haven't seen the bottle next to the stove in a long time. I was wondering where you hid it. Were you hiding it from Haasi? Dhruvi would have given it to me but he's so busy preparing for his entrance these days. Why do you make him study so much, Vani?"

"Oh, you haven't seen it in a long time? How come the last time I found it in your cupboard among your clothes and files?"

"Vani, why would I take the sugar into my room? And have ants eat up all my important files? Maybe Haasini hid it in my cupboard. She was always a naughty child. Not like her friend, that girl who's in America now, who was always polite. I forget her name. Has she been to Washington as yet? Met President Carter?

"Haasi kept it in your cupboard? My God, she's no longer a child! And imagine, he can't remember Malavika's name and that child asks about him in every letter she sends us."

"Your mother is going senile, Haasini. What is she talking of sugar in my cupboard? I'll be in the verandah. Bring that awful concoction she gives me in the afternoon outside. I'm expecting somebody. I'll wait for him there. Are my pants too crumpled?"

"Visitor? But no one's come to see him in the last ten years. He thinks he's still an important official of the Andhra government. He keeps imagining that the government will call him back."

"Ma, the two of you are like spoilt, squabbling children."

"Yes, he's a child, the child of my old age. Worse than Dhruvi when he was a young boy."

Haasini picked up the tumbler of coffee with the ends of her dupatta and retreated into the room. Her father had been diagnosed as having dementia, and had become as difficult as a child. He picked fights on the phone with the telephone or water departments, or people he met during walks in the park. He even accused the postman of stealing his fixed deposit checks and threatened to report his insolence to the postmaster general.

"The postmaster general is a friend of mine. A fellow much junior to me, but I know him. I'll talk to him to terminate the services of swindlers like you. Cheating good citizens of the country who worked to make Gandhiji's ideals come true. Look how they treat us in our old age! No respect for the likes of us. At least, young man, you have the decency not to talk back. Look at the other fellow who comes in the morning, flinging our letters when I've shown him the postbox I've tied to the gate."

He, Seshagiri Rao, the former Secretary of Industries in the Andhra Pradesh government, had begun to believe the world was against him. He would warn Vani against opening the door to strangers who he believed were builders wanting to buy his property. When two young boys came to collect donations for a Sai Baba puja near their lane, and had rung the doorbell to give Vani a pamphlet, he became furious.

"Vani, I know you'll sell the house behind my back to those good for nothing fellows who'll pull down my house and build multi-storeyed apartments. Do you know, when I was in government we brought stay orders against buildings higher than three floors. But some fool of a minister changed all that. There's too much corruption in the country. That's where the problem is..."

"But Mr Rao, I'm not selling the house. Those are boys who sometimes carry my bags when I go to the market. They are performing a puja in our colony. They wanted 100 rupees, not your property."

"Erecting pandals on the road, and creating traffic problems! It's people like you who encourage rogues to fritter away time when they should be building the nation. And Vani, what were the papers they gave you. Was it property notification?"

"Property notification? My God! No one wants this house, don't worry."

By early evening he would wear an ironed dhoti and jhubba and sit on his easy chair waiting for visitors. When no one came, he would grumble that fellows these days never stuck to their appointments. For some time, he had a student come and type letters for him, but when he too disappeared, he wrote letters in long hand, or had Haasini take down dictation.

In the nights he would complain of chest pain or discomfort in the stomach, and wake up Vani who would in turn wake up Haasini. Haasini would promise to take him to the hospital in the morning. In the morning when Haasini took the car out of the garage to drive him to the doctor, he would begin to weep wondering where Haasini was off to so early in the morning. On being told she was taking him to the hospital, he would refuse to get into the car, saying he was alright and he couldn't understand why the women of the house made such a fuss over his health.

Sometimes Haasini felt acutely the powerlessness of ageing parents. At the hospital when the doctor asked for the blood reports her father would look at his wife who was carrying a file in which she kept his medical history. But she had dropped it somewhere on the way and they would begin to argue till the doctor appeased them.

"I headed the Industries department in the Secretariat, Dr Mathur. My department was known for its efficiency. Not a single file out of place. And here my wife can't find my reports," he thundered. The doctor asked him to sit down and not to worry about the report, that he would ask the diagnostics centre for another copy.

Haasini's shoulders would hunch in weariness at the vulnerability of parents. Hers, and everyone else's. She wanted to protect hers from the cruelties of the world — uncaring doctors and callous public servants.

So our hearts are broken, she thought. Not at any precise moment of the death of a loved one. But much, much before that, when you know and understand that your parents are growing old and nothing you do will ever stop your mother or father from dying.

A few evenings later when Haasini came home from class, she couldn't find her parents anywhere in the house and panicked. Where could they have disappeared without telling her? Just as fear was tightening her heart, she saw the two of them in the backyard. Her mother was pouring hot water from a huge brass gangalam, and giving her father a bath.

She turned away, a smile on her face, moved by the affection between them that stayed even after so many years.

Dearest Haasini,

Thank you for your birthday wishes, belated as they were. Do you think we are the only ones in this day and age, when people have little time to even make a call, who still write to each other? But, I so believe in the romance of writing letters.

We belong to another time and age, you and I. We are two old fashioned girls, surely. And what shall we do, we two old fashioned women when we become old old, ladies? Sit under Siraj's mango tree and read stories to each other? Or shall we hold hands and look for the girls who played hopscotch on those large squares in the veranda of his house? No, I think we will wear soft, flowing skirts and blouses in cotton without bras and vests, with no slippers on our feet, let our hair fly, and sing the songs our grandmothers sang!

I know what! When we two are old, we shall do things we have always wanted to, and do only those. Not because something is right or because it's good for our families. But because it's what we want to do.

On summer afternoons we shall lie on our bed and do nothing but read our favourite books, and during summer nights go out and smell the jasmines and raat ki rani in the garden. And on full moon nights go out into the courtyard and bathe in the moonlight. We shall look at the tulasi there and remember the tarnished gold mangoes on the ochre kanjeevaram saris our mothers wore when they prayed to the tulasi every morning. Remember all that, and hear the resonances of Kasturi tilakam lalata palake that my Avva taught me.

As ageing women, we shall sit in my room. You will move in with me, of course, and we shall talk to each other and look out of the window for Siraj, Ma, Pa, your parents, and all those who have left us physically, but will always sit in some corner of our minds. We live after all, as long as we are remembered. Look for them through the windows among the stars, and look among the same stars for our unborn grandchildren, whose bellies we will tickle just to hear them laugh. When they grow up a little we will teach them how to play Snakes and Ladders and Ludo, and recite to them silly rhymes we have made up. We'll laugh, we'll sing, we'll cry together and nothing will seem so sad, because we will have each other.

What a silly, happy card you sent. As you said, we are all born gifted, and probably it's our so-called culture that kills our creativity. When I was young, actually much before you moved in, we had a little girl who came from the village to be my playmate. She was a few years older than I, but do you know, before I even woke up in the mornings, she would be busy drawing elaborate muggulu in the yard! She would even fill the half empty notebooks I gave her with these drawings and patterns that she would work on endlessly. I guess since she did not have an opportunity to go to school or have a childhood, she poured all her longings into art.

And you should have seen the number of ways she'd do her plaits. One day there'd be a simple plait, another day she would coil it with ribbons and flowers. She often wanted to style my hair but was too afraid to ask if she could. What was her name – Dolly, was it? It wasn't, actually. It was Subbalakshmi or something, but in my arrogance I decided it was not a nice name for my playmate, and changed it to Dolly, and she didn't even protest at this change in identity.

At least she was happy with us for a while, before they took her back to the village and got her married, which was the only time she cried. When we asked Dolly what the matter was, she said she didn't want to go back and get married, but was too afraid to say so because her father was a tyrant who had beaten her and her sister frequently for being disobedient.

I remember telling her that since Amma had promised her father that we would send her back in a year, she was obliged to do so. But Amma assured her that if her in-laws did not treat well, she was welcome to come back to Hyderabad and live with us.

I am not sure Dolly was reassured but she was too afraid to protest, and went back to her village where I am sure she married, and I trust was happy. Her name must have been changed once again. From Lakshmi to Dolly to Parvathi or Padma.

As I wrote a few months ago, I have started to write poems and stories. I am thinking of enrolling at NYU for a course in creative writing. More importantly, I have begun to do something that my mother had always wanted me to, go for Carnatic music classes at the temple. These are basic bhajans, but at least my mother will be happy that there are other things I can do besides reading.

I miss India. To me, it's not a country, but a dear person that I love very much. So many faults and disasters, but when you love someone you forgive them for everything, don't you? One day, I hope I will be able to come back, and if I'm lucky, be near you once again.

Is your mother recovering? And I am sorry to hear of your father's onset of dementia. I think if there is one thing more sad than a sick child, it's a sick parent. At least, in the case of the child, you know the child's natural immunity and strength will enable her to get better, for sure. But with a parent you know their bodies and energies are flagging. And it is agony for them when they realise they cannot move that swiftly any more, or that their memory is failing them. We feel the pain and realise we have to let them go. But how do we muster that courage? How can we let them go when we've not even acknowledged their presence fully in our lives?

I miss Ma and Pa and I feel heartbroken knowing I am not there for them as they age. Do keep an eye on them for me, Haasini.

Ever your friend,

Malavika

CHAPTER 19

Malavika leaned back on the small quilted flannel cushion of the rocking chair, thinking how not doing anything for a few minutes, but just sitting and rocking like this had become a luxury she so yearned for. She uncoiled the toes of her sore feet, stretched her aching fingers and closed her eyes. She wanted to finish the new book that everyone was raving about, *Zen and the Art of Motorcycle Maintenance* or at least one of the *New Yorker* magazines that were piling up, but decided all that could wait for another time, when her daughters were in bed.

For now, she wanted to not only to rest her body, but her mind as well. It had been a tiring, tiring year since Anisha's birth. But just as she was beginning to doze off, Anisha woke up, wanting to be carried. Malavika lifted her from her bed, cradled her in her arms and surfed the television channel for *Seasame Street* hoping Miss Piggy would keep the girl quiet for a while so that she could have her nap. Miss Piggy was singing a song about crossing the street, when she felt Anisha climbing off her lap.

The lightness was a relief, and Malavika dozed off once more when she heard loud screams. She opened her eyes, sure that Tom was chasing Jerry on the cartoon channel, which was always followed by all sorts of thuds, crashes and screams. Too much violence on American television, she thought sleepily, till she realised the screams were Anisha's.

All of three years herself, Avantika was entertaining the one-and-half-year-old Anisha, and everything was going well, until in a moment of anger she picked up a diaper pin and pierced Anisha's chubby thigh with it. Avantika had pressed the pin so deep that Anisha's face turned purple from the shock of the large pin in her body. Malavika jumped out of the chair and scooped up Anisha, not sure if she should quieten her first, smack Avantika, or just get on with the job of dislodging the pin from the baby's skin. She wanted to call Vikram and tell him to come home to help her tide over the chaos. But then, he would say there was a crisis of this kind every day at home and she must learn to cope.

Just a few months ago the two children had stood strategically poised on the staircase ready to jump through the gaps in the railings. Malavika had stifled a cry of horror, and calmed down in time to pull them away before they injured themselves. When Vikram came home, she had wept hysterically. He'd hugged her and promised to take her out for dinner for saving his two mischievous daughters.

Vikram came from a family of two boys, where despite the rough and tumble of childhood, they had grown up healthy and had survived. So he never felt their daughters were in any real danger. He was only irritable that Malavika had so little time for him, or rarely went out with him, even to the movies that she loved.

Malavika lifted Anisha to rub antiseptic cream on her leg, putting off punishing the older one for the moment. But Avantika was already looking sorry, and she decided not to be harsh on her. Anisha was a mischievous elf, but a pretty one with curly hair and a dimple on one cheek. In the turmoil of being a suburban mother raising two children on her own, it was difficult to abide by her mother's advice: "Malavika, treat the children as gifts, the biggest gifts God has given you. Do not punish them and bend them to your will. Nurture them so that they grow up into good human beings."

"Yes Ma, I'll be kind to them but not before I catch up on my sleep," she would tell her mother in an imaginary long distance conversation.

For Avantika's delivery, since it was Malavika's first, Rekha had arrived in Connecticut to be with her daughter. But she was aghast at the American doctor's attitude. The gynaecologist had told Malavika that since the delivery was a normal one, she could go home the next day. Her mother was shocked at this cavalier attitude.

"Devuda, how can we expect Malavika to manage the baby and the house on her own? What do these American doctors think, not wanting to keep mother and baby in hospital for longer? Mothers stay for three whole days in India, but who is going to listen to me here, not that American doctor for sure."

"Do you remember, Ram, when Malavika was born, not only my mother, but her sisters and sisters-in-law all turned up in Hyderabad!" continued Rekha over a long distance call to Ram, getting teary-eyed.

"Yes, they didn't give me a minute with you or Mala," he had said.

"That doesn't matter. What mattered was that they took care of every need of mine and Mala's. The only time they brought Mala to me was when she needed to be breastfed."

Rekha remembered how her mother would not even let her get down from the large four-poster bed on which a mosquito net had been tied. And when she complained that she was gaining weight, putting on so many kilos around her waist and hips, and that she should be going for walks at least in the nearby park, her mother had become angry with her saying, "What, and tear the uterus and not be able to have any more children?"

Instead, one of her aunts gave her an oil massage, every day, pressing her stomach down hard till she cried with both pain and the pleasure of the massage. If the uterus did not go back into position in the first 45 days of the delivery and the stomach was not flattened, the bulge would stay forever, she was warned.

Even the baby would be given a massage to strengthen her limbs. Malavika gurgled with pleasure during the massage, but wailed during the bath that followed. Here in America, however, Vikram wouldn't hear of a massage for the baby or his wife, and Rekha had to be content with making fresh food for Malavika. She certainly didn't want her to be eating canned vegetables and frozen foods, which Vikram advocated when all of them were tired after a long day with the baby.

Rekha had been excited when Malavika told her that she was expecting her second baby because it had been her lifelong regret that Malavika was an only child. She was set to go to America to help Malavika again, but Ram wasn't keen, and with his recent heart problem and diabetes, she didn't want to leave him at home by himself.

"I love our Mala but I cannot be locked up in their suburban home, Rekha. I will miss my routine here of walks, and movies on Saturdays with my friends," Ram said as they had dinner. "You go. I will get you the ticket. Surely now you are a seasoned traveller and can travel by yourself."

"It's not a question of whether I can travel by myself, Ram. Mala will need my help. And Avantika will need caring. She's only five years old, so tiny herself. But if you won't go, I won't too. I can't leave you alone. That's final," Rekha said firmly, feeling sad nonetheless.

She wrote to Malavika asking her to come home instead for the delivery, but Vikram would not hear of it. Hospitals in India were far too unhygienic, he ruled. Rekha wept reading the letter.

"But all the best doctors in America are from India. What is Vikram talking about? So many are from Andhra, especially from the Osmania and Gandhi Medical Colleges. More importantly, there are thousands of women here who deliver babies at home, and in small hospitals, and no one is any the worse for it. Mala herself was born in a small nursing home in Hyderabad among people who loved her, and continued to love her. But Vikram and his American ways... Poor Mala..." she murmured at her own helplessness.

Some months later, Malavika delivered a healthy baby girl. When photographs of the two girls were sent to them, Rekha began to feel sad once again. She wondered how her girl would manage to take care of two children by herself in America. Like most husbands there, Vikram would help, but Malavika would have to cook and take care of Avantika and the newborn too. She hoped, even in her sadness, that Malavika didn't take the easy way out and eat frozen foods – worse, give the little one Gerber and other bottled foods that everyone abroad seemed to do. Next time Malavika called, she would tell her to breastfeed her baby for as long as she could, and then right away switch over to home cooked food – mashed rice, pappu with soft vegetables.

Malavika's father walked into the room just then, wanting to know if that was a letter from Malavika; instead she vented all her anger. Thrusting the letter into his hands, she said, "Yes, it is. Here, look at the photographs of the baby, Vikram's mother says she looks like you." Ram couldn't understand why his wife was so angry with him, when she should have been happy that Malavika had delivered another normal child. Women, he thought, shaking his head in disbelief and walking out of the room.

Malavika, too, missed having her mother around at home for the new baby. After Avantika was born, when she wanted to sleep, she would just hand over the baby to her mother. When she craved for something to eat, she had to only to ask her mother and she would go into the kitchen to make it for her, even rustle up a quick gaajar ka halwa, her favourite. In the months since the second baby arrived, she was so tired coping on her own, she barely had the energy to walk into the kitchen to shake out some cereal from the box and pour milk into it. Mostly, she ate Avantika's leftover rice and dal that had become cold from sitting on the kitchen counter for so long.

She had spent so much time sterlising bottles, opening readymade baby foods, mixing feeds and feeding the two children in Donald Duck bowls, that she began to wonder if babies did anything in life besides eat and throw up, and if she would do anything other than tell them another Dr Seuss story and read anything other than Dr Spock herself.

It seemed such a long time since she had read a book or a magazine, or even the newspaper. By the time she got past the front page of *New York Times*, some child would cry for her attention. If she didn't give that attention on time, the newspaper would be grabbed, torn and flung into far corners of the house, which meant more work for her. When one of them screamed, she had learnt to drop the newspaper or the book she had just picked up to read without further ado, and give the child her immediate and complete attention.

She always hoped to finish reading the newspapers on some weekend when Vikram would take the children out, and had hungrily begun to save the features section. They accumulated in such large piles in the basement that one day Vikram took them out and junked them in the garbage.

A suave husband who made enormous amounts of money, cherubic looking children, and a lovely suburban home in the US were not part of Malavika's adult goals. Babies, especially, had been far from her mind. Even if marriage did enter her mind occasionally and children did manage to crawl into the outer fringe of her vision, they were children who wore polka-dotted dresses and ribbons in their hair, who she would take for walks in parks where everyone would smile at them and tell her what angels they were. The only effort on her part would be to read aloud *Winnie the Pooh* stories and play peek-a-boo. Mashed potato being spat onto walls, and unending bedtime stories had not figured in the dream at all!

In fact, nobody had told her that children routinely spat food, messed up the house, refused to be toilet trained and pulled at the pink satin ribbons she braided into their dark hair. She had never been warned about the tantrums – the way a child could hold her breath till she was allowed to pour water into the telephone. Certainly no one had told her that a little daughter, of all people, could break your heart when she looked at you with those beautiful eyes and cried, "Mama, you are a horrid witch. I like Dadda more."

This, when it was she who had cleaned up after the brat had thrown up all over the car on the way back from the Bronx Zoo, while the Dadda merely rolled the windows down and sat with her on his lap after she had been cleaned up.

She shook off her reverie to realise that Avantika and Anisha were sitting quietly in front of the television, the frenzy of the cartoon characters having calmed them down. In a corner of her mind, Malavika knew she must not let her children watch so much TV. But the Society to Curtail Excessive Television Among Children, if such a society existed in America, would have to forgive her. She had no more energy to play with them, trying to find them hiding behind cupboards or living room drapes.

She stretched her long legs, and closed her eyes again holding the diaper pin that had caused such havoc a short while ago. Thank god it was the end of another hectic day, she thought – till she realised she was through only half the day.

Where was the father of the children? Why was he always at work? Why was he never around for coughs and fevers, tantrums and crises? How did he manage to appear only when the girls had gone to sleep and looked angelic as all children do when they are asleep.

But really, she had had enough of this life with no one for company but the girls. She didn't want to see another stuffed toy in her life. Not another diaper pin. Or another cartoon channel. She rebelled against the shapeless clothes she had begun to wear because she was feeding the baby. She wanted to wear saris or at least smart Anne Taylor dresses and remind herself of the woman she had forgotten she was.

Above all, she wanted to read a decent adult book.

Dear Malavika,

Are you surprised at the British postal stamp on the letter, or have you by now got used to letters from me that come to you from across the globe? Well, I'm in London to work with David Abraham. Yes, the very same director who had Alec Guinness play the dark Iago some years ago. This time it's an international star cast for a production of Ramayana. The story is told from Sita's point of view, and we have a black actor, Julian from Nigeria, who is playing the mighty Hanuman. Rama is the British Michael Brooks. I shudder to think what my grandmother would have said to this casting. Even Amma, who was also upset that I was leaving her for a year or more at least, was aghast at the nationalities of the cast. Of course there is no rule that only Indians have the right to play our gods. Do you remember the Raja Ravi Varma prints in our homes with green faces, gold crowns and red saris? Well, considering how avant garde everything in this production is, it may not be out of place if some of them used body paint and tattoos. I'm the only Indian, and more importantly, the only dancer. The others are all cross-cultural international stage actors.

When I was summoned to London for the auditions, I was surprised as I had no idea how David had even heard of me. Only recently, Julian told me that he had seen me dance many years ago at the Festival of Indian Arts in London, and sent his agents to India to scout for me. Though I'd heard of him, rather read about his flamboyance and various marriages in magazines, I was reluctant to come to England, especially Ma being the way she is now with cancer.

Believe me, they wouldn't take no for an answer and dragged me here literally. Short of sending the mighty Raavan to carry me off here! Now I am not only in awe of the director, but overwhelmed by the magnitude of the production. Costumes from the runways of Paris, Tokyo and Milan, but you should see the shapeless robes I have to wear. Props from America. Sound system from Japan. It's all so magnificent, but what I am petrified of is the acting. I'm a classical Indian dancer, whose alphabet is gesture and movement. I have never had to speak my part, the mudra has conveyed everything. I've had no voice training. Do you remember what a squeaky Lady Macbeth I was in school? I was assured that I didn't have too many lines to say, and that David wanted his Sita to tell the story of an oppressed woman through dance.

So I've forsaken country and home to learn another language anew at the feet of a master.

Amma being ill and needing to go to the hospital frequently for the chemos was unable to come with me. She has moved to Bombay with Dhruvi, and I have no doubt the doctors at Tata Memorial are very capable.

Amma, incidentally, thought I shouldn't abandon classical Indian dance for acting at this stage of my life.

"Dancers younger than you may need such breaks and gimmicks. But not you who've built such a reputation in classical Bharatanatyam," she said even as she helped to pack my suitcases.

I have left behind not only Amma but my students for this new life – that is exciting, I have to admit.

So I'm going to be here for the next year-and-a-half at least, staying in a lovely studio apartment. Finally the dream of living by myself has been fulfilled, though I don't know if I really enjoy all this cooking and cleaning of the house.

But Amma's pachchadis, Hyderabad's churans and homoeopathic pills from Dr Ajay have followed me even here. I am often so tired after rehearsal that I don't cook. I just eat a cheese sandwich with some pickle thrown on top.

You know, this David Abraham is a tough guy, a taskmaster. Most of the time he just sits on his director's chair quietly and doesn't say anything till you begin to wonder what emotion or expression he wants from you. He said nothing nice about the way I was performing for the first few days, and I began to wonder if I should request that I be allowed to quit the production and go home. If I am not the Sita he wants, I should go home and not waste his time, or mine.

Julian, the Hanuman and my only companion here, assured me I was good and should continue interpreting Sita just the way I was doing. He explained, silence was the essence of David's style, and I mustn't be put off by it. By letting us interpret the roles the way we want to, he also puts tremendous responsibility on us to give our best.

Finally, just last evening, David said I was good. Good? I was magnificent! You know the Ashokavanam scene where Hanuman visits Sita with Rama's ring and tells her she must be patient and wait for the Lord to rescue her? Sita becomes angry and tells him: "Patient? How long am I to bear the burden of sorrow as the cosmic battle between good and evil is being played out in the world?"

Something got triggered at the moment – maybe it was the costume, maybe it was seeing Julian as Hanuman, maybe it was the enigmatic look on David's face – whatever it was, I executed some brilliant mudras and all that the great David said was, "Yes woman, you are good!"

I, who have been depressed for almost a fortnight – being away from home and Ma, the cold and the terrible weather here, this man not saying anything about what I was doing – am finally able to write to you once again. God! I've been in London for the past two months, and I have been trying to write to you from Day One.

If I had the time I would go sightseeing. I've been only once to my most favourite museum in the world, the Victoria and Albert, to see the India section with some of the finest examples of Indian textiles: I saw such fine Kalamkari panels and indigo Ikats, and so well preserved, that while I was angry that the Britishers had raided and plundered our country for wealth and artefacts such as these, at least they treasured what they stole I felt. Why is it that we think so little of ourselves that we have never valued our heritage?

I love London. I love walking in Hyde Park, and sitting in Trafalgar Square watching a mother take pictures as the pigeons sit on her daughter's shoulders. But there is a restlessness inside me, Mala, that maybe I'm missing something in my life. Rather, I feel I should seize more from life. Even this role in David's play hasn't had me in any ecstatic state. I now hear that there were many dancers who'd have given anything to be in this production, at least for the recognition it will bring them.

Julian who thinks Indian women are graceful and exotic has taken me out to pubs where we hang out and chat about our common interests of dance and theatre. And, he has been a good friend to me, almost as good a one as you. Well, almost!

But it is David who intrigues me. Who is the man behind the great director the world is in such awe of? They say he is a caring and kind person, though I personally feel he is the kind of man who wouldn't weep at his own mother's funeral! I know, I know, that's a cruel thing to say. But I really think this man who says so little has no emotions. At least not the extreme ones like love and hate. He's just indifferent, which is worse than the hate he might feel towards you.

Right now all that I'm praying for is that he'll approve of the final rehearsal before the curtains go up at West End. In a few weeks' time we'll be in Paris, Rome, Athens even New York, if critics approve of the production and the audiences like it. Not sure if we will ever go to India, as this is too expensive a production to take there.

Pray, pray to your favourite god, the mighty Hanuman, to bless the production.

Yours as ever,

Haasini, as Sita

CHAPTER 20

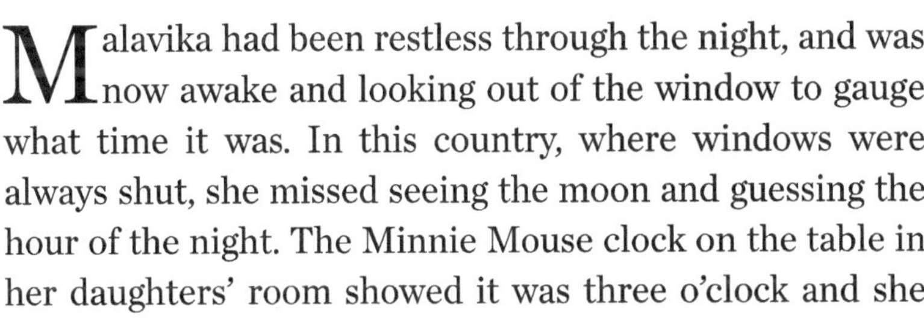

Malavika had been restless through the night, and was now awake and looking out of the window to gauge what time it was. In this country, where windows were always shut, she missed seeing the moon and guessing the hour of the night. The Minnie Mouse clock on the table in her daughters' room showed it was three o'clock and she wondered what dream or fear had woken her up.

She felt restless even lying between the innocence and plump softness of her two daughters. Both had wanted her to lie down beside them, a conflict she resolved by sleeping in the middle.

Malavika wanted to get up and fetch herself a glass of cold water, but she could not do that without pushing away either one of the girls who were clinging to her like baby koalas. She sat up finally, and gazed at the childish contours of her daughters' faces, familiar to her even in this faint light of the night. It was during moments of repose such as these, when they seemed to be energising their bodies and muscles, that Malavika liked them the best.

The two were becoming chubby like so many American kids, Malavika thought, feeling the hollow of Anisha's knee. She leaned towards Avantika, and pulled the comforter over her. She was one who slept in total abandon, holding dreams close to her chest. Malavika pushed her hair back, the fringe that covered her broad forehead, unable to understand the child's need to keep her hair so long. But Avantika's friends in class said they liked her long hair, especially the way she braided and tied them up with ribbons behind her ears, and after that it was impossible to get her to even listen to an argument about getting it cut to a manageable length.

Anisha whimpered in her sleep, and Malavika quickly turned towards her. There was residual anger and sorrow still in this little daughter of hers, even in sleep. The previous evening when Avantika had refused to play with her, wanting to draw and paint in her room, Anisha had spilt her baby glass of Coke on the painting. Avantika hit her, and both began to cry. Vikram, who was having a drink and watching the seven o'clock news, emerged from his room, to yell at them.

"Why is it that a man cannot have a moment of peace in this house?" he thundered, striding up to the girls. Before Malavika knew what happened, he was dragging Anisha out of the room, twisting her arm till she howled in pain and in fear of having angered a parent.

"Vikram, let go. She is only three. What's wrong with you?" Malavika said, as she saw the look of terror on Anisha's face, and more terrible, the rage on Vikram's face.

"I am tired of this noise and constant squabbling of kids in the house, Mala," he said letting go of Anisha.

Malavika stood pulverised by the violence she had witnessed. Vikram was saying something – in her shock she couldn't comprehend what. She vaguely imagined he was apologising for hitting the child, but no, he was now shouting at her.

"Don't look at me that way, Malavika. Don't protect the children and spoil them. Look at Anisha, forever creating chaos in the house. She's becoming a monster. She has to be disciplined!"

"But Vikram, she's a child! How can you ask me to be hard on her? She's our baby, your little girl. My father never once in his life touched me. Discipline? Look at me, what's wrong with me?" she heard herself yelling, surprised at her own anger now.

"What's wrong with you, Mala? Everything! You don't have time for me, for this house. Why, you don't have time for yourself. Whatever happened to the Malavika I married?" he said.

Angry, she carried a weeping Anisha out of the room with an already contrite Avantika following her. All three went into the children's bedroom and locked themselves away from Vikram.

Later, he had wanted to know where dinner was, but Malavika didn't answer. He had sat at the dining table and eaten a frozen pizza all by himself, as Malavika gathered when she went to get some milk for the children who had fallen asleep on empty stomachs. The lights were not turned off and Vikram had left pizza crumbs and his glass on the table. She sat down on a chair, put her head down on the dining table. And wept.

In her own home in Hyderabad, her parents had never raised a hand on her. A gentle reprimand was enough to have Malavika sulking for days and not speaking to anyone. Clearing the table, she began to wonder if there really had been no fights between her parents, or was it merely that she had not been allowed to witness the disharmony.

Deciding to give the girls a treat to make up for the traumatic evening, she changed her mind about the milk and scooped out some ice cream instead, crushing chocolate chip cookies onto it.

She switched off the lights, wondering at Vikram's anger or the reason for the outbursts that were becoming more frequent. Had it anything to do with the occasional drink he'd begun to have in the evenings, or was it his job? Was everything alright there?

She knew so little of his life these days, she suddenly realised.

In the past, she'd thought of him as a kind husband, and an even more caring father. She could not understand how in moments of rage he would become another person. A stranger.

He constantly told her that she had begun to complain too much. True, she had to admit to herself, she too was losing her temper often these days.

Once, recently, she had yelled at him to say she was lonely without him, being in the house with the girls for long stretches, and that she didn't like it that he left the care of the children to her even on weekends while he socialised.

He had not come home that night. She had called his friends to ask if he was with one of them. When even they said they didn't know where he was, she'd become frantic with a worry she didn't want to show the children.

He came back the next evening, but would not give her any explanation except to say he had gone to a friend's house to watch football. Seeing that he looked dishevelled, tired and hungry, she said nothing more. While he had a shower, she cooked a dinner with his favourite dishes. She lay next to him that night hoping he would say something, talk to her.

But he had instead reached out for her with an unfamiliar hunger that made her forget all the questions she wanted to ask. She moved to his rhythm, imagining like most women that making love was a way of building a bridge between a husband and wife, that it would annihilate the distance that often crept between them.

Carrying the tray to the children's room, she woke the girls up and tried to tempt them with the ice cream, which out of childish pride they refused to eat at first. Anisha still looked hurt, and hearing the sudden, quiet sobs inside her Malavika was saddened to realise how as parents they had failed her. With a bit of gentle cajoling, Avantika finally reached for her ice cream cup, and Anisha too, once her mother managed to push a spoonful into her mouth, ate the rest greedily, hungrily.

Malavika smiled thinking how easily children forgave, especially a parent.

Once the ice cream was eaten, the girls slept, and emotionally exhausted, Malavika too slid into slumber between them.

Some time early in the morning when it was time for her to wake up and get breakfast going for Vikram, she decided to go into their room. She wanted to forget her anger, relent, be embraced by Vikram and make things alright between them. But she was too embarrassed to admit what she wanted even to herself, and pretended she was looking for the *Times* she was reading.

She found Vikram sprawled on the bed with clothes and shoes still on. He had even left the light on in the bathroom. She bent to take his shoes off, pushed his long legs that were dangling out of the bed, and covered him with the duvet they usually shared. Vikram never felt cold, even in winter. After all these years in America, Malavika herself still could not get used to the East Coast winters. California... She would love to live in Los Angeles with sunny palm trees and fashionable women who didn't have to wear heavy jackets. She might even be able to grow her Indian Indian herbs, especially coriander and gongura.

Pulling the thick comforter over Vikram now, she switched off the bathroom light and geared herself to get on with the day. She would have to punish him, she decided, remembering Anisha's screams as he twisted her tiny arm.

Yet, there was such goodness on Vikram's face as he slept, that she couldn't believe he was the same man who had been livid with all of them the previous evening. Lying sprawled, he looked so much like her daughters. The girls did take after their father, she thought, smiling despite herself.

Malavika remembered him as the man who had kissed her so hard a long time ago, that it seemed earth and heaven had come together. He was the one who taught her to make love, who had given her the girls. She came back to the bed to look at her husband, her children's father.

She still felt she didn't know what love really was. But she slipped under the comforter, moving into the crook of his body, feeling his warmth. She turned and kissed him. Vikram opened his eyes and smiled at her, stroking her face.

He made love to her then, and she thought she would forgive him after all.

Dear Haasi,

What a lovely, lovely surprise it was to get a letter from you after such a long time! I've been wondering where you had disappeared, frantic, wanting to call Vani Atha to find out your whereabouts. And that's such great news about your work. Wow! Our own Haasini working with the great David Abraham! I can't stop talking about you to my friends who, incidentally, are all dying to meet you. I do hope your travels include New York, when I will be able to not only bring my friends but see you perform after such a long time.

Friends? Are you wondering who these newfound friends of mine are? They are Susan and Richard from the writing classes at NYU. I know we sometimes lose track of each other's lives, thanks in part to these postal delays. But I am working towards a Master's degree in creative writing, and taking classes at the NYU. Not a full load, just a few classes a week.

I have to admit, I do feel odd sitting in a class with 15 or 16 other kids from New York and parts of the East Coast who are looking for meaning in their lives through great literature. I am not that young anymore, and I do wonder what the hell I am doing in these classes – I, a mother of teenaged daughters. But I am still the Indian, still seen as the exotic species, in my silk jackets, and pants and long hair.

I find it so hard to make friends. I was always the social nerd, preferring to sit on window sills and trees and read books. I find it harder to make friends even now. Especially with these 20-somethings who are my classmates. I had Siraj. I had you. Enough, I would think, for one lifetime.

I notice, however, that you have made new friends. Julian. David (don't, dear girl, fall in love with him, for heaven's sake). You were always the extrovert who had the ability to strike up a conversation with utter strangers.

I have to admit though, it's so, so exhilarating to study in an university in the US. It has been so great, in fact, that I think I should have done this years ago, when I was in my early twenties, when I'd first come here.

But marriage then seemed so blissful, almost the nirvana one dreamt of. If only I could talk to every girl who is on the verge of getting married, I would tell them there is a life beyond marriage, and it does not always have to include your husband. In my case, I think the children came too soon, and where was the time after that for anything? Anyway, I feel young again, sitting with these youngsters, most of whom want to write the great American novel which will get them the Pulitzer Prize if not the Nobel for literature, and their pictures and interviews in the newspapers. Such dreams. I find this so amazing in this country, that they make you feel anything is a possibility, and that any dream can be a reality. This, after all, was a country built on a dream.

My professor, Dr Patrick Dempsey, is a New Yorker with two novels to his credit. He wants to know what's stopping any of us from telling our stories. He says to sit still, be quiet and take a pen and commit to paper. True, what is to prevent us from embarking on the great adventure of writing a novel, except the fear that we will get lost in the maze of characters who will come to seem more real than the people we know. To begin with, life itself is so confusing, with all its complexities and sorrows. Why take on the added burden of other lives as well for the sake of a story? But which writer thinks of all that before embarking on novel writing?

Every one of us in class fears writing, the effort of publishing our stories, and finally the critics. No wonder we writers (at last I feel like one) put off writing a novel, or when we do write, we are shy of showing our work to anyone.

I quote Professor Dempsey, who quotes Picasso: "Painting is freedom. If you jump, you might fall on the very side of the rope. But if you are not willing to take the risk of breaking your neck, what good is it? You don't jump at all."

To be a writer, you have to write, Dempsey says. But if you don't want to write, go bungee jumping at least. Learn roller blading on the streets of Manhattan, anything that makes you challenge yourself. Dare, he says. Get rid of all your fears and inhibitions. He is like a Zen Master almost, full of wisdom and aphorisms. True, we have only one life and God knows how much more of it we are left with. All of a sudden I feel I haven't lived at all. I have this urge to experience every delight life has to offer – the love of a good man, travel with a friend to Tuscany, Prague, even across to India to the great temples of Tanjore or Chidambaram (how come we never travelled anywhere together, ever?) and a few glasses of wine, and conversations with my favourite people.

And what else? Yes, certainly, I want to smell once again, the first drops of rain on the parched earth of Hyderabad, see a red beetle dragging patterns on the ground in my backyard back home. Listen to MS Subbulakshmi's Suprabhatam *in the mornings, and smell my Avva of unctions and unbridled love.*

But you need to be blessed for all this. Have the Devi smile on you to be a writer. I imagine, to even be able to rollerblade like these daredevils in mid-Manhattan without your heart skipping several beats, you have to have grace. And how blessed you are to be able to express yourself through the language of classical dance!

Prof. Dempsey is full of this devil-kiss-you kind of adventure. I have overheard that he was in Japan where he lived in a monastery with Buddhist monks for a year. He often tells us this story which I repeat to you. (His first name is Patrick, but I can't get myself to call him by that, like my American classmates do. I like to call him Prof. Dempsey. He's a teacher, and I cannot be disrespectful towards him.)

Well, the story is, three Zen monks while travelling meet a beautiful woman standing helplessly by the river, unable to cross. The seniormost monk, without hesitating, carries her across the river and deposits her on the other side of the bank.

Days later, the two younger monks are still discussing the woman, and asking themselves how the senior monk could carry such a beautiful woman on his shoulders and not be tempted. Unable to bear their curiosity for too long, they go to the senior monk. The monk smiles and tells them, "Ha, I see you two are still carrying the woman. I took her across the river, and left her on the bank of the river that evening itself."

He had emptied his mind of the incident and moved on. It was the younger monks who were still carrying her!

Before you write, Prof. Dempsey says, you must empty the mind and sit quiet so that you hear the story inside of you. Like meditation, I guess?

That's about the professor. Here is something about my brand new friends, Susan and Richard. Richard is married – rather, was married, before his wife left him and his son. He brings up the little boy on his own, teaches math in an elementary school, and takes the creative writing classes in the evening. Susan is a journalist working with a New York news agency. I am not sure if she has a partner she is living with currently, but it is her ambition to write the story of an American who goes to Communist Russia to find her grandmother. These Americans are so obsessed with communism and Russia!

Susan and I are friends, I suppose, because we are very close in age. We sit many times at Washington Square Park, listening to cello players, and watching the jugglers, often unable to move away from the dazzle and drama of New York on a sunny afternoon, to do our creative writing exercises for the next day's class. Sitting like that, I sometimes forget who I am – an Andhra girl who has been brought up conservatively, married to a banker, and is now the mother of two demanding daughters. That's the liberation of being in New York and being anonymous – and to think I've not even begun the writing part as yet. That will be another exhilaration, to express myself in writing. Imagine writing a book. I guess Siraj would have been proud of me.

I have to go. I have to finish the assignments for tomorrow before Vikram arrives and demands I give him my time. (Ah, now he wants my time, when I'm busy.) He thinks I am crazy to be commuting to Manhattan for the classes, and do you know, I had to fight with him for these classes? I know I have to take a train from New Haven to go to Manhattan to reach NYU but why doesn't Vikram understand, it's my life, and I want to live it the way I want to? I am getting old, old. And I want to do the things I have never been able to do either because of my parents, my husband, my daughters.

Sorry, I got interrupted. That was Susan Bunney on the phone. She wanted to know if I could walk around Greewich Village tomorrow, do a Happy Hour, and work on an assignment sititng in some café. She said she would ask Richard to join us if he could get away from his school. Already my mind is conjuring up parallel images of Jean Paul Sartre, Ernest Hemingway and Simone de Beauvoir in Paris cafés of the thirties talking about their work.

How exciting it is to live the life of the creative artist, Haasini. No wonder you always have happiness writ so large on your face. I am sure it comes from being a dancer.

I love you so.

Yours, writer-in-the-making,

Mala de Beauvoir

CHAPTER 21

When she woke up late on a Sunday with no rehearsals, Haasini discovered it was raining outside. Rain on the tulip buds in the box window, rain on the sycamore and oak that lined the street, rain on glass window panes, rain on the street outside, all of which made a dull, London afternoon even duller. In India, they called them unseasonal rains, downpours such as these. But in London it rained anytime and people always carried umbrellas. Haasini was too vain to be encumbered with umbrellas and raincoats and refused to carry them around like a hardcore Londoner. Many a time, therefore, she was saved from getting wet only by Julian's kindness and his large blue umbrella that he unfurled unfailingly over her.

She went over to the window to look for a rainbow. As a child in Hyderabad, she would wait for the sun to emerge after rain, and run out in the freshness of the wet afternoon chasing a rainbow. But that was so long ago and home was now here in London, she reminded herself.

She sighed and turned back from Hyderabad to realise that on this muted evening where darkness would fall soon, she was in someone else's apartment. In David's home, in fact, where he had invited her for an early dinner.

The evening's fading light gave a softness to the room as if it were from a Impressionist painting. The drapes, the cushions, the sofas, were all in shades of green – even the eyes of the cat that lazed around on the sofa were a brilliant shade of the colour. Was she called Ophelia? Or Juliet? Haasini couldn't recollect, but this cat had often accompanied David to the theatre during rehearsals and slept in the director's chair. Sometimes she would stare at the actors, yawn and go back to sleep. David paid more attention to her whims than to any of them. When he took her in his lap and stroked her, she purred in delight.

"She's a diva, that cat. She is more arrogant than our director. We must poison her one day," Hanuman would hiss into Sita's ear. While everyone thought he was whispering a message from Rama, he plotted ways of murdering the cat and Sita tried to look appropriately mournful.

Haasini felt a bubble of laughter well up at the memory but quickly quelled it, awed by the apartment she was in. And she certainly didn't want to wake up the cat to be subjected to its unrelenting gaze. She strolled around the room instead, noticing the oddness of objects around. A large malachite tortoise from Central Africa. Green again. An Indian miniature painting of a nayika on a dark and rainy night. From the Raagmala series, she conjectured. A painting of a mournful, introspective Matisse woman in luminiscent shades of blue, and three statuettes of Degas' ballet dancers.

She stood entranced before the statues wanting like them, to throw an elegant leg up to disturb the quiet space of the room. She remembered being told that Degas watched young dancers for hours in Paris before he began working on these models. These were preludes to the paintings he did of them. One statue in particular caught her attention, and she wanted to hold it, and feel its history.

Who had given David these statues? Or when did he buy them and where? Perhaps when he was walking on Champs-Élysées, with some pretty young actress? There were rumours of a French woman he was seen with once, in the south of France. They had caught her fancy and he'd bought them to humour her, after which she walked out on him, leaving the Degas dancers behind! She was amused by her conjectures, but then, David was eccentric. Haasini wondered what he had paid for those miniature statuettes – that must have been close to a few million dollars. What she could not understand or imagine was how he could love someone that much, this man who did not seem to have any emotion.

She felt a rustle of movement behind her and turned from her contemplation of those exquisite statuettes to face David. He had vanished after letting her in, leaving her to browse around. She had thought of the apartment as being small till she remembered Julian telling her that he had several homes, in America and Europe, one even in Cannes where his daughter Marguerite lived. There was a lovely photograph of Marguerite on one of the rosewood tables and she wondered which of the beautiful women in his life was the mother of his daughter.

"Looking at the Degas dancers? Bought them a long time ago because a woman I knew had got into a sulk wanting them. The one in the middle is beautiful. The others are worthless."

"They're lovely. I've always admired his work. Seen them in museums." She didn't want to tell him that she had postcards of some of the paintings in the room, too, that she treasured.

"You know, Haasini, you're a good dancer. Many years ago, I watched Martha dance. Her body was dance, all line and geometry. You are more rounded, more curvaceous, graceful like a breeze blowing through large oak trees. Maybe this has something to do with the chaos and contemplation that is part of your culture."

"You actually saw Martha Graham perform?"

"Yes, though I can't remember where. Every dancer moves to a beat. With her, the beat found her. She had the most wonderful body. She was what she was because of that body, made lithe through discipline. We learn by practice, whether it's dance or life. We all become athletes of god. Or so she said."

"You knew her, David?"

But he wasn't going to answer everything she asked, and she decided that very minute to dislike him, and his arrogance. And that there was nothing like having a conversation with him.

He brought out two cups and a coffee pot, and placed them on the table. She wasn't even sure if one of them was for her. He didn't ask her to pick up a cup, and she realised he hadn't even asked her to sit down. Instead he had poured a cup for himself and moved with it towards the window. Well, since cats didn't drink coffee the other cup must be for her, Haasini reasoned, and if she didn't have it, he might be offended. She always felt on edge with him, not entirely clear what she should do, or say. He had asked her to come to his apartment before they went out for supper and she hadn't dared to ask him if there was an occasion or if she should be formally dressed. She wore a silk sari anyhow though the rain had made the sari wet.

The cups looked like Rosenthal, and she wanted to see the English garden scene painted on them more closely. More than drink the black coffee that had neither milk nor sugar, she wanted to see the signature at the bottom of the exquisite bone china cup.

"Salvador," he said, not even looking at her. Flustered, she put the cup down hastily. Better be careful with it, she thought, for these were not her mother's steel tumblers that had survived many disasters on the floor. Viennese coffee and cups painted by Dali himself. Indeed! Where had the small-time South Indian dancer arrived?

He walked towards the large French windows to open them and let the rain intrude on the room. She liked the stillness in him, the drops of rain were now falling on his body that was wrapped in only a bathrobe much to her embarrassment.

She wondered what he was looking at outside. At the trees? At the falling drops of rain? Or into other gardens beyond this day? She wanted to touch his face turned towards that vast horizon where night was breaking. "I want to know what lies beyond the horizon," he had once told a television interviewer. She moved and stood beside him watching the rain fall on his face.

She had hesitated when after the rehearsals he had asked her to visit his apartment. Seeing that she was reluctant, he had asked rudely, "You don't have anything more important to do than seeing me in the evening, do you?"

Such arrogance. She was furious.

The hair just above the nape of his neck was wet, and she wanted to run her fingers on the wetness. Why was there such anger in him, such fire? He was rude with everyone, even to journalists, telling them there was nothing he had to say to them. His films and plays were his autobiographies, he told them dismissively. When someone wanted to write his biography he had raged at the lady: "What? And expose my life to someone who has no understanding of my work. And let you make money on my life?"

As a boy growing up in a small province in Italy, it was said, his mother had abandoned him and his father, and run away with another man. His father was an usher and had brought him up on high doses of cinema and circus. David went to work early in life, and had lived with the circus, doubling up sometimes as a clown.

She wanted to reach out to the vulnerability in him. The boy who grew up without a mother. A man from an era of black and white cinema, when stories were told with such passion.

He was intolerant of mediocrity and fools. One false note in his actors and he would growl at them asking them to go home, retire and become farmers. "Give up acting," he had yelled at her once during rehearsals. "You, you Indian lady, go home, become a mediocre dancer who will carry the audience with her because of the gaudy Indian costumes and loud make-up. Become another pretty dancer whose dance is a pack of lies. And when you age, teach dance, begetting other mediocre dancers who will be a shame, not just to themselves but their profession..."

That day Haasini had wanted to quit the play, and go home to her mother. But she hung around, encouraged by Julian who said this growling didn't mean much, and she should stay back if only to prove to this man that he was wrong, and indeed she would shine on stage.

She recalled that humiliation now, his contempt, and suddenly felt tired. Of the play, of London, of this man who wanted to take her out for dinner which meant more time with him. She moved away from him and picked up her bag to leave, even if it was rude.

David noticed her turning away, removing her presence from his orbit. His gaze arrested any further movement from her. She also realised, if he did not drive her home, at least to the tube station, there was no way she could reach her apartment in that downpour.

"David, I have to go home..."

"Why the sudden anger, love? There is no way you can walk to the station in that sari..."

He walked up to her, held her hand and pulled her towards him. Then lifted her stunned face and kissed her.

David? Wh-what...?" she heard herself stuttering not sure if she wanted him to go on kissing her or stop at that very moment.

"Haasini, stop looking so shocked and talking so much. If I thought you were a mediocre dancer would I have wasted my time on you?"

He let her go from his arms, withdrawn once again. She was puzzled. He said so little, as if words were precious things that had to be measured before they were given away. Did he not know that talking was seductive? But with him even the silence was erotic.

She strained her ears to listen to the music wafting in from somewhere, possibly his bedroom. Strauss... Vivaldi...? She couldn't make out, but hoped the music would make him move to her again. He looked at her instead. She noticed a piece of lint on the sleeve of his bathrobe, and stretched her hand to remove it. It was such a familiar gesture, as if they had known each other a long time. She wanted to melt into this arrogant man's arms, and be kissed by him again.

She had not been aware of this physical hunger in her that had lain fairly dormant all these years. Dance exhausted her physically and emotionally and there was never any time for men or love affairs. Her life was fulfilling enough with dance, her students and her parents. Journalists often asked her questions about marriage, and she would laugh and tell them that she was happy as she was, and there was no question of marriage making her happier. Maybe she should stop giving interviews. It might add to her enigma, as it did with this man. Ageing – past his days of glory – but still intriguing. Who was he? What did he want from her, and what could she give him who had known some of the most beautiful and talented women in the world?

Istanbul, the thought came randomly to her. Yes, that's where she wanted to go with him. On the Bosphorus. Just the two of them, or he could take the production. She wanted to say something to him, but with David, words didn't come that easily. Besides she didn't want to sound foolish with this man she suddenly wanted so badly. As a lover.

Her mother had wanted her to marry a doctor, a surgeon. But why was she thinking of a doctor, a heart surgeon at that, when she was being held by this man who was asking her to open her mouth, pushing his tongue in, holding her breast and sending her into a tillana mode. She wanted him, his approval, his love, so that she could bring another nuance to her dance. She would go to Paris, to Istanbul, to New York, and they would create together. She would be his muse and he would write plays and make films for her.

Was he married, or was he divorced? She didn't even know that. No one really did, there were only rumours. But how did that concern her? He wasn't exactly asking her to marry him, or even inviting her to visit him in his various homes across Europe. He, in fact, was not offering her anything.

But David was not saying anything, just nuzzling her long neck and kissing her face. She imagined he was murmuring something, and she tried to hear him clearly. Was he saying she was beautiful? Not likely, she thought petulantly.

Her sari was now swirling around her like waters of a whirlpool. Her one thought before she let this man take control of her was that her mother would not approve of this. Nor would anyone else she knew in Hyderabad. But then none of them had met David Abraham of *Sita's Sorrow*.

She herself wanted him to know her. In turn, wanted to know who he was. The man behind the mask who bellowed like that. She wanted to be enlightened by him. She wanted to plunge into self-discovery, even as he was exploring her body.

Ah, Bovary! That was the cat's name – she was sure of that now. Not Juliet or Ophelia. Madame Emma, he sometimes called her, stroking her beautiful body.

Dear Haasini,

I haven't heard from you in a long time, and I'm assuming it is your rehearsals and production that is keeping you busy. I was reading The New York Times *the other day and guess whose photograph I saw? David Abraham's! Good looker he is, isn't he? In that classical way of the older men we swoon over, like Peter O' Toole or Balraj Sahni. In fact, even Siraj.*

From what I read of David in the article, he sounds interesting, even intriguing. As you age, he says, you realise you don't have much time at your disposal, and don't postpone the things you want to do. He seems so interesting, it's a pity you don't get along with him. Oh, by the way, there was even a line about an Indian actress playing the lead in his new play, Sita's Sorrow. *That's you, of course, but since when did you become a beautiful Indian actress? Just kidding, as Avanti would say.*

My creative writing classes are going on just fine except for an illness that made me miss a week of class. But Susan and Richard came home to visit me. Susan brought me a lovely potted hibiscus plant – to remind me of my country, she said. Richard came with a bottle of rosé wine. We put the hibiscus plant near the kitchen window, poured a little water, and since it was a sunny day, waited for the bud to open. We remembered Patrick's class of a few weeks ago when Patrick had read to us excerpts from Slyvia Plath:

"I took a deep breath and listened to the old bray of my heart.

I am. I am. I am.

Kiss me and you will see how important I am.

Is there no way out of the mind?"

Suicidal woman (that's what made her write so intensely, I guess), and after that told us to forget the world around us. He asked us to shut our eyes and ears to everything else but the sound of leaves falling gently on the green grass of Central Park.

In the meantime, Richard brought the chilled wine that they drank with the cocktail samosas that I deep fried for them. I ate a samosa, of course, but stayed with soothing chamomile tea. We held hands in the kitchen and sang some Harry Belafonte songs. I sang a Rajesh Khanna song, the one from Anand, Zindagi kaisi hai paheli... a song whose refrain I taught them even if they didn't understand Hindi!

In that intoxicated moment, we even imagined the hibiscus flower had bloomed and began to laugh like children. Like we were high on drugs. That's what I hear. Promise, only once I've tried weed..

And who should emerge from her room right then, but my own 14-going-on-50 Avanti.

She looked at me as if to say, Mom, when I leave home and go to college soon, is this how you will be, going crazy? Susan and Richard thought she was beautiful and told her so. They wanted her to sing a film song for us. She sang Piya tose naina lage re, jaane kya ho ab aage re... the Waheeda song we so loved, and that we too sang as teenagers from the time we saw that morning show of Guide. She must have learnt it from listening to those tapes I play every other day to keep my spirits up.

Susan and Richard were having such a good time that they were reluctant to go home. They finally left when they realised they had an assignment for Patrick's class the next day, about 'The historical period I would rather be in'!

Now here is a time I'd rather not be in – in bed, sick! I'd been having excruciating pain in my stomach for some time and tests revealed stones in my gall bladder, and before I could say gall bladder, the surgeon cut me open, took out not only the stones, but the gall bladder too. Maybe I should write a story about the gall bladder that left a stomach for a writing class! Patrick of course got to know of the surgery and called to wish me a speedy recovery. He said, remember Keats, remember he was ill but that did not prevent him from writing that lovely poetry.

The illness has been a shock, since I have been healthy as an ox all my life, with even the deliveries having been so easy. All of a sudden it looked like my body was saying to me, "I'm tired, don't make me work so hard, let me sleep and rest." I've never felt so tired in my life and all I wanted to do was to lie in bed, read and sleep. Be irresponsible, as in childhood. Let someone else do the cooking, the washing up and cleaning. Is illness a metaphor, Haasini? The child in you needing to be loved, stroked?

It was so comforting to be holding hands with Susan and Richard and connecting on the one hand to Susan's American-Indian past, and on the other to Richard's German ancestry. Ultimately, whether we are middle class Americans or simple South Indian brahmins, poets or bankers, we all want to connect and feel human. We want to be able to share our stories, and in the sharing know that we are never really alone in this world.

I was reading somewhere that when the old feel neglected, they fall sick so that they can be 'taken care of' in the hospitals. Horror of horrors, I who have loathed hospitals, wanted to be in the hospital for a little while longer to be touched and soothed by the doctors and nurses, and the healers of the world. God bless them.

Amma, when she heard of the surgery, became agitated and worried, naturally so. But when she called I told her, Amma, Avanti here is my mother now who loves me and takes care of me much like you did. She not only makes sure I take my medicine on time but makes gulab jamuns that were disintegrating in the syrup but were as delicious as the jamuns you make for me. In fact, I told Amma, she made the jamuns from a ready mix that you showed her how to roll out and deep fry!

My illness made Vikram helpless and unhappy. When I was nervous before the surgery, he just kept patting my hand and saying it'll be alright.

How do we connect with men? How do we talk to them and how can they not talk to us without one of us feeling a bit hurt each time? How do we tell men that tears and anger are not a sign of our weakness or theirs but a sign of our vulnerability and of all that makes us human?

Men are incapable of intimacy, it seems to me. Why is it that I can't open my heart out to Vikram and tell him the sorrows of my childhood? Of you and me, and of how we fought many times but never gave up on each other! I believe a man must love you completely, you with all your intimate secrets, sad stories, and grey hair and these now spreading lines around the eyes.

I'm tired but I yearn to see you again, to sit and talk for hours with you. I'm sorry I'm not communicative on the phones. At least I get to hear your lovely voice that takes me back to a time when we'd read out to each other! But it's all never the same, is it? Half the time we are interrupting each other, and for the rest of the time, I'm baffled by the physics of the half-minute difference that occurs when you say something, and when I actually hear what you have said.

These letters are much better, what do you say? Though I'm worried that you might have left London by the time this one reaches you.

Incidentally, the NYT article says you will be coming to NY and maybe LA for big openings. In NY at the Linclon Center. Which means I will see you very soon, won't I?

Do you know what I need Haasini, today? A hug! I will ask my Avantika and Anisha for one.

Much love, I am yours, in sickness and in health.

Mala

CHAPTER 22

There was still a month to go before *Sita's Sorrow* would open at West End, but after six months of rigorous rehearsals with David, Haasini was exhausted.

That sunny afternoon she decided to get away from the play and the moody David. She went to sit by herself in Covent Garden looking at the *Punch and Judy* show, and at the children with candy and balloons in hand laughing at the clown on stilts. She sat there looking at the mothers who were content that their children were happy, but who held the little ones tightly by the hand lest they get lost in the Sunday crowd.

Haasini was happy to be out on the lovely London day, even happier to see the flowers in boxes – chrysanthemums, dahlias and phloxes. A gypsy was predicting someone's future, but no, she herself didn't want to know what the future held for her. She was content to let the energy of Covent Garden consume her, to let the children's chocolate-fudge-dripping laughter fill her.

A little girl smiled at Haasini, and her mother politely asked if she could keep an eye on her for some time while she stood in line to get the girl popcorn and an orange drink. When Haasini said she would be happy to do so, the girl climbed the garden chair to sit next to Haasini.

"My name is June and I am six years old," she volunteered.

"And my name is Haasini."

"That's my mum who's gone to get me a hotdog. She's nice though she won't let me buy that Raggedy Ann doll there. She says I've got far too many dolls. My Daddy buys me things. But he doesn't stay with us. He likes someone better than Mummy, and has gone away to stay with her. Her name is Christina."

"The other Mummy's name?"

"She's not my Mummy. And Christina is her daughter. Do you like the name?"

"Yes, but not as much as June. What a lovely name."

"And Daddy loves Christy too..." June was saying wistfully when a clown in stilts walked up to them, picked up June and did a jig with her.

June began to giggle, her flaxen hair bobbing up and down with the movement. The clown put her down next to Haasini and said, "A pretty girl ya have there, Ma'am. Very pretty, just like you!"

He courtesied to the two ladies, dancing to the music, amusing himself and amusing them. Haasini held June's little fingers and began to laugh. It occurred to her that she had not laughed in a long time, that wholesome laughter from deep within your belly.

June's mother was back with the popcorn. Haasini watched June being carried in her mother's arms and waved to her. From over her mother's shoulder June waved back, and Haasini realised how simple it was to love someone if you kept these arms and heart open.

She wished she could continue to sit there in Covent Garden and watch the pageant that was London in summer. But she had promised herself she would go to the Tate, where an exhibition on Van Gogh had just opened. After the warmth of young June's company, however, she did not want to enter the subterranean world of tube stations which made her depressed, and decided instead to take a bus.

When Haasini reached the museum she was overwhelmed by the sight of American, Japanese and Italian tourists at the ticket counters, all no doubt eager to see the same Van Gogh exhibition. She was reluctant to go in with any of the tourist groups and be led by a guide. Today at least she wanted to be by herself, look at the Van Goghs on her own. She wanted to observe each painting from the wall, enjoy the sunflowers and the self-portraits, admire them in quietness by herself far from the rush of tourists and crowds inside the musuem.

Looking at the paintings, she wondered what it was that gave the sunflowers, the irises and the wheatfields the luminosity that only Van Gogh could see, which others in their sanity could not. Did we have to be insane, too, to be able to see colours like that? Was it this madness that enabled Van Gogh to see the fire in flowers and fields but that also drove him to cut off his ear?

Haasini turned instinctively to talk to David about the strange insanity that made the artist both creative and destructive. But of course he was not with her, and she felt a sudden ache at the absence. Was this what they called love? In which case, why on earth had she fallen in love with an enigmatic man and that too at this age when she should have known better? Why was she so willingly blind to the fact that this relationship had no future, that he was a man who would move on with his life and films? Did she seriously imagine that he would marry her, or that they would ever live together?

To distract herself, she turned her attention to the self-portraits. Why were the eyes red like that, she wondered, almost like those of the wood ducks she had seen in St James's Park some days ago. Blood instead of tears, and tears and pain had a colour too.

"Pain. There is no pain, no pain of longing in your dance. Haasini, you have to let love, pain, death and other emotions touch you. You can't be smug with your dance. I see that you have to grow up, feel emotions and not be that surface dancer," David had told her, as she lay stretched against his body, a hand clasping his.

She liked lying against him after they'd made love, exhausted like she would be after an intense tillana. He liked the vigour of her young body, and the playfulness that was in her. He also liked the quiet contemplative moments in her when she lay against him like this, like an exotic bird with her captor.

In a moment of tenderness he turned her face towards him, and kissed her on her nose. She parted her lips wanting to be kissed, but changed her mind to look at him instead, to piece together his enigma. She drew circles on his cheek not knowing what tragedies in his life had made him so quiet.

"David, tell me a secret. If you tell me one, I'll tell you two."

"Secrets, love? Let me see now. The greatest director of that time, Fellini wouldn't let me work with him – said I was too raw, too much of a lad and that he didn't have time for the likes of me."

"And when you became famous as a director, did you meet and tell him that he had once rejected you?"

"No, no Haasini. By the time I made my first film, he was already an old man living with his dreams. There is something sad about nostalgia. I will not live in the past, never. And this is the last play I'm going to direct. Too much time, though I'm glad for one thing that it brought you to me..."

"More films then, David?"

"I'm an old man now, Haasini. And don't have the energy to make masterpieces or experiment; though I do want to make a film set in a monastery in Tibet. I want the movie to be like their thankas, convey the simultaneousness of life in those circles. Life is not linear, but moves in circles, round and round towards the same thing – the same things that cause us pain, happen again and again..."

"I love you, David..."

"And I love you too, my beautiful Indian lady. But you have to feel some more here. Live life, fall in love and be demolished. And demolish someone with your passion..."

'Oh, here's my secret. Ever since I met you, ever since you made love to me last time, I can't think of anything other than wanting to be held by you, to be kissed by you."

'And what's the other secret...'

"I've never fallen in love before. Well, not in the real sense... few crushes..."

"Never fallen in love to have your heart broken! My god, woman! Now I know what's missing in your dance. Passion. You have to live life with all its highs and lows. Fall in love, again and again. Fall apart, and start all over again. Be surprised. Be fearless. Always."

"David, can I tell you one more secret?"

"One more? My God, so many! Why am I the privileged one tonight?"

"I want to convey emotions in another art form that is not dance. There is no permanence about dance. Writing, but my friend Malavika is already a writer. Maybe paint? I want to create something more tangible that people can hold and admire centuries later, like those Degas dancers. Or Van Gogh."

She fell silent. He discouraged chatter. Well, she thought, let him unravel the mysteries of her person. Let him discover things about her that no one would know, except a lover. The way a mole sat above her left breast. Like she saw the boniness of his elbows that showed his age. Those stitches from an injury on her thigh. There was still so much about him that she did not know. Or he about her. Each was like a foreign country whose geography remained unexplored because the other didn't know the language of that country. She sighed. Why another, we are a mystery even to our own selves!

He had shut his eyes, and seeing that he wasn't watching her, she sat there mesmerised by the nakedness of the body.

Its vulnerability. There were no birthmarks or scars that she could memorise for a later time. There was nothing tangible about this man that she could hold on to, and remember.

She wanted to hear him laugh now, beside her at the Tate. Hold her around the waist and talk to her about creative madness. Everyone would look at them and wonder who she was. And when everyone looked at them like that, she would just raise herself a bit on her toes to kiss him on his shoulder. For such a larger than life director who you expect would be huge and towering, he was not that tall, she thought, moving away from the Van Goghs. She didn't want to see any of the Impressionists, or Modernists. This longing was enough for one afternoon.

Should she go back to Covent Garden once again and make friends with maybe another little girl like June? But why did she always want to live in the past? Like David, she decided she had had enough of nostalgia. She would sit in the park right here near Tate, and send a postcard to Malavika.

She took out a pen, a Mont Blanc that she had borrowed from David and not returned because he had forgotten to ask her for it. She kept it because she had wanted to possess some part of him, even if it was only his fountain pen. Haasini scribbled his name on a piece of paper, and let it fly in the wind. She wanted the whole world to know she loved David, and hopefully, he her.

A London Bobby who was passing by raised his baton and said, "Good afternoon, ma'am. No littering our gardens, eh? Beautiful day, isn't it? You from India? Want to go with my missus there one day to look at the Taj Mahal. You taking a holiday here, ma'am?"

"No. working on a play with David Abraham…"

"Eh? That great 'un, ma'am? I'm impressed. Have a nice day, ma'am. And be careful of the pen. It is expensive."

Yes, it was expensive and she wondered how David hadn't missed it yet.

If love was an act of self-discovery, this much she had discovered about herself – she could be a thief.

Dear, dear Haasini,

Thank you for calling last week. It was good talking to you, though I do wish the circumstances had been better. Don't feel sorry that you are not here with me. I know you've been busy with shows, and travels.

I'm still in Hyderabad trying to sort Ma's things.

Ma's passing away… she was felled swiftly like a tree in a storm, and it has left me so bereft and helpless. I will never again have the comfort of a mother's love. That was one place I knew I could rest protected from the hurt of the world. However, I do feel good that I was in Hyderabad to spend time with her, and be with her when she passed away. What a horrid thought this is, that I will never see her again. Somehow when I used to see all those obits every morning in Deccan Chronicle *I used to think, this will never happen to me – my father's or mother's photo will never be in the papers like that – those souls who have passed on. Still wanting some part of their life.*

Except for high blood pressure she had no other health problem. But one day when I called her, she sounded depressed saying things like that she found living by herself without my father difficult. I think she missed my Pa way too much after that glorious life of decades.

The way she was talking didn't seem right, so I left the girls with Vikram, and took the flight to be with Ma. Even if I had made a trip to Hyderabad when Pa passed away just at the beginning of the year. And I'm glad for that because we spoke and did many things that seemed to make her happy, and which made me happy too.

Every other evening I was there, we went to the Venkateshwara temple. Once we'd offered our prayers and prasadams to Shiva, Ganapati, Vishnu and other deities, we would sit in the temple courtyard listening to an elderly lady recite the Vishnu Sahasranamam while stringing garlands of jasmine and kanakambaralu. She was too old for us to ask her her name – besides it was not America where you shake hands and introduce yourself. We began to address her simply as Amma whenever we spoke with her.

One evening, Ma too stretched her legs, looped a thread on her toe and began to string the flowers. She told Amma one garland was for that goddess Lakshmi in the temple who would bless her granddaughters, and the other was for her daughter who had come to spend time with her. That day I had worn an off-white Khadi sari, gold bangles and a nice gold chain with a ruby pendant, which pleased Amma no end. I had also put up my hair in a bun that of course kept coming undone.

She told Amma, "She's a mother of two girls, and still she doesn't know how to do up her hair."

Amma smiled and said, she too had a beautiful daughter who lived in Malaysia, and a son and daughter-in-law who lived in the city, but they hardly ever came to see her. So she had begun to live in the temples stringing flowers for the gods, eating prasadam given to her by the priests and sleeping in the courtyard. In the end, one did not need anything except the protection of Narayana, she murmured sadly.

She had been living in the temple for years now, she told us, yet even Amma said she had never seen her before. Nor had I.

It is these remembered gestures of Amma that I so treasure. Ma leaning against the pillar of the temple and beginning to recite parts of the Vishnu Sahasranamam with Amma in the hour of dusk. I was moved to hear them raise their voices and sing in consonance so melodiously invoking Vishnu. In recent times, with Pink Floyd and Eric Clapton bombarding my ears, I had forgotten how beautiful Carnatic music is, and how it still has the ability to move me. I joined them in chanting verses in praise of Vishnu.

I was tempted to capture the moment in true American style with photographs, but I let it go. Now the moment etched in my mind has even the smell of jasmines, incense and camphor. I can still see the colour of Amma's pink silk sari with little temples on the borders, moving with the wind. And the gentleness and simplicity of that elderly lady, she with her coarse, faded cotton sari worn with a white blouse. The evening etched so vividly in my mind. For Avanti and Anisha, it would have been just another photograph of their mother and grandmother in the temple that they remembered having walked barefoot when they came many winters ago to Hyderabad. Of course, they asked a thousand times if they had to wear lehengas to the temple, and why they couldn't be allowed to wear their shoes inside so they didn't have to walk on the cow dung and water around the temple.

Another day, on Ma's request, I took her to a Jaya Bhaduri film which was playing at a theatre. After that we went to Tank Bund and walked on the pavements, wind in our hair. Ma and I wanted to eat the makka buttas. But in the glitzy new city that Hyderabad has become, we hardly saw any moophalli sellers or buttawalas. Finally we chanced upon one and bought ourselves roasted corn and ate walking up and down Tank Bund Road, happy to be together like this.

Ma later made me buy her a Kwality's chocobar from a bandi fellow. She told me she was not going to share the bar with anyone, least of all me.

When she was young, being the oldest, she said she always had to share chocolates and ice creams with her sisters and she wanted something entirely for herself. Finally.

We sat on the stone bench looking at the water of Tank Bund, wondering when the hyacinths had overtaken the lake with such abandon. I remembered the many walks I had on the road here with Siraj, and wondered how time had passed. Where was that girl who had walked on these roads unaware of what life had in store for her?

It was getting dark but we were reluctant to get back to our car. Ma sat like that looking into the lake, holding my hand. Had she been afraid? Had she known that her end was near? Do we have a premonition of our death?

All of a sudden she touched my shoulder gently, and told me that before her parents insisted she marry the banker who was my father, there was someone whom she liked in Madras, a boy from the neighbourhood. She said he had lent her a copy of Tagore's Charulata.

"I don't know why I am even thinking of him now, but that was a beautiful book. I never saw him after we got married and moved to Hyderabad. Or did I? Oh yes, I do remember seeing him again when I went home to see my parents in Madras. When I saw him I realised, he wasn't half as good looking as your father and I wondered what I had seen in him. Maybe I was fascinated by his love for Bengali literature and his ability to quote Tagore in Bengali."

"Ma!" I said.

"Now Mala, don't be shocked. There was nothing between us."

Haasi, it was wonderful to think of my mother as a young girl in love with someone just like you and me. It was fantastic talking to her like that and I am glad for the conversations.

The following few days we would sit in our courtyard, I on the swing, and she some distance away on an easychair, neither of us wanting to say anything for fear of shattering a beautiful moment.

Only once, she looked over her glasses and said, "Mala, I've gone back to reading the old classics. The Bronte sisters, Jane Eyre and Wuthering Heights. For some reason, though you've been writing about modern writers, I'm not able to read all that modern fiction, magic realism and fantasy. Especially what comes out of Latin America and America."

I told her I liked some of the feminist writers from India, and that I too was doing a book of short stories, mostly on the expatriate experience in America. And you know what, she smiled and said: "You were always a dreamer, Malavika. What else would you be but a writer!"

She said she wanted me to send her the first copy when it was published. She also wanted to see Anisha and Avanti married and live to see their children.

"I want to see my great-grandchildren. Your grandchildren. Your father passed away too soon. It's been lonely after him, and you living so far away."

"You should come and live with us, Ma. Wind up this house. It's going to be a long time before Avanti is married. She's just joined college. And who knows, she may marry someone from America. Not like the Telugu boys you and I married."

Then she told me something that broke my heart. She touched my face and said, "Mala, you were always a beautiful girl. Your father told you that many times. And you did like him more. Somehow this young mother did not know how to show her love for you. All that I did was to be critical of your clothes and hair."

"Ma, never mind. That's why at least I comb my hair now and wear these lovely saris of yours. Can I take back some? And you are coming back with me, aren't you?"

She then came and sat with me on the swing, put her head on my lap and lay quietly there while the swing rocked us both gently. It was that very night that she passed away. I am not sure at what precise hour though. And I don't want to know. There was no intimation, no warning for the daughter to be prepared for this loss that would make her an orphan once and for all.

There was only Herman Hesse's Siddhartha *bookmarked at a particular page that she had placed on its spine, hoping to finish the chapter the next day. I found that by her bedside along with her reading glasses.*

Your mother was there the first thing in the morning, consoling me. Holding me she said, "Child, don't cry like that, be brave like your mother. Look how lucky she was to have died the way she did in her sleep. And she was not alone when this happened, you were there. How would you have been able to forgive yourself if you knew she died alone? Why should you cry? She had such a complete life, so active even after your father passed away, the woman's club, the Ramakrishna Mission, always made time for me and her friends and relatives. She is blessed and so are you to have been born as her daughter."

I have to leave for America in a few days, but as yet I don't have the heart to give away her things, or disturb the order of her clothes, books and puja room. Especially the puja room. I don't want to remove the remnants of the camphor on the aarti plate, or the wilted jasmine flowers she had hung on the Devi vigraham. I hope when you come back, you will light a lamp every day in this room for my mother, for me, for my daughters, Haasi. The only things I will take with me are her books, a few of her saris and maybe some of our old photo albums.

It will always be a mystery to me what exactly she was thinking that night when she kept the book away, turned off the light and went to sleep.

I hope you haven't found this letter too disturbing. I had to unburden myself somewhere. No one except you will understand the loss I feel.

Yours,

Mala, the orphan. And as always relying on you for comfort

CHAPTER 23

Susan and Richard had not come for the class, and Malavika was sitting by herself. She had not had many conversations with anyone in her course, other than Susan and Richard, though she thought some of the things the good looking Ralph had to say in class about India, writing, were interesting. She had not had a word with him so far wrapped up as she was with Susan and Richard. Today he was in the library as she was browsing, and she smiled at him tentatively as he raised a hand in greeting.

She had heard that he was a financial analyst who was taking time off from his job at Chase to do these creative writing classes. Patrick had once mentioned that he was one of the few in the class who were published writers with a book of poems to his credit.

Patrick had decided many weeks ago that the class would go on a walking tour of mid Manhattan to stop over at the New York Public Library. She was excited about the walk today, and had wondered why neither Susan nor Richard had turned up. She had spoken to Susan on her return from India and told her of the passing away of her mother, though she could not speak her heart out about the anguish of losing parents as she could with Haasini. There was only that much you could tell American friends, Malavika thought, hanging up the phone. But of course, she told Susan that she'd got her a silk dress from India, which was a kaftan!

It was Susan who had asked Malavika not to miss this walking tour with Patrick. She said these turned out to be the most interesting parts of the creative writing classes that he taught. They sometimes sat at the sidewalk cafés and read out each other's work. Or they drank beer, ate pizzas and played word games. Sometimes he just told them to quieten down and imagine Manhattan as it might have been a 100 years ago.

Maybe Susan and Richard would meet up with them somewhere in Manhattan, she imagined, walking out of the library, all of them following Patrick like schoolchildren. She looked at her shoes, glad she was wearing her walking shoes, and not the flat Kolhapuris she often wore at Susan's insistence, who also liked to see her in a salwar kameez, the 'Punjabi', as she called it.

They were out of the New York University campus, walking in pairs or three or four of them together. She found she was the only one walking alone until Ralph hurried up to catch up with her. "Hi, I'm Ralph. We've never met. Though we're in the same class with Patrick."

"Yes, I know. I'm always in a hurry. Coming in for the class and rushing home to Connecticut."

"That's a long distance to come for a creative writing class, isn't it?"

"Yes, it is. But I had to do this sometime. And what about you, Ralph? Heard you were the head of a financial division in a bank."

"Yes a sort of TS Eliot slaving in a bank and imagining *The Love Song of J Alfred Prufrock*, when all that I wanted to do was to write. It's strange isn't it, the writing business. When you announce you are quitting your job to write, they think you're weird. They act as if you've announced you're shaving your hair, only worse. Though even that doesn't seem so strange here in New York. But to announce you're giving up your half-a-million-dollar-plus job at Chase certainly sends shivers and shock around."

"You quit a million-dollar job at Chase to take Patrick's course? Ralph? Come on, you're kidding!"

"Not a million, but half-a-million. And am not kidding. With one thing or another, I got pushed into the bank, when all that I wanted to do was to teach, read and write. As you said you have to do it sometime. I'm 48. How old are you? You look so young. You're here for graduate studies?"

"Do I have to tell you my age, Ralph? I'm just as young as I look. I'm not here for graduate studies. I am married and have two teenaged daughters who act like they are my mother. It's just that after all these years, I thought that I should do something about my urge to write, to tell stories. And I love this about studying in America that you can do it anytime in your life."

"That's true, when it finally comes to writing, you have to do it by yourself. Sit on a favourite chair behind a nice writing desk, look out of the window, see the snow fall relentlessly but imagine it's a sunny afternoon in India and write. Where are you from? Bombay? Ma-laa-vika. Is that how you say your name? Such a beautiful name for a beautiful woman. That was a play by Kalidasa wasn't it?'

"Ralph! But how did you know? This is the first time that someone in this country knew who Malavika was. A Kalidasa heroine."

"Well, I studied Sanskrit in a liberal arts programme at Harvard many years ago."

"Harvard! I'm impressed."

"Come, lady, we have to walk faster. Hope Pat isn't thinking of taking us to the Met today, to ask us to write a poem on those African heads or Grecian art. It's my favourite place, but not today when I want to be on the streets of NYC on a great afternoon. Did I tell you I grew up close to here, in New Jersey, and did all sorts of wild things in NYC. Of course not – how could I, when I have never met or spoken to you before?"

"That's the New York Public Library, isn't it? Is Patrick going to stop there?"

"I think so. I don't mind sitting on these steps if you will sit with me. Kalidasa's Malavika sitting next to Ralph of New Jersey. Wow! Was I born lucky, or did I just get lucky this morning?"

She smiled at him. He was so amusing and well read, even muttering lines from Eliot or Auden under his breath. Occasionally even Tagore's *Ekla Chalo* or some other Bengali poem. From the nearby kiosk he brought lemonade, saying he hoped she liked it since this was the only thing he could drink in this weather.

"Patrick there, you know, Ma-laavika, he's a genius. Even published two novels. But has too many weird ideas that he tries out on his students to loosen them up. He is like the Zen masters who beat their disciples with sticks when they say they are enlightened. There, look at him, he wants us to stand on the steps, and say aloud, I'm a writer! Not just a writer, say, I'm one helluva great writer!"

"I can't stand like that, with my hands stretched! I couldn't..."

"C'mon honey, if you can't stand like that in front of millions of New Yorkers who, on any given day, really don't care what you do with your life, how will you sit down on the kitchen table – is that where you write?"

"No, at my desk, in my study."

'Oh, at the desk in your room. How will you sit there and shed your inhibitions and say what you really want to say, instead of being discreet and saying the right things? C'mon, stand up! And here, hold my hand, though you're not an old woman who needs my help to stand or sit."

"Okay, I'm standing. But Ralph, I can't say it, I can't."

"Close your eyes, it helps. He would know, though, he has a hawk's eye. Hold my hand and say softly so that only I can hear, Ralph, I'm a writer."

"Ralph, I'm a writer."

"Yes, Malavika, I know you're a writer. Though I haven't read a line you have written. All that is festering inside you, inside your heart, inside that head of yours let it come out in your poems and novels. I know you'll write..."

"Ralph, I, I...."

"What is it?"

"My mother died recently. And I want to cry when I remember the Hesse she earmarked to read the next morning, afternoon..."

"But what a nice way to remember a mother, Malavika. I hear you. I feel your loss, right here. The only way to honour those we love is to live the way they would have wanted us to. Be a good mother, a wife and a writer!"

"I want to sit down. I'm tired."

"Okay. You can sit. Just for a little while, though, because it looks like Patrick is anxious to make us walk some more. The fiend will stop only at lunchtime. Maybe we could suggest an Indian restaurant in your honour?"

"Indian restaurant? I eat that day in and day out. I want pizzas."

"Pizzas! My God, where did I meet a pizza eating rakshasi? Oh, the others are walking on. We'll sit here for a while and see Manhattan pass before us. Have you ever wondered why these New Yorkers walk in such a hurry? I am convinced their houses are on fire or some child is being strangled somewhere. I am sure it's something like that."

"And in India, everything moves so slowly. It seems as if nothing moves really, not our cars, or cycles or buses. You've been to India?"

"Yes, as a student. I'd like to go there again to wander around the country, take a dip in Ganges in Benares, study more Sanskrit somewhere with a teacher. Find another reason to do a book of poems, maybe like those Sanskrit love poems I like to translate. I should read them out to you one day..."

"And where were you in India? Bombay..."

"Bombay, but mostly Calcutta..."

"You must have been appalled by the poverty..."

"No, not really, Malavika. Calcutta is throbbing with life. The music, the poetry, the art. I even felt a kinship with the people there. Watching Bengali movies, sitting in addas eating mishti doi and discussing Satyajit Ray, Tagore, Bengali cinema, book fairs... All of which I liked hearing more than the World Bank discussions for which I was there, sitting in Writer's Building. I even wanted to marry a Bengali woman because they were so beautiful. You're not Bengali, are you?"

"No, no. South Indian..."

"That'll do for me. I'll settle for a South Indian. You do know some Bengali though, don't you?"

"No. Not at all! Don't make me laugh! I think, we'd better go..."

"Yes, Patrick and his flock have disappeared. Where are those two friends of yours? Susan and Richard, always around you as if they were your bodyguards. Haven't seen them around, but I'm happy if they found other things to do today. I haven't had a more enjoyable day, really. Come, be quick. I think I know where Patrick is heading for now... To his favorite Greek restaurant some streets away, where he'll order gyros."

"How do you know so much about Patrick? You haven't done this course before, have you?"

"He's my brother, that's how I know all about him. He was the crazy one in the family. So it was alright for him to write and teach and do the things he wanted to. I was the smart one, so I had to go to Harvard to do a double major, in Sanskrit and finance, some combination that. But I was expected to become a banker and make money. Then I realised, I was making the money and he was having all the fun. You know what he'll ask me this evening? What was I talking about to a beautiful woman like you? I think I'll go home late to avoid his questions..."

"He thinks I'm beautiful? But does he think I'm a good writer?"

"Your British spellings confuse him thoroughly. And he thinks you're much too shy in your writing."

"So you discuss me with your brother?"

"What do you think we did as teenagers? Play baseball and discuss girls! Here is Pat now. He's glaring at me for having lured you away. Well, now let's pretend we don't know each other while he talks about his favourite poet, Dylan Thomas."

"Who's your favorite poet, Ralph?"

"Yevtoshonko. Then Keats." And my most favourite play is *Malavikagnimitra*. Don't look so shocked, Malavika!"

Dear Mala,

My condolences to begin with. My heartfelt apologies for not writing to you earlier. At least I spoke to you over the phone though it's tough to say anything worthwhile over these international calls. I hope, hope you are feeling better now?

From my end, finally my friend, we are through with the London premiere, and all of us are relieved because London is the acid test for David. Well, the play got mixed reviews, and there were more bad ones than good, I must admit. Some critics thought the play was the dying gasp of a spent genius who had reached the end of his creative period. Some ridiculed the inclusion of elements of Indian traditional dance in a Western play, even if the story was an Indian mythological story and the director, avant garde. One or two had the gumption to say that in an otherwise dull play, it was my performance that gave it strength and lifted it from the mere banal to clever!

However much as I'd like to pretend that these critics and their criticism don't matter, I think they do, especially when you consider the amount of hard work and thought we all put in – especially David, poor man. Although I am not suggesting even for a moment that because we worked hard the creative effort has to amount to something.

This is akin to the paradox that always puzzles me. Do you have to be a good human being to be a great artist, or do we judge a work by its merit irrespective of the character of the artist. What do you think? I feel the kind of person you are is organically reflected in the art, whether dance or painting. Though from what I've read of Charles Chaplin, he was not a good man but what he produced were works of pure genius. Was it not the same with Picasso who we hear was cruel to his women? But what does it matter when you can paint like that?

As for David, not only is he impenetrable, but his films and plays are puzzles, raising questions without giving any answers. I didn't think the reviews would affect him that deeply, but they did, because I could see that bewilderment on his face, wondering where he had gone wrong. There is so much creative energy in him that even until the last day he kept changing dialogues and positions which put immense pressure on us. I am always a bundle of nerves before a performance, but this time round I was so worked up I couldn't sleep for nights. In the absence of Amma's care, in the absence of her hot chocolate, some hot upma always, I've had to resort to tranquilisers to be able to sleep. Not a good thing, I know, but what could I do, Malavika? Even this world famous director who you'd think would be used to openings and curtain calls, was somewhat he disappeared somewhere after the beginning of the play and appeared only during the last curtain call.

At curtain call, when all of us were called on to the stage along with David to take a final bow, I was elated. I expected David to have a special word of praise for me. Or at least say he was grateful that I had dropped all commitments in India to be part of his production. But no. Even later when all of us were having dinner, he praised and critiqued everyone's performance except mine. And there I was looking at him hungrily hoping he'd say something to me, about me. No, not a word, not even a glance in my direction. I was naturally hurt because I had put in so much effort into this performance.

If you haven't guessed from all this 'David said this and David said that', I'm in love with him, Mala. Hopelessly and madly in love. I, who thought I would never feel passion, am like an adolescent who walks with Puccini music playing in the background. And these feelings for a man like David, who is far from being sentimental and emotional. Anyway, when I asked him later if he my performance was any good, he said bluntly that he didn't expect anything but the best from me! He says so little, really.

Begin with music. It's a good way of meditating on emptiness. He says.

I say I'm in love with him but the sad thing is I don't know if I'll see him again after we finish the travels with Sita. He says we'll meet again, in Venice or in Paris. But I know he's already working on his new film, and once he becomes obsessed with a film, he will forget everything, even me, especially me. Does love exist at all in the monomaniacal obsessiveness of the creative artist?

I have to confess though, it is I who have become obsessed. Who knows this may not be love at all but the crazed feelings of a middle aged, repressed spinster. Because if I really loved him would I let him go as I am doing? But what do I ask of him, Malavika? Marriage? It's such a middle class concept for the insecure, as he said once. It's so clichéd in the artistic world of Europe that I dare

*not even ask him for it. He has been married before, of course –
twice, to two of the most beautiful women in the world. He even has
a daughter, Marguerite, who I hear is an artist, and has an atelier
in Paris or Cannes. He has told me he's too old for anything now and
the only thing he wants to do for the remaining years of his life is to
make one last film, or if he's lucky, two.*

I love him and I want him, Malavika.

*Someday, I want to be able to sit in the front row and watch him
as he receives an award in Hollywood. And watch him become
emotional receiving the award and acknowledge the wayward life
he led, and the mother he missed having while he was growing up.
Later in the evening, sit with him by the fireplace and read a book
while he writes.*

*But I know I will have to let him go for I love an insane, creative
genius who must find his destiny. I also know that he will make love
to other women – women who will fall in love with him and hold him
in their arms as I have done. Only I hope with as much affection
and love as I have. There will be days when he will sleep alone in
all those homes he owns across Europe, and I will feel sorry for him
that he does not have me with him. Importantly, I will feel sorry for
myself that I am not with him, sharing his life.*

*I already feel the heartbreak of parting as I sit by the gardens
and museums in London, thinking of love, friendship and death.
The meaning of dance. Such cruelty of destiny, Malavika, that I
may never see this man again, only read something about him in
newspapers.*

*David has told me often not to look too much into the future but
to live in the moment, knowing change is inevitable. Brave words
from someone who has liberated himself. But what about me? I still
feel foolish. There's no wisdom in me at all, even now, not where love
is concerned at least.*

*There is such fragility about our time together, even the moments
I have with him – those especially – in fact, seem to pass all too*

soon. But maybe it's the transience that lends this relationship a special charm, so that instead of frittering time I am grateful for every moment we are together.

This is a gift, I am sure, that I have known this man and shared his life, even if only for a year. It makes me happy too that I have touched him in some way, that I will find a place in his memory. And I hope that memory of me will bring a smile to his face. Finally, we are the sum of the people we have known and loved, don't you think, Malavika? When I perform now, how can I not but strive to touch a moment of perfection, knowing that this is the way he would have expected me to perform, with discipline and clarity. And the joy it must bring. Anything less would be a failure of our love.

Of course it's my fault for falling in love with a man who's as elusive as the sand that passes between your fingers. What were those lines in Capote's Breakfast at Tiffany's: "Never love a wild thing, Mr Bell…" That was Doc's mistake. He was always lugging home wild things. A hawk with a hurt wing. One time it was a full grown bobcat with a broken leg. But you can't give your heart to a wild thing: the more you do, the stronger they get. Until they are strong enough to run into the woods. Or fly into a tree. Then a taller tree. Then the sky. That's how you'll end up, Mr Bell. If you let yourself love a wild thing. You'll end up looking at the sky."

I think we should be in New York and LA. I'm not sure if David will come with us too. He says the production will now have to move without him. We feel like orphans already.

Guess what? His cat, Bovary travels first class with him everywhere. I hate her. Naturally.

Love, Haasi

CHAPTER 24

Vikram was travelling, Avanti was in her sophomore year in college, and Anisha was finishing high school. The house was quiet. Malavika stroked Charlie Brown, their beagle. She remembered when she first moved to the country how lonely she had been, hungry for company, to cuddle something, even a teddy bear. She would beseech Vikram to take her to her friend's home, where there was a puppy. She wanted to stroke a dog, feeling the soft fur of another living thing. Vikram had resisted having a pet for so long that she had given up hope. Till Charlie Brown leapt into Anisha's arms one day. One of her school friends's dogs had littered, and even without asking her parents, Anisha brought him home.

"I said we'd like to take care of him, Mom. He's adorable, isn't he? I know you'll like him! If we don't like him we can always give him back to Sarah's family, Ma! Please?" she pleaded, looking more the waif than the homeless dog. Secretly delighted, Malavika let her keep Charlie Brown, though she knew ultimately it was she who would be left to take care of him, as everyone else went to school or college and got busy.

Charlie Brown was now lying at her feet, content, though he was happiest when Anisha was at home. Anisha was applying for colleges on the West Coast, too far away from home for an 18-year-old, Malavika thought. She told

Anisha that Charlie Brown would miss her, and maybe she should find one closer home, with so many of the Ivy League colleges nearby.

Avantika was more like her father – indifferent to animals, though she would let Charlie Brown lie on her bed, with her two feet resting on him. To the hyperactive Anisha, he had been a calming influence. She would lie on the carpet on the floor with Charlie Brown, talking and reading to him. He would miss Anisha if she left home, thought Malavika, as she rubbed the soles of her feet on the dog, reading Salman Rushdie's *Midnight's Children* that everyone was talking about. Even Patrick.

She had to finish a bunch of short stories by the end of the term, and she had not even done four. Susan had bravely embarked on a novel about her Russian grandmother, and Richard had chosen to write a science fiction fantasy.

She wondered what Ralph was going to submit for his class project at the end of the term. She closed her eyes thinking of him, not reading what she was supposed to, this novel on which she had to also write a report on what made this Indian writer so sensational. But she wasn't even halfway through yet. Her eyes were troubling her and she was finding it difficult to decipher the fine print. Maybe she needed to get a pair of reading glasses. Taking a break, she picked up the *New York Times* and wondered why she had offered to write about *Midnight's Children,* a book that she would have liked to discuss with Siraj at this very moment. She should have chosen a classic instead. Even *Anna Karenina* that Siraj introduced her to, and that she read later in college. She was looking at the Sunday magazine section of the *NYT* when the phone rang.

It must be for Anisha, or a telemarketer, she thought. To answer the phone, she had to get up from her rocking chair, startling Charlie Brown who had dozed off.

"Hello?" she said.

"Hello?"

"Hello. Yes?"

"May I speak with Malavika, please?"

"This is she."

"Malavika, hi, this is Ralph. I'm not disturbing you, am I? Not in the middle of making samosas or rasagollas and stuff?"

"No, no. Just reading the *New York Times.*"

"Oh, that epitome of good, even great, journalism. Listen, have you finished the book report? You're writing on Salman Rushdie, or is it *Anna Karenina*?'

"No, not *Anna,* but Rushdie. I've no idea when I'm even going to finish reading it, I am still on page 135!"

"You should have offered to write on *Anna Karenina*. Pat likes the book. I've not known him to give anything but an A+ to anyone writing a report on that one. So what were you doing when I called?"

"Reading *NYT* and taking a break from Rushdie, like I told you. But mostly wondering how alike both you and Patrick are, though I would never have guessed you were brothers."

"You know, he's the better looking one. He used to get all the pretty girls, and I got to date all those 'hot' girls in glasses who dressed like Julie Andrews in *Sound of Music.* You know the women who did all the finance programmes, while girls who went mooney over him were writing poems and looked like Audrey Hepburn. It took me this long to figure the fun he was having. Look at me now, finally talking to a beautiful Indian woman. Would you have spoken to me if I were a banker, Malavika? Tell me the truth."

"I don't know. I would have, whatever your profession was in fact!"

"If you take the subway in the next half hour into Manhattan, and you come to the World Trade Center we could have lunch. You're a vegetarian, of course, all South Indians are vegetarians. I knew a family in Jersey once. They did a lot of pujas and gave away yummy rice pudding to eat – prasadam as they called it."

"No, all South Indians are not vegetarian and, Ralph, why do you talk so much?"

"I talk a lot? That's because of my deprived childhood. Patrick got to do the talking, and reciting all poetry he wrote, and guests saying he was so adorable..."

"A traumatic childhood, is that it? I don't believe it, of course. But what about the World Trade Center?"

"Well, if you come there, we could have lunch, and I could show you all the bankers and Wall Street stockbrokers looking so sombre in their grey suits, as if the world's financial doom lay in their decisions. Will you come, Malavika?"

"Will I come now, just like that?"

"Yes. Just like that. If you want, you could bring your copy of the *NYT,* we could read the paper together."

"But…"

"I promise, I'll be more interesting than brother Pat. I'll even help you with Rushdie. I could even see what brother says about this interesting novel emerging from India after so long. I mean after Raja Rao, RK Narayan where were the great Indian writers?"

"Malavika…?"

"Yes, yes. I'll be there by noon. Is that okay?"

"Yup! Thanks, love. You made my day!"

Malavika began to laugh. She had begun to do strange things in the past few months. Imagine standing at the NY Public Library and yelling, "I want to be a writer!" She must ask Ralph, if Patrick was inspired by the movie, *Network*. Was that the film? Well, she thought, brushing her hair, putting on her tiny diamond earrings, and pulling on a brightly coloured kurta over her jeans, she felt like doing some more crazy things these days. She would make the hour's journey into Manhattan just to meet Ralph. He made her laugh. More important, he made her feel good. She stroked Charlie Brown, whispering, "I'm going into New York, and I'm excited." She left a note for Anisha in the cookie jar that she was sure to see; and drove to the station.

Even the usually sombre New Yorkers were looking at her. She wondered self-consciously if she should have avoided the diamonds, and opted for a less colourful kurta. Why did she wear orange? But she was tired of all those jeans and shirts she wore. Mercifully, the subway station was at WTC itself. She looked at the other commuters, at the poetry on the subway trains, the black men in dark glasses, people collecting money to save the starving of the world, the yakkity-yakking Chinese family, and that girl with her eyes closed. What was she doing, reading aloud from the notes? Auditioning for a part in Broadway? There was life outside her home and family, she was only now discovering. The subway, especially even at mid-afternoon, did look menacing, but she wanted to see the world for herself. Not through her children's eyes, not the inner parent's, not her husband's – especially not his.

She had to discover life and living in her own way, on her own terms, she decided. If she got mugged and her diamonds were stolen, that too would be a learning. She would then not wear diamonds and Indian clothes on her next trip to Manhattan, so she didn't look like the unsure tourist, even after all these years in America, on the way to seeing the Times Square for the first time.

The girl who could be reading her part in Broadway, looked up and smiled at her. Malavika smiled back. There was happiness everywhere, only she had not known it, complaining about being lonely. She wanted to tell the girl that she genuinely hoped she would make it on Broadway.

But it was the girl who spoke first.

"Important day for me, you know. I have to get this part, want it badly. Have you ever wanted anything badly?"

"Yes, sometimes..."

"Well, then you know how it feels, the butterflies in the pit of the stomach..."

"And you can't eat before and after that for two days..."

"Yes, that's it. You're a classical dancer from India, aren't you? Is this your first trip to New York?"

"No, I'm not a dancer. But my friend is. She is in a play with David Abraham in London."

"David Abraham! Wow! Your friend must be really good to have got the part. Is it the new play, *Sita's Sorrow*?"

"Yes, that's it. I do hope you get the part and that you become a famous actress. This is where I get off to go to WTC, right?"

"Umm, yes, but be careful which exit you take. And have a nice day. Thank you, you've made me less tense."

Malavika got off the train and looked apprehensively at the subterranean station. Her Indian clothes were a sure giveaway. All the muggers would think she was a tourist and go for her.

"Hello, pretty lady!" She was startled by a voice. "I was going to hang out at the station for the next 20 hours, but you made me wait only two. But you look just lovely in that colourful kurta and scarf."

"You've been waiting for two hours in the subway station for me, Ralph? Are you crazy? And what is that rose doing in your mouth? Is it for me?"

"I'll pass your questions. But yes, may I present the rose to you? Come, let's get out of here. I feel I'm in a sauna. And all these ladies with umbrellas looking at me suspiciously as if I was going to attack them. Now that's the problem of looking like Woody Allen, and not Al Pacino."

Hurrying commuters jostled past them, pushing Malavika so close to Ralph that she could smell the cologne that reminded her of the NY Public Library. She held his hand once again, and grasping hers, he whispered, "I've just got my prayer to Kali Ma come true."

Several escalator rides later, they were at the square in the World Trade Center where in summer months such as this one, there was music in the courtyard. He steered her to a seat near the fountain and asked if she minded listening to the jazz concert for a while. He then pulled out a sandwich from a brown paper bag and handed it to her.

"It's vegetarian. I promise. Peanut butter sandwich that I made for you."

"Peanut butter sandwich! How do you know I love them?"

"Pizzas. You told me you like pizzas. I'll get you one, when we walk to the South Seaport restaurant."

"Ralph, about Rushdie and *Midnight's Children*..."

"Forget Rushdie for an hour, will you Malavika? And stay quiet. That guy who's playing the sax, he's particularly good, don't you think? I'll let you into something."

"What?"

"I used to play the sax when I was in high school. Before I became the banker. That reminds me, look around you. Have you seen more poker-faced bankers anywhere in the world? And the grey, black suits. All Brooks Brothers, no doubt. They're the only ones who can afford them. They make all the money, but don't seem to like whatever it is they are doing. Poets and writers don't make money, but at least they look happy because they don't have to file boring taxes."

"But I'm going to write a book that'll be a bestseller and bring me lots of money."

"Ambitious lady. I know you'll do it. You're smart. Then you'll be one of the few who are rich and happy and do what they like. One of the lucky ones."

"What is it that you want to do, Ralph?"

"Write a book that's better than Patrick's..."

"And? You were going to say something else..."

"Not now, later. I'll tell you later. Finish the sandwich. It's a long walk to South Seaport. I don't want you complaining on the way."

They walked together, she slowly and he a little quicker. Ralph often had to remember he was walking with her. Why was he in such a hurry to go somewhere? And why had he asked her to come to Manhattan on a day like this when he was busy? He knew he had to teach a class at Columbia that afternoon. But he had called in to say he had taken the day off. He had not played truant like this in a long time. Why did he do it?

They had to cross a street and Malavika froze. She did not know when she would learn to handle the traffic of Manhattan. Ralph had already gone across when he noticed she was still on the other side. He crossed back, took hold of her hand and almost dragged her through to the other side. She looked around, hoping none of the Indian families she knew had seen these acrobatics. She began to complain. She was tired. Her feet hurt.

"I forgot to tell you to wear a good pair of walking shoes. That we were going to walk around. We could always take a cab. Would you like that, Malavika? But it's such a nice day."

"Oh, we'll walk. But not for more than another five minutes. What is that you're crooning…"

"A Bob Dylan song, *Blowing in the Wind,* a song from my generation."

"Were you at Woodstock?"

"My dear woman, I'm old, but not *that* old?"

"No, I just thought… Woodstock, it was a big thing for us in India when we were in college. I remember, a whole lot of us went for the film – documentary or whatever – wearing those peace pendants and torn jeans. That too ten years after Woodstock."

"Oh, here we are. Just another two steps and we'll be at the restaurant. And I'll buy you the world's largest pizza."

Suddenly worn out from the long walk in the mid-afternoon sun, she thought of the journey back home she would have to make. Anisha would be home in a few hours. And here she was with this man with whom she was feeling such kinship. She hadn't come to Manhattan to look at serious bankers. She had come all the way into town to see Ralph once again. There was no doubt of that.

"Ralph."

"Yes, sweetheart? It's the pizza, isn't it? I've asked for a lot of broccoli on yours. Will make you strong, all that iron."

"Well, I'm not that hungry now!"

"After I ordered that large pizza?"

"Ralph, were you married ever?"

"Umm, yes. Still am. But she wants to call it quits. She thinks I've gone crazy, giving up my job in the bank. She's a banker too. She says she doesn't understand me. She won't listen to what I have to say. We haven't been listening to each other in a long time..."

"I'm sorry. Any children?"

"No, that's the sad part. She didn't want any. And I wanted lots. Especially daughters. You know what, at one point, before I did my Master's I wanted to become a professional storyteller."

"Storyteller?"

"Yeah. You know, the ones who wear masks and carry puppets, and go to public libraries and schools and tell stories. I've done that too, you know. Which school do your daughters go to, Malavika?"

"They went to the public school in New Haven. They're grown up now. The older one is in college."

"Well, I haven't been to that one. But when I don't have to go for these writing classes, or teach at Columbia to keep body and soul together since I gave up being a banker, I go to schools and tell stories. You want me to tell you a story now? You look as if you are going to go to sleep anyhow. Do you know this Indonesian story of a monkey, a lion, and crocodile? I don't have my glove puppets. But I guess I could manage. And we could have a nice audience around too. Maybe they won't charge us for the pizza!"

"Oh god, Ralph, you make me laugh! If your novel doesn't sell, you could become a professional storyteller. You know, in India, the whole village gathers in street corners or temple courtyards to listen to stories from the epics."

"Every community has its stories. It's sad that we in America have forgotten ours. Our only mythology is the television which insulates people and makes them even more neurotic. What better way of bonding, Malavika, than for the whole community to come together to keep alive their dance and music. All traditional cultures have this – in Africa, in Mexico, in Bali, in India..."

"Ralph, do I have to finish the pizza all by myself?"

"Yes, and all the broccoli. Okay, I'll take a piece."

"What is your end of the term project going to be? What sort of story?"

"You know, Malavika, Patrick is a tough cookie. He'll be especially hard on me. So I have to make mine very good. It's about the banker who goes to India looking for a Bengali beauty, instead goes to Hyderabad or some other South Indian city..."

"You're kidding! But will you be my friend?"

"Of course, I'm already your friend."

"If you're my friend then you have to help me with Rushdie."

"Forgive me, dear girl. That's too serious for me. I have my weaknesses – Proust's *Remembrance of Things Past*..."

"It's so nice here, and posh, isn't it Ralph? If I tell you something, will you believe it?"

"You don't look like a very truthful person, but I'll believe you this one time..."

"I've never done this kind of thing. Sit with a male friend and have a pizza."

"You should do something a little more brave next time."

"What? Have a martini at the restaurant on top of the Empire State Building?"

"Yes, and make love after that."

"You're embarrassing me…"

"And you lovely Indian lady, I'm falling in love with you."

Dear Haasi,

I have not heard from you for a long time, but will forgive you, since presumably you have a busy schedule. I'm not sure if you got my last letter, which I wrote to London. I hope these letters are reaching you, wherever you are. We must talk more on the phone if you have the time. Because with Ma passing away, I feel this pressing need to be more closely connected with you. You are, after all, my one link to my past, to my childhood, to Hyderabad.

Everything is changing in my life. Even my two girls are growing up way too quickly for my liking. They're so unlike each other, but each with so much of their own quirks and intelligence. Anisha is the outdoor one, a swimming champion in school who loves animals. Our latest acquisition, a beagle called Charlie Brown, is her love. Avantika is like me – quiet, an introvert, making us all wonder what she will be like when she grows up. Everyone thinks she looks like me too, though I think I was never so pretty as my two daughters. They all take after my mother. I miss her so, Haasini. Somehow even when Pa passed away, there was not this overwhelming feeling of being disconnected. But with Ma, I feel so much has been taken away from me that cannot be replaced or retrieved.

I now wish I had been more attentive to her needs. Why did I have to make all that fuss when she asked me to go to the bazaar with her, or to a relative's house? What was it I was doing that was so important that I couldn't please her? I often think we should all be given a second chance to redeem ourselves by doing the things we didn't do right the first time around.

I heard from your brother that your mother is not well too. You must hurry home. It was so good to spend time with her in Hyderabad. You won't believe this, she told me to bring my hairbrush and combed and plaited my hair and put flowers in them, just the way she used to many years ago. She is the only one who can quell this curly hair of mine. She's terribly proud of you, Haasi, but becomes sad every time she realises you are still not married.

She said, "Now that our children are gone, even Haasi, my husband and I have to take care of each other. Daughters-in-law are nice enough, but we can't go to Bombay to live with Dhruvi. I think of your mother, and how bravely she lived by herself. And died just the way she wanted to, at home." Your mother says that doctors these days don't let you die in peace. All the radiation and chemotherapy has left her weak and debilitated and, she says, denied her her dignity.

"I can't eat, my hair is falling, and I feel tired all the time. And Haasini's father, he has been of no help for a long time. He doesn't even know I have cancer and still expects me to take care of him," she told me.

It is true, she has become frail. I remembered the first time I saw her, from the window of my house. I thought she looked so traditional and beautiful in the Vaira Oosi sari, like a dancer. You now look exactly like she looked then. I saw some of your photographs. Not dance photos where you are transformed, but those that your mother has kept all over the house – of you in front of and behind famous monuments all over the world. I especially liked the one you sent with the London group. Julian, David and the others.

(I tried to look into the eyes of your famous director, but couldn't make out much, except that he looked old.)

Then after plaiting my hair, your mother touched me and said, "Why should I feel sad that Haasi is not married? You are like my daughter too. And your daughters are my grandchildren. Next time you come home you must bring them with you."

Before I left, I touched her feet, and she blessed me with a long married life. She sent gifts and sweets for my daughters... that kind mother from my childhood.

Why was marriage so important to women of our mothers' generation, Haasi? Why do Indian mothers think their girls are incomplete without a man, a husband?

Even my daughters think marriage is important. Growing up in America, you'd think they'd have more liberal views on these things. But guess what, Anisha is already worried about whether she will marry an American boy or an Indian. And Avantika screams she'll kill herself if we ever bring her an Indian boy and ask her to marry him. Look at the Indian doctor they brought for Mridu (one of their cousins here), she said. He turned out to be such a wimp, asking her to cook and refusing to help with the housework. Everytime she took the car out, he wanted to know where she was going.

Oh, they don't want to marry Indian men from India, but want to get married to guys similar to them who have been brought up in America. Coconuts as they call them here – brown on the outside, but white inside! Although, to think of an arranged marriage for them is obnoxious to me. I'm afraid this is one mother who will not help in finding boys for her girls. They have to find their partners, though already the soul quivers to think what I'll do when Anisha too moves out.

When Avanti left, it was heartbreaking to say the least. Now when Anisha goes next fall, I will be so very lonely. What will I do then, Haasi? Maybe I should move back to India or travel with you.

Vikram, I'm not sure will want to settle down in India. He's much too rooted in this country, his job, his golf, his weekend football. But I've about had it with the life here. Especially with Ma passing away I feel the need to go back to Hyderabad and be comforted and be held by the house I grew up in.

Vikram and I will have to work something out. Even if we do not love each other any more, we've grown to need each other. He's been a reasonably good husband. A kind one even. But I'm not going to hang on to a relationship that is only comfortable and convenient. I too, I guess, have found him convenient, enjoying the luxuries he has provided me. But enough of this.

I want to be on my own. Do the things I have wanted to do. Read, write, travel – and sometimes do nothing, without feeling guilty about it.

I don't want to hurt Vikram or the children. But I want to live for myself after all these years, Haasi. Am I sounding selfish? I'm in my mid fifties. And that's a lot of life I have lived for others.

There will be a time when Vikram or the girls won't need me. But before that time comes, I will set myself free.

Love, as always,

Mala

CHAPTER 25

Haasini wanted to be alone. Seeing her look as forlorn as Sita without Ram, Juilan had offered to take her out for a walk to the park, but she had refused. They were just done with the tour of Europe, after playing at Vienna, Rome and Paris, and in a few days, they would leave for America.

David had told her he'd been called to Paris and would not be travelling to New York with them. She'd asked him several times if he couldn't change his plans but when he said no, she let it go. He was not the kind of man you could coax, let alone nag or bully, she realised.

These were her last two days in London, and she wanted to walk around and explore the city by herself. She knew, however, that in reality she didn't want to explore anything except her own feelings. She wanted a re-run of her life, the past year or so when she had changed so much, not only because of her exposure to an international stage, but mostly because of David. Being with him personally and professionally had altered her in many ways. She wanted to think about all that.

She decided to go to Hyde Park. She took a taxi there and tried to find a bench where she could be by herself. But finding a bench to herself in Hyde Park on a brilliant day such as this was impossible. It was late afternoon, and there were people playing the accordion, the banjo and so many other instruments. She listened to the music, but was unable to pay any attention to the songs. A man asked her to join in the dancing, but she declined and he shrugged politely and went away, leaving her alone. She half-wished he had forced her to dance, for she wanted to laugh and be part of the crowd, forget the ache that was sweeping within her. But then the British never did believe in imposing themselves.

She wanted to think of all the good times she had with David. She remembered with a smile her time in Vienna when she and David had sat in Strauss Park, drinking wine. When the music began, he wanted her to waltz with him, and she had glided shyly into his arms, not sure if she could move with him the way he wanted her to. There was a formality about him, and a certain courtesy. He was so European in so many of his ways. She knew that instant that there would be only one David in her life, she would never meet another man like him. She raised her face to look at him. He kissed her, and she felt giddy with pleasure and too much red wine. How did Europeans drink so much wine without their heads swirling, she wondered deliriously. There was still dinner to go to, she couldn't get drunk before that, she told herself.

They were going to Paris the next evening, and back to London before he flew out. But for now, they were together.

Not wanting another bowl of onion soup or another pizza, she asked David if they could have dinner at home. She wanted to cook for him.

Not surprisingly, he had his own apartment in Vienna and that too in Kinderland. David had been amused at the shock on her face when she first entered the place.

"The architect – or shall we say, the artist – of this colourful building is a friend of mine. He let me have the apartment for literally nothing. See that column? Columns are an important part of architecture. According to him it's like standing under a tree."

"As a child, I had my favourite tree too. And I had a friend who sat on trees and read books, and the first time I saw her I thought she was a tree elf..." She wanted to tell him all this, but when he was telling her about a renowned architect she didn't want to pour out girlish confidences.

"And you see these boxes of flowering plants on every window? He used to say we must give back to the earth what we have taken. These plants are his way of giving back to the earth that we have plundered."

To her the building looked bizarre, even if it was a tourist site in the famous city. She wasn't sure if she liked his Vienna apartment. It was less homely than his London one, but she didn't want to tell him that.

"David, in this very modern house, not to say a piece of art, is there a kitchen where I can cook something for the two of us," she asked as they returned to the apartment.

"Of course, there, in that part of the house, you'll find the kitchen. I wanted it out of my vision. What is it, my beauty, that you want to cook? There are only all these herbs, and probably a few tomatoes, carrots, broccoli and cheeses in the fridge. Just open the fridge and see what's in there..."

"Only lots of wine. Are we going to drink *more* wine?"

"Yes, why not? And waltz some more. *Blue Danube,* that's what you like, don't you? Though when we were young it was not Strauss who was popular, but Beethoven. Now Strauss is all the rage."

"Oh no. No. I can't drink more wine. I want to cook something for us. I really can't eat any more of those

Viennese vegetables or that awful coffee that you seem to like so much. I wish I could have rice and pickle."

"I agree! German and Viennese food is possibly the worst in the world. Give me Italian any day. What is it that you want to cook, my love?"

"I want to eat Indian food. But there's nothing here with which I can make it."

"Indian food? Too pungent, too spicy for the likes of me. Shall we settle for some soup? And we can rustle up a salad. See what you can make out of the tomatoes and zucchini and the herbs. You could throw in some goat cheese too. If you don't feel like cooking, I can still take you to a restaurant. I can find you an Indian one."

She looked into the fridge and found there was nothing much in there except for some cheese, vegetables and fruits. She might want to eat her mother's pachchadi with rice and ghee, but for the moment she would toss a nice salad for the two of them, to go with a tomato soup. And she would make coffee – not the Viennese black, but with a lot of milk and sugar.

David had showered in the meanwhile and emerged in a blue bathrobe. Haasini didn't know too many men who could look that sexy in blue, like he did. And with hair that was wet.

He opened a champagne bottle, poured the bubbly into the tall and thin glasses and placed them next to the plates she had set on the table. She was standing at the counter, her back to him, cutting the bread into chunky slices and wondering why she was trying to make these connections with a man she knew would go away to Nice, Cannes or wherever in a few days. Why was she trying to smother him like a wife, when she knew he was perfectly capable of taking care of himself?

He was sitting on a chair and writing notes. He had already forgotten *Sita's Sorrow* and was working on a film that that had obsessed him for long, on the life of Buddha. He looked up to find her still cutting bread. What was taking her so long to cut up some bread, he mused. Why was she looking so forlorn? Did she want something from him, this Indian woman so exotic but who was still a child? That was her charm, he thought, twirling the champagne in his flute glass.

"Lady, if you're done with the bread, could you come here and sit with me so that I can look at you while we share this champagne. And yes, eat that wonderful soup and salad that has taken you 45 minutes to make?"

"Forty-five minutes? I took so much time because I couldn't find the peeler to skin the avocados."

"Avocados? You've put avocados into the salad? Now, now. You'll work out all the calories in your dance but what about me? I don't ever want to see that British heart surgeon again, who cut me open some years ago. Telling me not to eat half the things I like. That's better – come, sit. Here. So I can look at you."

She sat in front of him playing with her glass and looking at the sparkling bubbles.

"Haasini, my beautiful Sita, what is it that you're thinking? Why this sudden sadness?"

"You know I'm going to miss you, David. We've done too many things together. Forged too many memories... And after all that, to think..."

"To think what? That we'll never see each other again. That won't be true at all, Haasini. Our paths will cross soon enough, I am sure. You'll be the reason I come to India finally. To Bombay or Calcutta. You know they keep asking me to come for the film festivals as a jury member. But I was never interested. I was never one for awards, though once or twice my films got nominated for the Oscars."

"David?"

"I don't want you ever, ever to be sad. Be brave. Trust yourself. That we met, that we've known each other, lived together for so many months that have been so utterly delightful. Do you think I'll ever forget you? Don't look for permanence in anything, Haasini. Life is always in a flux. We each have to do what we must..."

"I don't want to go back to India without you. Even if I wrote, you'd never read the letters..."

"I would, if I knew they were from you. There are so many letters I get that it really is humanly impossible to read all the mail."

"I don't want you to be lonely. I don't want to be lonely and be by myself either..."

"What are you talking into my bathrobe like that! You, the articulate one, chattering so much. Although you've been rather quiet the past few days, haven't you?"

"I was thinking of how much I'd miss you..."

"Oh, now we are talking about my favourite subject – the loneliness of humans. I have always been lonely, despite my several wives and mistresses. Something to do with childhood insecurities. My mother left my father and me and ran away, you know. My father was an usherer in theatres. Whenever I came back from school, he would sneak me up into the theatre. That's how I saw all the great films. Charles Chaplin, Kurosawa. *Citizen Kane,* that's where I discovered the magic of cinema. I would sit on a seat at the back weaving fantasies. That's where I learnt to dream. I dream, my darling, I dream large dreams."

"But David, I don't want..."

"We creative artists are more alone than others. Painters, writers and filmmakers. Unless you've been shut into that fortress of silence how will you even know what you want to express, or for that matter know that you have something to say? Ah, there is magic to being alone and hearing no other voice but yours. I've been fascinated for so long by this, the individual journeys artists have to make. Even philosphers. Imagine someone like Siddhartha, the Buddha, how alone it must have been for him when he realised what Enlightenment was. What detachment meant. What it must have been for him to say he knew how human beings could break from the cycle of rebirth and suffering, and not have anyone understand what he was saying."

"David, I love you..."

"I adore you too. But you're so much like a mother. All you Indian women are fecund like the many mother goddesses you worship. You must dance like those goddesses, with your spine erect. Love a man believing you are his equal, not be the forlorn nayika pining for her man. You're a strong woman, you'll be alright."

Later that night as she slept wrapped in him, she heard the sound of footsteps on Vienna's cobbled stones. Someone heading home after a tryst. Or a Beethoven going home in the silence of his deafness. She stirred, wanting to wake him up. She didn't want him to sleep, on this, their last night together.

"David, is your daughter beautiful? The one in Paris?"

"Yes, very beautiful. Her mother was a beautiful woman."

"Italian?"

"No. She was French and she was an actress. But was too wilful, too arrogant, which I found charming then, of course. She's the only woman I have loved, but she didn't want me, just as my mother didn't want me. Maybe that's why love doesn't find an entry in my dictionary."

"Do you see your daughter often? What's her name?"

"Marguerite…"

"As in Hemingway?"

"Ha, precisely. Yes! Michelle, her mother, was a huge fan of Hemingway. You can see Marguerite's photo there on the shelf. Can you see it? She was very young then, but she's grown into a lovely woman now. God alone knows whom she's dating currently. She calls long distance, and says, "Papa, guess what…" and the rest I have to read in the newspapers."

Haasini moved closer to him, putting her ears to his.

"What's that you're doing, eh? Have you been reading the *Kamasutra* lately?"

"No. Just wanted to hear those voices that make you write those fabulous movies that Julian and I saw in London."

"What is it you hear now, Haasini, my darling?"

"Just the music of Amadeus."

"Want to dance?"

"No... no. I want to have a daughter with you. Like Marguerite."

"I couldn't get that lucky. Not twice. Now close your eyes. They give away too much about you, your longings especially."

"Why is it, David, that you don't ask me anything? My life before I met you...?"

"What's important is that two human beings have connected. But it's Buddha who fascinates me now. Buddha and suffering, not so much enlightenment. That could come with a bottle of wine, *ma cher*!

"Know you? Of course I do, some. What I need to know. I know when you lie in my arms like this, waking me up like a child... How old are you? It doesn't matter. I know you love your ears kissed and your feet tickled. And I know what makes you close your eyes like that and turn your face away from my gaze. I know then that there is sadness sweeping through your body. Your honesty I can taste on your lips, your strength in your body. Your kisses will never lie to me. I know what makes you happy..."

"What do you think makes me happy, David?"

I make you happy. Staying near me makes you happy. Creating dance with me makes you happy. ... thought David.

But he didn't say that. He walked out to see why Madame Bovary was whining.

Dear Mala,

I've been on the move Mala, and apologise for not writing to you often enough or being there for you in when you're going through difficult times. Of course, I feel sorry for you, but grieve for my own loss too, because she was so much a part of my growing up years in Hyderabad, and later took the place of an older sister. She was someone I admired because she didn't seem so old fashioned like my own mother.

I loved her. I remember the first day when I came to your house to meet you and she hugged me and said, "Now my Mala will have a playmate." I didn't know what to say but was excited that such a sophisticated woman like her had thought of me as a playmate for her daughter. And the many times she stood by us when we wanted to do something wild like staying out at night or going to see a movie. She always reassured my mother that we were sensible girls who wouldn't do anything wild.

Once when I came to her asking for a home remedy to cure the acne on my face, she told me to just wash my face regularly and not worry about anything. But I persisted, wanting an instant remedy.

She simply said, "Child, these are small things that will disappear as you get older. Look at Mala worrying about the dark circles under her eyes. You will realise as you become mature young women, that these are trivial things that won't matter in the larger scheme of things. One day, your hair will become grey and the skin around your waist will sag. You will be aware of all this, but you will still love yourselves more than you do now, in fact. You know there are other things in you that are more precious – those are the things that have to be nurtured and taken care of."

How wise she was to have told me that, so long ago. I do love myself more now despite the lines on my face and my hair turning grey. To me these are the signs of the life I have lived.

The advice she used to give when some boy didn't look at us and we were heartbroken!

"Don't worry," she said. "There'll be other admirers. You are still not what you are meant to be. In fact, you might well be a character from a film or book that you admire. I know Malavika at one point wanted to be like Jo from Little Women, *and that you admired Grace Kelly. How did I know? It was obvious, the way Malavika cut her hair and wanted to wear long collared gowns. And you suddenly walking around in that stilted manner! But one day you will discover yourselves, find what you were meant to be, and then some other girl will want to be like you, someone else will want to laugh the way you do. And you will find a man who'll love you for what you are. Even if there is a pimple on your nose, or if your hair has turned grey."*

I wailed out loud: "Please, Rekha Atha, I can't wait that long, till my hair has gone grey, to find a man to love me." She laughed and said, "Till you meet that one man who'll have to be grown up himself to love you for what you are, you'll keep looking and falling in love."

After you got married and moved to America, she used to miss you, and wonder if she should have allowed you to go so far away from home. But she would also say Vikram was such a perfect match, they couldn't refuse. "Maybe we should have waited for a while but the family seemed so cultured and educated. She is happy, isn't she, Haasini?" she would ask anxiously. "She writes to you so often. If there is anything amiss, do tell me." She wished you had studied more, got a Master's degree. She felt you had children way too soon, like her. She wondered if you had been embarrassed by the fact that she was a young mother while all your friends' mothers were older.

Whenever I was not busy with dance, I'd sit with her, and we'd watch a film together, or sing a Thyagaraja kriti. Yes, on the favourite place of hers, the swing.

I used to think, when I age, I want to age like her – gracefully, without even acknowledging the burden of the years. She always wore such gorgeous Gadwal and Venkatagiri saris, and always an ornament to adorn that long graceful neck of hers. In all my life, I have never once seen her in a crumpled sari or a strand of hair out of place. Such grace! She was truly beautiful. If we were not so obsessed with ourselves and our problems, we would have known the number of hearts she must have broken till the very end. I don't know about other men, but your father at least was truly besotted with her.

I shall feel Rekha Atha's absence when I go home, more than you ever do. As I said, in later years she became more of a sister whom I looked up to. So many times, we both have sat through the night, looking through Sanskrit texts to find appropriate verses for the dance pieces I was choreographing. I will miss that companionship.

I just got your letter. Did you get mine? If you haven't I won't tell you about it now. Waiting to see you in NY. Incidentally, David will not come to your country. He has been called to Paris by his daughter. That's one woman he can't resist.

Take care. I want to talk to you so much. Some things are best spoken in person.

Yours in sadness,

Haasini

CHAPTER 26

It was past midnight but Malavika was working furiously on her computer, editing the last few pages of her collection of short stories. For the past one week she had been working at this feverish pitch so that her manuscript would be ready by the end of the term. When had she begun to procrastinate work like this, she wondered. She'd always been one of those who handed in her assignments before time. Too much to do in the country, she thought, turning her eyes from the monitor that was green. She still preferred writing longhand when the mind, heart and hand all connected, but the computer was undoubtedly useful for editing and reworking manuscripts.

The PC, as they called this unwieldly machine that was now occupying half her writing table, had arrived at the girls' insistence. But she had to call Avantika often to help her save files or find them. Avanti and Anisha's generation was so fearless with technology. If she could, the adventurous Avanti would be thrilled to go to the moon in a space shuttle!

Her own generation had seen so much, Malavika thought, closing her eyes to rest them briefly. She remembered the time when her paternal grandfather travelled to Japan and brought back the first transistor – they had all been so awestruck that they could hear Lata Mangeshkar sing, and that too on an instrument that needed no wires. Thereafter, the transistor was given a pride of place in their Madras home, next to an array of important gods. When she was growing up in Hyderabad there was not even the black and white television sets. In the cacophony of US television, she sometimes longed for the peace of a home without TV.

There was hardly any technology back home in India, and now she was expected to make that leap of mind and type away on a computer with the constant fear that one wrong button pressed and she'd lose all she'd written.

She could even send mails to Haasini on the computer, if only she knew if her unreachable friend had one or several mail accounts, and if so, whether she checked her mails and remembered her password. Malavika herself had to write her password and paste it on top of the computer screen.

Ralph had been telling her that people were even writing poetry on the computer. But she couldn't magine reading poetry on a monitor. She wanted to feel the rustle of paper as she turned the pages, savour the pleasure of reading lines of Neruda's poems from the bound volume that was almost always by her bedside. She wanted to close her eyes and imagine the woman who had hurt the poet so much that he created such a wonderful poem,

Tonight I can write the saddest lines.

I loved her, and sometimes she loved me too.

Through nights like this one I held her in my arms

I kissed her again and again under the endless sky..."

Sure, she could read any number of stories from the Indian epics on the computer, but how could it compare with what she'd heard from her grandmother! She could still recall her fear as her Avva described the snake coiled around young Krishna, how she'd move close to her for comfort, how she had to be assured that the child was none other than Vishnu himself, so how could any harm come to him?

Enough of rumination, she told herself, stretching her legs. It had been decades since Avva died. The father she so admired, had passed away, leaving her and her Ma bereft. She didn't even have a mother now. Wiping tears away, she thought it was Ralph who made her feel like a young girl who needed to be hugged and taken care of. It was all his fault.

She forced herself to get back to the last few pages of her 13 stories that had to be handed in the following day. What would the title of the book be? *The Purple Lotus and Other Stories* or her favorite *Talk to Me and Other Stories*?

Summer was drawing to an end, and classes were concluding. After writing the stories, she had closed her eyes and tried to hear her voice just as Patrick wanted them to. They sounded like her alright, but she had no idea how good they were. All she knew was that she had in some way connected with herself, a self that was only part of this family or the family she had grown up with.

The other afternoon Susan and Richard had disappeared immediately after the class, and it suddenly occurred to her that they might be dating each other. Of course they were, it was now so clear!

That was the afternoon she and Ralph had gone out of the NYU campus to go to a café for sandwiches and coffee.

"Malavika, you are looking lost. What's the matter? But then you always look as if you've wandered in by mistake when you wanted to be somewhere else," Ralph said holding her hand.

"My mother, she used to say I dreamt a lot. She believed I was always in another world. That irritates my husband now. Do you know what happened one day, when the children were very little? The kitchen practically caught fire, as I had left something on the stove to cook and forgotten all about it in the excitement of reading out stories to my daughters."

"But if you didn't dream you wouldn't write, Malavika. Sometimes the financial analyst gets the better of me, making me wear a grey suit, which kind of freezes my brains from any flights of fantasy. I then have to rip off the grey suit, wear shorts and a tee or something else to get myself to think like a poet."

"Where are we walking to now, so aimlessly?" She had asked when they left the café.

"Let's just get lost in Manhattan. Though with me you could never get lost. I know these streets like the lines on my palm that palmists in your country like to read."

"I like walking with you. But could you walk a little slower? I have a feeling that everyone's watching us..."

"Yes, woman. Because you're so pretty – and you don't even know it. You haven't been told that enough number of times, have you?"

"Am I? Still, after two daughters?"

"Yes. Not pretty but beautiful. So beautiful that everyone is looking at us, and is thinking you are my wife. And I'm proud of that."

"Oh, stop pulling my leg! What's big brother Patrick saying about the class assignments? I am so scared to submit my final thesis of short stories."

"Well, he thinks this has been a great class. He thinks some of us even have a chance of being published. By the way, he wants to know if there is anything going on between us."

"I hope you told him the truth..."

"Truth?"

"Ralph, do you think you'll have time to read one or two of my stories. Just tell me if I'm on the right track..."

"I've seen some of your work with Patrick, though he doesn't know about it. He would massacre me if he knew I had seen other students' work. But I couldn't resist looking at yours. I saw some good stuff in yours. But you're not saying what you want. Or are you? What are you afraid of?"

"Family... husband, children..."

"They are all there, an important part of your life. But treat yourseslf as the priority, Malavika. Eat delicious food. Walk in the sunshine. Be silly, be kind. Be weird even. Play, play a little, don't be so serious about life. Let some man adore you, and make love and teach you what intimacy should be."

"I'll miss you when these classes get over, miss talking to you. All these walks... They've made my leg muscles strong, though!"

"If I may be permitted to give you a gift..."

"What's this? A picture of me? Oh, at the New York Library with my arms raised like that – Ralph, how terrible I look! But who took it? The professor?"

"No, you look just lovely. And I'll tell you a secret. I have a copy of that picture that stands on my desk, and I love looking at it, every evening when I go back."

"My photograph on your desk?"

"And remember to look at the world in a different way. Otherwise, we can't be writers. Even now, my friends think I'm crazy wanting to sit here and write stories. Look at it this way, Malavika. There are such few people reading books, especially fiction. How foolish we must seem that we not only want to spend money on buying books to read them, but also want to spend our life writing books. I mean, when people out there are doing important things like sending guys up in spaceships, making nuclear weapons, and running over small unarmed nations...think of it, Malavika. When you think about it, it does seem a bit smug that we should spend so much time writing. How wasteful that activity must seem to the others."

"I know, I always have a sense of guilt when I sit to write. I tell myself, maybe I should bake a cake for Anisha. Or clean the cupboards, or put away the dishes. Sometimes, you know, I have to do strange things, just to be able to give myself over to this pleasure of writing. I clean and scrub the bathrooms or the kitchen so that I can say, I've done something for my family, now let me sit at my computer and work on the stories. Or even allow myself to sit and read, ah!

just to give in to that pleasure. It's the ultimate indulgence that I have cherished since childhood."

"It only seems natural that those who love books and stories will want to create their own. Listen, this is sounding like one of my brother's classes. What do you say to taking a walk to the Hudson Bay?"

"Ralph, why do you always make me walk? I think I've seen more of Manhattan with you than anyone else."

"My pleasure, lady."

"Could we go to Central Park instead? I've always wanted to walk there, but been too scared of getting mugged!"

"It's a myth that you'll get mugged in Central Park. The chances that you'll get mugged in Central Park are about as good as you getting mugged in New Delhi."

"Thank you for that bit of information."

"Don't worry. I may not look huge, but I'm strong. Especially after eating all that broccoli you left over from the pizza last time."

"Ralph, you're the dearest friend I have, apart from Haasini."

"Haasini? Who's this new character who's been introduced into the play in which I thought you and I were the main protagonists with Susan and Richard as the sidekick characters?"

"Haven't I mentioned Haasini before? She's a childhood friend and a very special person."

"Malavika, you are such a special woman that it takes a very special person to love you."

She was going to open her mouth to say something, when she saw two girls roller-blading past them, oblivious to everything but their speed. How she'd love to do that one day. She was about to ask Ralph if he would teach her roller-blading, when he lifted her face up and kissed her.

"No, Ralph, you shouldn't... the story..."

"Woman, be quiet. Open your mouth and kiss me..."

Malavika shook herself from her reverie and looked at the photograph on the desk, next to the computer, and said as loudly as she could, "Yes, I want to be a writer. And Ralph, I do love you."

Dear Haasi,

I am writing immediately as I read your mail.

Thank you for finding the time to write about my mother. She was special, only I didn't realise it then. Do we, as girls, idealise our fathers and take our mothers for granted? Have you realised how unforgiving and exacting we are of our mothers, while with our fathers we are more generous. But I can see that bond, a strong, unspoken bond that connects my mother's mother, her mother before her, me, my daughters and theirs one day. Our collective womanhood, in which we will not only carry common genes, but many of our individual hopes and dreams.

My daughters may have been brought up in America, may even marry men who aren't Indian, but there will be within them a part that is not just mine, but their grandmother's and her mother's. A certain grace, a tradition of lighting a lamp at sunset, that will be embedded in their subconscious. Like I did, they too will tell their children how, because Krishna slayed a demon, we in the

South have an early morning bath before we burst crackers on Deepavali.

We may think we have forgotten those traditions, which in the rebelliousness of youth we said we would never follow. But these days I do light a lamp in the evening, if only to remember Ma and her gentle ways. For Avva who told me that by lighting a lamp we are dispelling darkness around us, even within us.

At some point, many years from now, I know my daughters will teach their daughters to draw rangoli patterns, if not at the doorstep – since most likely Avantika will live on the moon – at least before a deity. They will cherish this all the more for living in the Western world, so far from that of their parents.

I have finished my book of short stories and would like to have revised some of them, but there was absolutely no time. So, I have had to submit them to Patrick, unfinished as they are.

There is a good chance that some of the best work from the class may be published. It has happened in the past, and anthologies of students have been brought out. But that's a distant dream really, Haasini, to get published. What matters is, I have discovered new things in the journey that I had never hoped to make, and I have been surprised and delighted to discover new things about myself.

But trust me, delightful as it was, it was also a difficult journey, Haasini, because there are no maps to guide you in this journey inwards, no one to hold your hand and take you around in a world where you have face truths about yourself. Speaking for myself, I am now committed to an exploration that will lead to something, I don't know what. My roots? My home? A spiritual path even?

What shall I say about your other letter, about David? Except that I'm so happy that you found someone like him to love. My mother had told us many decades ago – do you remember? – that there would come a time when we know who the person is we are destined to love. Yours was to love this intriguing man. But there is also something sad about loving such men of destiny because they will never belong to any one person. Painful as it is, we have to *share them with others. Though these days I realise these fleeting moments of love are better than a whole lifetime of marriage that does not mean anything.*

I can also understand your pain – your incomprehension about the surge of happiness and the equally swift loss. But that is the nature of happiness, isn't it? Such pain is inherent in happiness? Somehow we know happiness will pass, and we will be left only with memories.

It's these memories of pain and longing that makes you want to create. Imagine how passionate that fleeting kiss must have been for Rodin to want to recreate it in sculptures again and again.

I'm looking forward to seeing you in New Jersey. And to seeing you perform. Haven't seen you on stage for such a long time. Hope you can take a few days off to spend time with me and the girls, before you leave for India or back to Europe for some other festival. I can't even begin to tell you how happy I am for you. And how much I want my two daughters to meet you. You've seen them when they were very young, when I used to come to Hyderabad on and off. But now they are quite the young ladies. Sometimes, I think, a little like you and me, with secrets and laughter, and a life still ahead of them. When I hear them cry over a bad hair day, or a boy from their class who hasn't called them up, I want to tell them, "No. No, this is not it. Don't be in such a hurry. There are things in the world more delightful, more important, than a teenage girl's anguish."

But as Vasudeva the boatman says in Hesse's Siddhartha, *we cannot protect our children from what we ourselves have suffered. We must let them discover the world for themselves. But for that, as parents, we must be brave. So brave that we can let our children fall and get hurt, when all the time we know we could have somehow saved them from it.*

In the meanwhile, I think it's so lovely that we have started e-mailing each other. Quicker, no?

Fondly,

Malavika

CHAPTER 27

Haasini sat in a cafeteria in a shopping centre in London, eating a large bowl of salad with croutons of which she had taken an extra helping. She picked up each one carefully with a fork, tossing them into her mouth and feeling in her ear the crunching sound of the crouton being split open between her teeth. She then rolled the lettuce and arugula leaves on the fork and pushed them into her mouth, relishing the taste of the crisp salad leaves. She searched through the salad bowl, looking at the assortment of vegetables and nuts. This was the punishment of being a vegetarian in a European country, she told herself. She saw sliced cucumbers, and decided she would leave their delicious familiar wetness for the very last, till she got through these innumerable leaves that her bowl was splayed with.

She wrinkled her nose at the black olives. However exotic those may be considered, she didn't want to eat them. But she pierced one with her fork and lifted it up to the light as if she were examining someone's coloured head. An elderly woman passed by her table and smiled.

"Don't like olives, dearie? Never liked them myself either," she said. "You're beautiful. And you stay that way," she added, and strutted away. "Look at that hat!" Haasini thought with a gasp. "With a feather sticking out. And that green dress and red lipstick!" There was such flamboyance in the woman, even at her age.

Haasini took off her shoes, and pressed her feet against each other for comfort. Rising waves of a sudden wistfulness swept over her and she closed her eyes to block the tears. The lady was looking at dresses in the Gucci store just there. Haasini didn't want her to see the tears. Olives. He had passed the olive from his mouth to hers. She'd protested that she didn't like them, but on his insistence crunched the bitter sweet fruit, wanting to taste him in it, his Italian heritage; wanting to love not only him, but anything that belonged to him and his country.

"Didn't you miss not having a mother, David?"

"Mother? Never even knew her, my love. When I was four or five, she went away and never came to see me after that. Carlos, my father, was everything. Never married again. He loved her too much, I think. When I was sick, he would sit by me and pray to the Lord. Stop drinking for a few nights then. Never knew he had any religion in him. But I actually saw him kneeling before the Holy Mother and weeping and praying for me once when I was very ill with fever. He cooked really awful food, and it's a surprise I survived all that. His cooking was just a little better than yours though."

"That's not my fault at all. There is nothing in your fridge. And David, when I'm gone will you remember me? Not like your mother..."

"What do you think? Would I remember you?"

"I don't know..."

"Every time I hear the sound of Indian cymbals and drums, I'll think of your beautiful face, of the lovely Indian I made love to in Vienna, in London, in Paris..."

"But where would you hear the sound of cymbals and Indian drums in Paris, for Christ's sake?"

"Very difficult, I agree…"

"So, you won't think of me then?"

"Difficult," he said, ruffling her hair. "But seriously, my love, you know what would be the saddest thing in life? Not death, but the fact that you are not remembered or stay in someone's memory. Like my mother. I hardly think of her. I don't even know if she is alive, though some years ago I heard she was ill and wanted to see me. That's why I think I create all those films, an arrogant and proud man's hunger to be remembered and known even after his death. But ultimately what does it all matter? Nothing."

"Then why create?"

"Men in their insignificance try to duplicate God's creation, foolishly imagining they have made a difference to the world."

"I think even falling in love is a way of averting the void that comes with the annihilation death brings. We think love will redeem us. We think because we matter to someone, our life must mean something," he was saying. Haasini was hungry to receive as much wisdom as she could from this man who was years older to her, had seen so much of world.

"And when I think of all that I've created, and think of Marguerite, I realise that nothing I've created is quite as beautiful as her."

"You really love her, didn't you, David? Your Marguerite…"

"Yes, the one person I love most besides myself."

"Ah, that's a fond father speaking. You're sure you're not going to come to New York with us?"

"Dear, dear lady. Marguerite wants me in Paris, and I can't say no to her."

A tear began to slide from Haasini's eyes as she looked down at her salad bowl once again, remembering how empty she had felt when he said that. Licking it, she decided she still preferred the saltiness of it to the olive at the end of her fork. The lady in purple clothes came out of the Gucci store with bags and waved to her.

Haasini waved back.

There were two lonely people in the shopping centre today. The lady came towards the cafeteria again. Let her, Haasini thought – she wanted to talk to someone. It wouldn't be long before she herself would be like that – wobbling around, shopping in the afternoons out of boredom. She hoped at least she'd be able to afford a Gucci bag.

David would soon be leaving for the airport. She didn't want to be there when he left. He would still be in the apartment now, though. Doing what? Packing? Calling for the taxi?

She didn't know that while putting away the papers David had found her anklets, (had she left them deliberately? he wondered) lifted them up, and laughed. Yes, it would be quite difficult to find another woman like her. He was missing her already. He tried to call her apartment and hung up impatiently when she didn't answer. She had refused to get a cell phone, he didn't know why. The car for the airport had arrived. He had to leave. And soon. He was beginning to like this Indian woman way too much. Maybe, he would go to India for the next film festival. And Buddha would take him in his footsteps to Sarnath, Benares, Lumbini.

Haasini put her hand to her neck to touch the platinum chain with a pearl hanging from it that David had given her.

"Thank you, David. Is this something very precious?"

"It's a Mikimoto. A rare piece, just like you."

Haasini smiled, remembering, and touched the pearl again. Would he come to India to see her?

The purple lady, with her bags and hats and feathers stood before her.

"Ducky, do you mind if I sit here for a while. My legs ache so. I want to show you the dress I bought. My daughter is going to be angry with me for being so extravagant. But I was too excited when I saw it, and I bought it on my credit card."

"You're welcome to sit here, ma'am. I'm Haasini..." she said, stretching her hand out.

"And I'm Elizabeth Brown. Thank you, love, for letting me sit here. I think I'll drink a glass of wine..."

"Shall I fetch you some?"

"That would be lovely! And very kind of you. I always liked Indians. And their temples. Been to one in Southall. Is that where you stay?"

"No, I'm visiting London. Worked in a play..."

"So, you're an actress..."

"No, not really, Elizabeth. I'm a dancer," said Haasini, and got up to get the wine.

"Never mind what you are, thank you for the wine," the lady responded appreciatively when Haasini handed her the chilled glass. "You don't drink wine or beer, do you? Nothing like a little drink to lift the spirits up and keep you happy. And buying a Gucci just adds to the pleasure. But tell me, Haasini – have I got the name right?"

"Yes, you have."

"Haasini, you look sad and lost. Missing someone...?"

"Mmm..."

"I know from the look of it. Been in love several times myself. Married twice, though not to the men I loved. Marriage, love, what have they got to do with each other? So tell me the rest of the story..."

"No story, Elizabeth. Except he's leaving London. And I love him very much..."

"Leaving a pretty woman like you and going away? Where to?"

"Paris."

"A glamorous playboy, is that what he is? Knew one myself who went away to Hollywood. Said he'd write to me after he became famous. Believe me, love, that was the last I heard of him."

"Elizabeth, you're funny, and I'm glad you chose to sit at my table. Now aren't you going to show me the dress?"

"I will. Here. Now be careful, cost me a fortune. Bought it all with my own money. Decided long ago, I didn't need any man's money to buy dresses. I don't think you do too, Haasini. I know you'll become a great actress. And rich. I like what you're wearing. A sarong, that's what it's called isn't it?"

"No, a sari..."

"Yes of course, that's what they call them. My uncle and aunt were in Bengal in the tea estates. They had a jolly good time there, with all those servants and chhota haazris. I have seen many Indian women wear the sari. But none have looked as elegant as you."

"Thank you, Elizabeth, and the dress is just lovely. Will you wear it and come to see our play at the Albert Hall tomorrow night?"

"Albert Hall, tomorrow night? Wait until my daughter hears of this. You're a star, and I know when I see one."

"I'm not a star as yet, but I'll be honoured to have you as my guest."

"And I would be honoured to see you on the stage. Who's the director?"

"David Abraham."

"Never heard of him."

"He's a film director."

"So what's he doing with a play...?"

"He likes to work with different media..."

"Eh, what's that? Before you leave here, you must buy yourself a box of delicious Godiva chocolates They just melt in your mouth. Here, you can have one of 'em. Salads!

They're good for your health but taste like sawdust. Look at me, would anyone think I'm 70 years old? I'm 73, really, but I tell a few lies, no harm in that. Here, take one more chocolate, lovey. Nothing like chocolates and a glass of wine to get over a love affair, take it from one who knows!"

"Elizabeth, I think I'm pregnant. And I want to have the baby."

"A baby! And he's leaving you and running away to Paris! All men are bastards. Here have, another chocolate. We'll think of what to do."

"He doesn't know about the baby."

"That's where you are being naive. Call him in Paris, Geneva, Germany, wherever he is, and tell him this instant about the baby. And he will marry you..."

"He doesn't believe in marriage."

"I'm sure he doesn't, no man does. You have to get them to marry. Though I don't believe in marriage either. But still, if there's a baby..."

"I think I'll go back to India and have the baby."

"You're a brave girl, sweetheart! It looks like it's going to rain. I'd better call for a taxi. And yes, I'll be there tomorrow. Take care, love."

"You too, Elizabeth, it was nice talking to you. I'll buy that box of chocolates and eat them all up tonight, along with a crateful of wine!"

❋ ❋ ❋

Dear Mala,

Only a few days to New York, before I see you! I hope we can sit and talk just like we used to, when we were young. I know it's less than a fortnight before I'm there, but I'm alone in my flat tonight and need to talk to someone who cares about me. I tried calling you. But you were not home and the phone went to voice mail. Thank god for these emails though.

We have come to the end of the season in Europe, and with David himself having left, as you can imagine, the enthusiasm of the group is flagging, at least mine is. I'm weary, Mala, tired of living and sleeping by myself. I'm tired of being strong, of everyone saying I'm such an icon. I'm tired of the drone of introductions before every show when they call me the best dancer the country has produced, a supreme example of the Kalakshetra tradition.

I want to dance freely like those Lambada women who would come home during Holi, and dance and sing, clapping their hands, their skirts with mirrors on them swirling, their silver jhumkas and bangles dangling, and the women themselves so happy, carried away by the rhythm of their dance. Do you remember them, Malavika, their colourful clothes and laughter, their dance? I want to be like them – dance and not be bothered about what the dance critic of Time Out *or the BBC will say. Or what* The Guardian *will write.*

Enough of the wanderer's life, Mala. I've travelled enough, seen enough. Danced at Avignon, at Canterbury, before the Queen of England, and the Pope. Now I want to lie quietly with a man who loves me, lets me lie in his lap, and lets me dream.

I want to wear silk saris with gold zari and mango motifs on them, rubies and sometimes diamonds in my ears, feel the sensuality of the moment in the rustle of a sari, and go with him to film premieres, letting its softness caress his shoulder. And afterwards, laugh at all those who remarked, "Why did she marry him?" How will I tell them that the dancer is in love with the director and wants to watch over him to make sure he doesn't die and leave her.

Mala, I no longer want to sleep in lonely hotel rooms, worrying about the musicians and the performance the next evening. I want to be a wife being chided by her husband for the extravagant shopping, and a mother fussing over the children's homework. I want to do simple things like every other woman. Decorate the house with diyas and flowers on Diwali and lean against the doorway to admire it myself.

I want to have a daughter who will come with me to the temple wearing a pattu pavada and flowers tucked into hair that I would have plaited myself. I will show her the mudras of dance and teach her the first few notes of Carnatic music, and my husband will look at me and say what a fine mother you have turned out to be. He will look at her and her faltering steps and realise she was not meant to be a Bharatanatyam dancer like her mother at all, but a ballet dancer, and suggest we send her to Paris to learn from the best teachers. When my daughter with her dark black hair and father's blue eyes sits with her friends and talks about how much she adores her father, he will look at me and say, Haasini, we did the right thing, we created her in a moment of love, listening to Mozart.

I want to have this daughter who is in my womb, and to whom I've already begun telling our stories, about the mango tree under which we sat, the games with cowrie shells we played, how we read Little Women *and then every Louisa May Alcott book one after another.*

Mala, I want to have this daughter. Give me the courage to have her. Even if its risky to have one at this age. You at least know who the father is.

Yours in joy and in anguish,

Haasini

CHAPTER 28

Neither Anisha or Avantika had ever seen their mother animated like this, talking and laughing so much as if she were a little girl. Avanti was waiting for a call and had to go out on a date, but she ran out of her room into the kitchen one more time to see her mother with Haasinatha. They were sitting at the kitchen table finishing a bottle of red wine, and munching nachos from a bowl between them, music playing in the background. Crosby Stills, Nash and Young. She had heard the music before – it sounded like poetry. No wonder her mother liked it, she thought. She looked at her mother's face again – she had never seen her so happy. Avanti wanted to go into the kitchen for a drink of water and maybe some of the nachos, but hesitated, not wanting to create a ripple on the scene.

She liked her mother's friend – she was so kind, and gentle. She had brought so many silk skirts and scarves for Anisha and her. And books, including one autographed by the film director David Abraham that she knew she would never part with, only auction it one day, if she ever needed big money! She stood in the arch of the doorway, shoulder pressed against the wall, when Anisha walked into the kitchen to be part of the conversation.

"Mala such fine young women we have here. I'm tempted I tell them how naughty you were. Shall I?"

"Do you know what your mother would do, in school, Anisha? She would spray chalk dust on the teacher's chair, so when the teacher sat the dust would fly into her face and nose and she would start coughing and sneezing, and there would be no class for the rest of the day. She would be an angel with the other teachers, but not with this one – I think she was our Hindi teacher."

"Haasi, no wonder my Hindi is still so bad."

"Ma! You were so naughty? And you're always telling us we are not women enough!"

"Wait until I tell you what Haasini would do to Dhruv Uncle who was much younger to us. While he was asleep, she would take a piece of rope, slide it through his pants, and tie him up to the window grill. When he woke up and couldn't get up, he would start howling, till Vani Ammama came to see what had happened!"

"Luckily, you know Mala, Dhruv doesn't remember too much of that torture. Or that time, when Amma asked me to take his temperature, and seeing he wouldn't open his mouth, I just shoved the thermometer in. What if it had broken in his mouth!"

"Wow! Haasi Atha, you guys were not all that angelic, it looks like. Maybe Anisha and I will grow up to be responsible human beings one day..."

"Yes, Avanti. And be kind and loving like your mother."

"Now Avanti, Anisha, give Haasi and me a hug and leave us alone. Anisha, you must have some school work, and Avanti you get ready. And make sure you don't come home very late."

"Don't tell them how your mother had to brush that hair and braid it into tight plaits since you never ran a comb through your hair all your life," Haasini laughed, whispering into Malavika's ear.

"Ma, what is Haasini atha whispering?"asked Anisha.

"Nothing girls. Can you leave us alone?"

"No! Haasi Atha, tell Mom about the film you're taking us to tomorrow," Anisha said, giggling.

"Film? What, on a weekday? And don't giggle so much, Anisha."

Looking at the two girls, Malavika wondered how, despite their own distinct personalities they were so much an extension of her, physically at least.

Yes, the girls were what she and Malavika had been as girls, thought Haasini. It would be nice to have a daughter like them. She'd never missed having a sister. She put her hand into Malavika's, who clasped it affectionately, thinking she would readily give up any man's love, but would be heartbroken if she had to ever give up Haasini. She was her person, as they said in America. Her soulmate.

Now it was the Beatles who were singing, *"Yesterday, love was such an easy game to play, Now I need a place to hide away, Oh, I believe in yesterday..."* and Malavika leaned across the table to pull out the pins from Haasini's bun. She wanted to see if her hair was still as long and thick as it used to be. As the mass of hair tumbled down Haasini's back, it reminded Malavika of the Cauvery river hurrying to the sea. She noticed strands of grey, the fine lines around the eyes, the shadow of age not just on Haasini, but on herself as well. Enough. She didn't want to think about the years that had gone by, or for that matter, how the rest of their life would span out.

Finally, there was nothing but the passing of time, all too evident when she saw the way the girls were growing up. Very soon even the younger one would leave for college, and the older one, already with a boyfriend, would announce she was going to move out and live with him.

Malavika held Haasini's hands and pulled her up from the chair, wanting to drag her out into the night. Drag her out of the room, into the expanse of the outdoors lit by the full moon. They both went out of the kitchen into the backyard. To them, everywhere there was the smell of jasmine and mango flowers, and the moon from a childhood night. It was drizzling, but they let the drops fall on them, drawing circles on their bodies.

Haasini reached out to touch the silver drops on Malavika's face, tracing their path. They remembered another time, beyond the moment in a country, a country even beyond the time they were children to a common ancestry they both shared, of being female, of being Indian, of having known each other for many lifetimes, and they held hands and danced, letting the rain drench them.

And the child entrenched inside Haasini's womb. Mala touched her friend's stomach affectionately. As if to say, welcome to the sisterhood, baby.

Anisha heard sounds and voices somewhere in the garden and peered out of the window. She couldn't see anyone outside, though the laughter that wafted up sounded very much like her Amma's. It would be foolish for anyone to be out in the rain, she thought.

Had she seen her, she may even have felt uncomfortable at the joy, at the abandon, the letting go, that was sweeping through her mother just then, like waves of an electric current.

✳ ✳ ✳

Dear Mala,

It was a long, exhausting trip from New York and it feels so good to be back home. It was lovely seeing you and you were the perfect hostess, taking me around, buying me gifts and feeding me all those elaborate gourmet meals. You were caring and you were kind. It's just that I felt the Malavika I was sitting with was not the same girl I had sat with reading forbidden romantic novels, or the Malavika to whom I poured my heart out. People grow, people change, for sure – it's just that our perceptions of them don't change and we refuse to see them for the people they have grown into.

Don't get me wrong Mala. When I say changed, I mean it in a good sense. You have become mature and strong. What was that Siraj would tell you to do – glide like a swan? You certainly carry yourself very much aware that you are a strong, beautiful woman like your mother, like his Lillette must have been too. Watching you in Connecticut, I recalled, not the scent of a flower, but a whole valley of flowers. Lilies, chrysanthemums, gladioli, roses, magnolias, jasmines... not only their scent, but their colours. Siraj would have been so proud of you.

You are, of course, as beautiful as ever. But now I'm even more envious of you. You have beauty backed by character and strength.

Your daughters are replicas of you – very pretty! But is everything alright between you and Vikram? I noticed a certain aloofness and reserve in him. Was he not happy that I was visiting you? He too has changed. Maybe he works too hard at the bank. But we should thank him for keeping you in such comfort all these years. You do have a lovely home. Of course, with books and paintings everywhere!

As I returned, Amma fell sick. She had to be admitted to the hospital, and is still in ICU. The doctors are giving her a 50-50 chance of survival. Even if she pulls through this time, she may not recover again. Anyway, I keep my fingers crossed. She will pass away soon. I have known this for some time now, but it is more than a little difficult to accept the truth, isn't it? I would like her to live forever. We would like our parents, who are our buffers against all the trials of the world, to live on and on. But that would be mean and selfish on our part. Like Eos who prayed for eternal life for her husband but forgot to ask for eternal youth, so that he grew old, deranged and decrepit, and could neither live nor die. I would only wish that Amma does not suffer more before she goes. It is already heartbreaking to see her like this, hooked on to all those machines. Whenever she sees me, I can see the silent plea in her eyes, "Haasi, take me home, I want to die in my house." Yes, what a cruel thing it would be to let her die like that among strangers, without any dignity. If the doctor says it's alright, I'll take her home very soon and put her in her bed, so that she can look at her tulasi.

And, let her look at all the trees she planted many years ago, when we first came here. The mango, the chickoo and the guava trees. The coconut trees grown so huge and old. Let her hear the fruit birds on the guava plants that she would shoo away many years ago trying to save the fruit for us, while my father would argue that the fruit belonged to the tree and the birds, as much as it did to us. I want to see her in her resplendent Guntur saris and not the hospital gown which doesn't make her look like my Ma at all.

I am sad and I am happy all at the same time. There is life here in the womb. With the losing battle for Amma, there is so much determination to hold on to the baby in me. I'm only waiting for her to be born, so that I can feel life. So that in some manner what Amma is, what I am, will continue.

One generation will pass on, must pass on to make way for another. That's what it's all about, isn't it? Just as I cannot prevent

Amma from dying, I can't prevent Ganga from coming into this world. Ganga. He loved that name.

Be well. And take care. We have grown up, growing old, but will never grow apart.

Yours,

Haasini

CHAPTER 29

Malavika unlocked the door to her mother's room. She kept that locked even if the rest of the house was open. The room seemed smaller than she had remembered it to be. She found a pair of spectacles on the table by her mother's bed that she had thought she had taken with her to America. They had belonged to her mother.

She picked up the spectacles and looked through them into an out of focus world. She wiped the smudges off them with the end of her sari pallav, and thought sadly how dusty they had become in the many years she had not come home. She put them on her nose and looked into the mirror. With a shock she saw her mother in the reflection, and hurriedly put the glasses back on the table. She resolved she must remember to find a nice spectacle case for them soon, so that she could keep them away safely with her mother's books and saris that she had stored in a trunk.

She picked up an exquisite Somaskanda bronze and held it in the palm of her hand. She had forgotten about this artefact that was part of her childhood: a Shiva and Parvati between whom sat the handsome Kartikeya or Skanda. She replaced it gently on top of the chest of drawers in the room.

She turned her head in a semi-circular motion and noticed a grand old map on the wall. Walking closer to it she wondered where in Hyderabad her mother could have bought this old map that had such intricate details of an earlier South India. It was a piece of art with illustrations of people, forests, rivers and mountains. And temples. She didn't remember seeing it the last time she'd come home, when her mother had passed away.

Trincomalee, Thanjavur, Kanchipuram, Seringapatnam, Masulipatnam, Chidambaram. Malavika loved the sounds of these towns and the images they conjured in her mind – of the British and the French who colonised them and set up trading posts. Now more than ever she lived with words as they flew out of books. She wanted to hear them just as Siraj had once read them out to her. She didn't know what she yearned for more. Siraj, his voice, or just the cadences of a Eliot poem?

More familiar than the map was the Ravi Varma painting of the Rama Pattabhishekam that hung on the wall. She wiped the gilt edges of the frame with an old piece of cloth, and bowed in gratitude to the gods. At least they had seen her safely through the passage of this life so far. She prayed her mother, wherever it was that she had taken rebirth, was happy and healthy, and she prayed for the health of her two daughters.

Close to the map of the world was a black and white photograph which had her mother and father along with a little girl. What a lovely velvet blouse with zardozi work her mother was wearing. And she did not remember when her father sported such a thin moustache. And who was that gawky looking child in the photograph, smiling like that, secure between her parents, quite unaware of what the future held for her, she wondered, squinting her eyes.

It was she, Malavika of course, she realised, who had grown up in this lovely old bungalow in Hyderabad. She laughed, seeing the little girl she had grown out of. Two pigtails like two coiled snakes near her ears, and a frock of velvet twinkle nylon. She touched her hair. Yes, it still wound itself against her fingers even if it had greyed.

She missed her two daughters but knew they were happy in America with their first jobs and colleges and their friends. Vikram... he too would be alright. He would be lonely without her, but would find things to do. Besides, he hadn't dissuaded her from coming here. She sometimes missed the company of Ralph. But he'd promised to mail her, when he could. Maybe visit her one day in India.

She had come to realise that, finally, our lives are made up of people who will not be with us. Avva, Ma, Pa, Haasini, Vikram, Ralph. Avanti and Anisha, of course.

We are the fragments of the many people, wherever they were now. The laughter of her mother. The father who was rarely angry with her. Avva and her cackles and fierce love of South Indian coffee. Siraj who moved through history of an ancient city and walked around Oxford. Haasini forever ebullient and wanting to dance. Her two daughters. Vikram. We are never one person, really, she thought. We are even the music we swayed to. The kindness of the last book. The clouds that move like wisps of old men's hair. The clear skies of the night. The intoxication of jasmines. We are all that. She was both, a part of America and India. Hyderabad and Connecticut. Yes, she was everything, and she wanted to embrace all aspects of her life.

Malavika sat on her mother's large four-poster bed that creaked despite her slenderness. She was becoming thinner. The maid who had recently joined thought she was the lady in the photograph, and wanted to know where she had left her little daughter. For a moment Malavika could not comprehend what she was talking about. But then she became aware that she had mistaken her for her mother. She looked at the photograph again and wanted to tell the young girl, "But my mother was much more beautiful than I. And look at the saris she wore. I want to wear each one of them during my time in Hyderabad. I want to tell Ma that I may not be all that she wanted me to be. Or half as graceful. But I have made something out of myself. I am a writer, and my first book of short stories, *The Purple Lotus* is dedicated to her and says, 'Amma. For the woman I want to be...'."

She wanted to slide into the picture and be comforted by the warmth and presence of her parents – those loving souls hugging her. These days, she was hungry for the touch of her two daughters. Their giggles and secrets that young women like them had. Their pouts and anger. They were wrapped in their own worlds. They couldn't understand why she wanted to go back to Hyderabad and live there for six months of the year, why their mother needed to be free. But she hoped just as she had given them her unconditional love, they would give her the freedom to be what she wanted.

Anisha had come from her college in California, and Avantika from New York City to see her off at the airport. If she didn't back come back soon, they would come to India to visit her, they had threatened her.

She would like that, having Anisha and Avanti in Hyderabad. Though she did wish they had come more often when their grandmother had been alive. Her daughters had never really got to know her mother and they just thought of her as the Ammamma.

If her daughters came, she would show them all the places where she and Haasini had spent their childhood. The steps on which they had sat and read books. The verandah and the large squares where they played hopscotch. Show them the dimly-lit room where Siraj sat listening to his old gramophone records. Show them the trees. Yes, the trees were important. The large mango tree which was like a great-grandmother now. Just as this house was, a great-grandmother who had loved her through her years, even when she went so far away.

Malavika got up and walked to the window to see if the large tree still existed. Of course, she couldn't see it from her mother's room, she had forgotten that. She had to go to the window of her room to see her childhood companion, the mango tree.

But that evening, she imagined that even from this room she could see the tree. What manner of tricks was her mind playing? She could see two girls there, and she wanted to tell them to be quiet, till she realised they were Haasini and herself as little girls. She wanted to go out and catch up with the two before they ran away and disappeared.

She ran out of the door in a hurry, tripping over the bed.

"Stop running like that, Mala. When will you learn to walk like a young lady?" she could hear her mother say. In the background, from her Avva's room she heard the sonorous chanting of Adi Shankara's *Nirvana Shatakam*.

Na Mrtyur Na Shangkaa Na Me Jaati-Bhedah

Pitaa Naiva Me Naiva Maataa Na Janmah

Na Bandhur Na Mitram Gurur-Na-Iva Shissyam

Cid-Aananda-Ruupah Shivoham Shivoham

She turned back to tell her mother, "Haasi is waiting for me, Amma, I have to hurry, I have to go."

Till she finally understood it had been an illusion. A magnificent illusion.